FLAME *Ignites*

AN ELIZABETH AND RICHARD LITERARY SUSPENSE
BOOK 1

DONNA FLETCHER CROW

Verity Press

First electronic edition 2015
StoneHouse Inc.

First print edition 2018
Verity Press
an imprint of Publications Marketing, Inc.
Box 972
Boise, Idaho 83701

Editing by Sheila Deeth
Cover and book design by Ken Raney

❀ Created with Vellum

"An enjoyable read that will activate your 'little gray cells.'" ~ Janet Benrey, The Royal Tunbridge Wells Mysteries

"Excellent, lighthearted, easy reading." ~ Dolores Gordon-Smith, The Jack Haldean Mysteries

"Looking forward to more in this series." ~ DeAnna Julie Dodson, The Chastelayne Trilogy

"A delight!" ~ A J Hawke, Cedar Ridge Chronicles

"Delightfully English." ~ Sheila Deeth, *Divide by Zero*

"An enjoyable read, with just enough plotting to keep the action going and the reader just a bit off guard. For a few hours one plunges into another world, and an enjoyable and believable one it is." ~ William Shepard, Robbie Cutler Diplomatic Series

"Extremely well done, and my evening of reading was very well spent." ~ Clark Crouch, *Rustic Ruminations*

"This book will keep your brain active as you follow the complex plot and interesting characters." ~ Hannah Alexander, The Healing Touch Series

"Engages the reader with a lively dialogue between the two protagonists in a complex dance of relationships." ~ Gwyneth Bledsoe, *Death Before Breakfast*

OTHER TITLES IN THE ELIZABETH AND RICHARD LITERARY SUSPENSE MYSTERIES

The Shadow of Reality—Elizabeth and Richard confront murder and find love at a Dorothy L. Sayers mystery week high in the Rocky Mountains

A Midsummer Eve's Nightmare—Danger interrupts Elizabeth and Richard's honeymoon at a Shakespeare Festival in Ashland, Oregon

A Jane Austen Encounter—Elizabeth and Richard, on sabbatical in England, discover that evil lurks even in the genteel world of Jane Austen

A Most Singular Venture—Elizabeth and Richard face peril in Jane Austen's London

To
Elswyth Thane
In Memorium

Looking Back

So long ago.
A lifetime.
Or was it yesterday?
You were so young,
So beautiful.
You were so cross.
You were wonderful.
Silly. Confused.
Autumnal leaves.
Apples in the trees.
Danger.
And unicorns.
Unicorns?
There are always unicorns.
We almost missed it all.
There but for the grace of God...
Yesterday.
A lifetime.

CHAPTER 1

October 1984
Newfane, Vermont

"*Y*ou have the right to remain silent. Anything you say may be taken down and used in evidence against you. You have the right to an attorney…"

This is insane. She, Elizabeth Allerton, was being read her rights by a tall man in a dark-blue sheriff's uniform with a hat that looked like it belonged to a Canadian Mountie. And it wasn't just some silly police show on TV. This was really happening.

Elizabeth shook her head to clear it. Well, all right. That wasn't exactly what he said. She wasn't actually being arrested. Yet. But that was what his accusing questions sounded like to her. Yes, she just told him she was driving a white Plymouth Satellite at the Newfane Market this evening. *So what?*

Anger rose to replace the fear. *What did he think he was doing?*

"Ed, what in the world is going on here?" Elizabeth's hostess, Susan, interrupted. "Come in and have some coffee."

"I'm afraid this is business, Miss Dillabaugh." He turned back to Elizabeth. "Would you prefer we talk alone?"

"Sue is my attorney as well as my cousin." She had the right to counsel, didn't she?

"What is this?" Sue repeated.

"Miss Allerton admits that she was driving a white Plymouth Satellite at the Newfane Market at 6:30 this evening."

Elizabeth nodded her confirmation.

Sheriff Edward Norris, as his name badge declared him to be, glanced at his notes. "With the license number—" He read off a number.

"White Satellite, yes. I don't know the license number."

"That's right," Susan spoke up. "It's my car. What's the problem, Ed? Elizabeth had my permission to drive it. And I can assure you the registration is up to date."

"May I see the vehicle?" It might have been a question, but there was only one possible answer.

Susan led the way to her garage and threw open the door. Even this late in the evening she maintained her crisp, professional air, every hair in place in her sleek blond bob. Elizabeth knew her own long, dark tangled locks only added to an appearance of guilt.

"I didn't speed or run a red light. I'm sure I didn't." Elizabeth's voice came out strangled with nerves and a sense of the unreality of the whole thing.

Sheriff Norris walked the length of the car and bent to examine the front left fender. A moment later he straightened and pointed at a tiny red smear.

"Blood?" Elizabeth cried. "That's impossible." Then she looked again. Not blood, but a dot of deep crimson paint. Right by the chrome around the headlight. It was smaller than a dime. But it was enough.

"There was a small red car parked next to you?" The officer consulted his notes

Elizabeth blinked. "Maybe. I—I guess so. It was getting dark. I didn't really notice…"

"Just a minute, Ed." Susan stepped forward. "I suspect it may have been the other way round—that the other driver bumped my client in the parking lot."

"We have a witness who says the driver of the white car hit the red one while leaving the parking space. That the driver observed the damage, then drove on."

Elizabeth made a strangled sound.

"How much damage was involved?" Susan asked.

"Not a lot. A dent, maybe five or six inches long. I'd guess about a hundred dollars' worth. It can be pounded out with a mallet, I'd say. The other driver probably wouldn't have noticed it if the witness hadn't left a note on the window giving the license number of the white car."

"You've seen the other car?" Susan knew her stuff an as attorney. Never had Elizabeth been happier for Susan's profession.

Norris nodded.

"And there is white paint on it?"

Again the officer nodded. "You were alone in the car, Miss Allerton?"

"No, I had Tommy with me—Susan's nephew—and the dogs." The official pencil scribbled. "And, yes, we were wearing our seat belts. I assume that's the next question."

The officer took out a smaller notebook and began filling out another form. "I'm going to charge you with leaving the scene of an accident where there was property damage. You will appear in court next Tuesday." He tore off the top sheet and handed it to her along with a small card. "You may call this number to get a copy of the accident report."

Elizabeth took the papers in numb fingers.

"I'll just see myself out." The sheriff moved toward the garage door. "Thank you for your cooperation. Sorry about interrupting your dinner."

The young women returned silently to the kitchen table, but the clam chowder in Elizabeth's bowl was cold and the lettuce in her salad limp, the croutons soggy. She jabbed at the dispiriting food with her fork. "No one ever expects the Spanish Inquisition, huh?"

"*Was* the other car there when you drove in?"

Elizabeth thought for a moment. "I suppose so. I don't really remember. We weren't there more than ten minutes—more like five... I ran in for the doughnuts for Tommy's Cub Scout meeting. He stayed in the car with his dachshunds."

"Well, there you are," Sue said. "Tommy would have noticed if there'd been any trouble."

"I'm not sure he would have. He was talking nine to the dozen and playing with Jesse and Joey. I was the adult in charge. I should have noticed."

Susan started gathering up the abandoned dishes. "You were— are—undoubtedly jetlagged from flying all the way from Denver to Boston, then our two-and-a-half-hour drive on up here. I was insane to let you run that errand with my bouncing nephew—to say nothing of those dogs. They diverted your attention for an instant. That's all it would take."

"How's that going to sound in court?" Elizabeth managed a wry smile and attempted to push her hair out of her face.

"I'm not sure I'd say that to the judge. He'd just remind you that it's your job to be attentive when you're driving."

"And he'd be right."

Susan nodded. "And he'd be right. But I shouldn't have let Atomic Tommy latch on to you your first night here."

"Oh, but he was so excited to meet 'Auntie Liz.' And I was pretty excited to meet my almost-nephew, too. Giving him a ride to Cub Scouts was such a small thing—I thought."

"Busybody complaining witness." Susan shook her head.

"Undoubtedly a gossiping spinster with nothing else to occupy her mind. She'll be sure to declare it was her public duty. Not enough people willing to get involved these days, and all that. She'll probably dine out on it for a month. Most exciting thing that's happened to her in years, no doubt." Then Elizabeth calmed a bit. "Of course, if I crunched her car, I *should* pay for it."

"Of course. But the complaining witness wasn't the car owner. Just someone else who happened to be looking on."

"Isn't the term officious intermeddler?" That pleased Elizabeth. It so sounded like the village gossip she was sure had signed that complaint. Her satisfaction faded at the next thought. "But they think I did it on purpose."

Susan nodded. "Hm, yes. The witness said you observed the damage. Did you look at something?"

"Of course I looked! Good grief! It was a tight space in a busy parking lot. You don't think I'd back out without looking? I looked backward and forward and to both sides." Elizabeth turned her head from side to side in pantomime. "Many times. All the time. Does she think I'd go out with my eyes closed? But I didn't see any damage."

"Well, if it's any help to you, as your counselor, let me explain that in order to be guilty of leaving the scene of an accident you have to be aware that an accident occurred."

"But I did it, even if I didn't notice. There's no other way it could have happened."

"That seems likely, but you're not charged with denting a fender. You're charged with leaving the scene of an accident. That's another matter altogether."

"Any chance we could get the charge changed?"

"To what?"

"Is there anything on the books about outrageous stupidity?"

One of the two television programs a week that Elizabeth enjoyed at home was on that night, but not even Masterpiece Theatre could hold her attention. Sitting in a chintz-covered, overstuffed chair in Susan's comfortable living room, she kept going over and over the events in her mind. She replayed the scene in slow motion: Hurrying into the market, then almost running back, jumping in the car, greeting Tommy and the twin dachshunds, who were yapping excitedly at the scents emanating from her bag... She'd started the engine while Tommy refastened his seat belt. Then, aware that the space was tight, she'd backed out. Almost out. She stopped. Pulled forward, and backed again, straighter this time.

Now, that's the crux of the issue, she told herself. *Why did I stop and pull ahead? Did I know I was against the other car?*

She raked her memory. *Did you know?* Something told her she had gone as far as she could go. Had she sensed hitting the other car, even subconsciously? Or was she just being careful in a tight space? *But surely, even if you knew we touched, you must have thought it was just the bumpers,* she pleaded with her confused brain.

And she always came back to the same answer: Whatever prompted her to pull forward, she absolutely had heard no crash, felt no thud, experienced no sensation of having damaged anything. But that was the only thing she was clear on. And at the moment it was very little comfort.

CHAPTER 2

"Oh, groan." Elizabeth opened one eye, then pulled the blanket over her head. Then the pillow. As if the sunshine coming in the window weren't bad enough, now the church bells had to start. And Susan would be expecting her to go to church with her. If there had been another pillow within reach she would have added that to the stack.

Maybe she could just say she was sick and have a nice quiet Sunday morning lie-in as she would have at home. Except when she was small and her grandmother was still living with them. She and Nana always spent every Sunday together: church, then the park or the sweet shop. Always something special. The memory brought a crimp to Elizabeth's heart. How she missed her nan. She was the one the small Lillibet had always gone to with her problems. The one person in the world she could tell anything to without fear of ridicule or reprimand. What would Nana say about her present problem? If only she could talk to her.

One thing was certain, though. Nana wouldn't have countenanced lying in bed on a Sunday morning. Reluctantly Elizabeth dug herself out of the cocoon she had fashioned and managed to find a not-too-wrinkled brown corduroy skirt and rust-colored sweater in her tumbled suitcase. Despairing of bringing her unruly hair into submission, she simply pulled it back with a silk scarf.

Doing the right thing should have perked her up, but a short time later neither the autumn-crisp air nor the picture-postcard perfection of the scene before her managed to raise Elizabeth's spirits. Black-shuttered, white buildings surrounded a village green dotted with trees turning fiery red and gold. She wasn't sure whether she was admiring the view or resisting going forward as she paused to survey the scene spread before her. The trees glowed like individual suns, and their fallen leaves had carpeted the grass with thick gold. The central fountain, turned off for the season, pointed to the statue of a Civil War soldier standing sentinel atop the war memorial, partially shrouded in leafy branches.

"Are you still moping?" Susan nudged her. "I thought I told you not to get this out of proportion."

"Sorry. No. I'm just trying to take all this in. I didn't really get a good look at it last night."

Susan surveyed the scene. "Yes, it is rather amazing, isn't it? I guess we tend to take it for granted when we see it every day." Then she pointed out each building: The Union Hall, with its square tower; the First Congregational Church they were heading toward, pumpkins and corn shocks beside the double black doors standing open below the tall steeple; the Windham County Court House, with a range of impressive pillars across its porch; the inviting double verandah of the Newfane Inn; the Country Store across the street.

Elizabeth was relieved when her hostess moved on rather than needlessly pointing out the Newfane Market beyond that. She tried for an ironic smile as she stuck her hands in the pockets of her tweed jacket and fell into step beside Sue. "Hardest thing in the world—living with your own stupidity. Besides headaches and depression, it produces restless sleep and very bad dreams that I can't even remember—which all add up to a terrible waste of time at the very least."

In spite of her megrims, however, Elizabeth found herself charmed with the eighteenth-century interior of the little white church. Tall stained-glass windows, burgundy carpet and white box pews made her feel as if she had stepped back to the founding of the village in 1753, although the plaque on the church said it was built in the nineteenth century. She noted that each pew bore a small brass plate with the name of the family who owned it. "Are some of the original families still using them?" She asked.

"Believe it or not, many of them still are. My family are upstart newcomers—we arrived after the Civil War, rather than before the Revolution."

Elizabeth was wondering where they would sit, when an ancient, baldheaded usher in a black suit held the gate at the end of a pew open for them. When the two women were seated he shut it with a tiny click. "Talk about a captive audience," Elizabeth whispered.

Elizabeth was surprised to find the quiet of the church and the formality of the traditional service soothing. She was fascinated when the offering was taken in a velvet pouch hanging from the end of a long pole with which the usher reached to the end of the enclosed pew. The choir, in the back of the church, sang an anthem. Then the black-robed minister went to the pulpit. "We are delighted to have one of our native sons returned to us this morning, as he does every year about this time. Richard Cabot Bracken Spenser will read the lesson."

The congregation stood, but Elizabeth sat in amazement. "Stand up," Susan prodded her.

Elizabeth rose and gripped Susan's arm. "That name..."

"Shhh," Susan signaled.

Susan's warning reminded Elizabeth that the exalted visitor had begun the scripture reading. But she couldn't concentrate on the words. Cabot, Bracken—two of Elswyth Thane's most beloved

9

characters. The author herself had admitted in a letter to Elizabeth that they were among her own "pets," as she put it. And the minister had referred to him as a native son. Here. In a village just a few miles from Thane's own Wilmington. That couldn't be happenstance.

At the very least his mother must have been an avid fan. Perhaps she knew the writer personally. Or was a distant relative. Was it possible that the childless Thane might have stood godmother to this man? Elizabeth must talk to him. What a boost that would be for her dissertation. She certainly needed—she would almost say deserved—a break. Elizabeth felt an aching hollowness as she recalled her devastation when she learned that the woman she had dreamed of meeting for so long had died just that July—only three months before her scheduled interview. It was so unfair. After waiting so long, studying so hard, scrimping to save money for her study leave...

In spite of the blow, she had carried on with her plans, hoping to ferret out original, unpublished information. This could be her big break. For the first time since the sheriff's intrusion Elizabeth's mind returned to the subject she usually held foremost. And her heart soared with possibilities.

When Elizabeth brought her mind back to the service she realized the object of her woolgathering had taken his seat in one of the front pews to her right, offering her a clear view to study his profile—especially since he was so much taller than those around him and sat so erect. But the most amazing thing—almost as if his mother had been prophetic in naming him—was the marked resemblance he bore to Elswyth Thane's Cabot. After all, he could have turned out short and pudgy and sandy-haired. Who knows what an infant will grow into? But this man was the image of the "Yankee Stranger" from Philadelphia who fell in love with a southern belle in Williamsburg and helped her entire family survive the Civil War even as she in turn helped him survive the horrors of a prisoner-of-war hospital. Elizabeth went through the items in her mind like a checklist: Tall; thin to the point of being gaunt; long, angular bone structure; thick, luxurious black hair; cool, but kind gray eyes... Well, all right, he was too far away to see about the eyes. But surely...

Yankee Stranger had been the first Thane book Elizabeth had read. Falling in love with that book and the entire Williamsburg Series was the beginning of what grew from teenage daydreams to a serious academic involvement for Elizabeth. *I can't wait to meet his wife,* she thought. *If she's blonde with a southern dialect I'll be in danger of swooning*—even if Elswyth Thane would never have let one of her heroines behave in such a spineless manner.

When the congregation rose to sing the Doxology Elizabeth realized she had daydreamed the whole sermon away. *It's no wonder you could hit another car and drive off without knowing it if you can get lost in your thoughts like that,* she berated herself.

Her impetuous, single-minded desire to waylay Richard Spenser, however, was thwarted by a wall of old friends who gathered around to welcome him home. And to her surprise, an almost equal number converged on her with welcoming smiles. Some of them even addressing her by name before Susan introduced them.

When they were finally able to break away Elizabeth caught her breath. "And I thought New Englanders were supposed to be stand-offish. How did they know my name?"

"I told you I've been looking forward to your visit. I only mentioned it to a couple of people in the office. The village drums did the rest."

Elizabeth, though, was more interested in learning more on the subject of her desired interview. "Tell me about your local celebrity." She nodded toward the tall man still surrounded by people as Sue turned to walk home.

Susan nodded. "'Local celebrity' about sums it up. Very, very old family—came over with William the Conqueror, so to speak, and they've been conquering everything in sight ever since." She paused as if looking at her own words. "I don't know why that came out sounding snide. They're really very nice people. The grandmother and an aunt live in the family digs on the hill, and goodness knows where this village would be without their support of every worthy cause that comes along.

"I don't know much about his branch of the family. His parents moved out west somewhere, I think. Richard oversees the family enterprises for his grandfather or great uncle or someone. The family's in publishing, I think. In Boston or Philadelphia or somewhere."

Elizabeth shook her head at the idea that this Cabot, like Elswyth Thane's hero, might actually be from Philadelphia, too. But one disappointing fact stood out from Susan's breathless biography. "So his parents don't live around here? What a shame. I wanted to talk to his mother."

"His mother?"

"Well, I assume she's the one who chose his name. It may tie in with my research."

Susan kicked at a pile of crunchy leaves, her forehead furrowed. "I haven't been back long enough to get caught up on local gossip yet, but there seems to be something of a mystery about it all. His family were social leaders here when I was a child. I remember hearing about great parties at the house and all that.

"Then it all changed. I think there was a crash in a private plane or something along about my second year of law school. I don't remember who was killed—family friend, maybe… Yes, one of the sons and a friend, I think. I have the idea that was when his parents moved. The great aunt or whatever still continues her charities, but no more parties."

"What about his wife?"

Sue pushed her oversized glasses frames back up on her nose. "There was a fiancée once. Or did they get married? Mary something—something unusual." She thought. "Eileen? Eleanor? Ilona?

I think it was Ilona. Mary Ilona." She shrugged. "I've been away too long. But what does this have to do with anything?"

Elizabeth opened the gate in the white picket fence surrounding Susan's house and paused for a moment to look at the brilliant red of the sugar maple trees on either side of the walk. "Do you realize how amazing this is? I mean, the Rockies are stunning, and our aspens turn golden as sunshine, but there's nothing like this red."

Once inside the house Susan repeated her question. "You still haven't explained your interest in our tall, dark mystery man."

"His name—the Cabot Bracken part—I think he must be connected to my subject in some way. I guess I haven't really told you anything about my dissertation, have I?" Elizabeth kicked off her shoes and sank onto the sofa.

"No, you just said that you needed to do research in the area and could you stay with me."

"I had planned to tell you over dinner last night. Before the roof fell in."

Susan turned to her with a concerned look. "How are you?"

Elizabeth shrugged. "It comes and goes. But I still feel sick here." She put her hand on her chest. "I feel so vulnerable—if I could do something like that in a moment of inattention and not even know it—what else might I do? Maybe I should just be locked up in a nice quiet padded cell so I could be sure of not hurting anybody."

Susan leaned over and hugged her. "What you need is a diversion. Let's throw our Sunday dinner in a hamper and make it a picnic. We might as well invite Tommy and those dogs of his, and while they run you can spend all afternoon telling me about your project."

"You are a glutton for punishment. I just might do that. Then you'd ask the judge to lock me up, too."

"Oh, don't worry. I said you can spend all afternoon talking. I didn't say I'd spend all afternoon listening. I was raised on the good old-fashioned virtues—high on the list of which is a Sunday afternoon nap."

Julia—sister to Susan, wife to Stuart, mother to Tommy, housemother to the dachshunds and heavily pregnant—was delighted to send her son out for the afternoon. Especially since the invitation included the floppy-eared Jesse and Joey.

So a short time later the small menagerie bounced in the back seat of Susan's car as they drove along a narrow, winding, country lane with colored leaves drifting down on them. Pumpkins decorated the doorstep of every farmhouse, and almost every lawn ended with a roadside stand selling apples, pumpkins, squash or homemade jams.

"I've been here less than twenty-four hours, and already I can understand why you chose to set up your law practice in such a far-off corner of the world."

Susan smiled. "Family ties aside, there's an unspoiled peace here that's restful all the way down to your roots. Vermonters aren't impressed with high-tech races. To them change and progress aren't synonyms. I suppose it's something elemental to do with hard winters and rocky farm land, as well as isolated geography. Anyway, after the frenzy of law school and two years of big-city excitement clerking in Washington, D. C., I'm plenty glad to settle into a small town practice."

"And come back to your childhood sweetheart?"

"Well, that's another story." Susan ran one hand through her smooth blonde hair as if she were thinking. "Ah, here we are." She pulled up beside a low stone wall bordering an apple orchard. Tommy almost managed to wait until the car had come to a full stop before he and his four-legged companions tumbled from the back seat, rounded the end of the stone wall and streaked off down the hillside.

Elizabeth and Susan followed at a slightly more sedate pace. They spread the picnic cloth and travel rugs on the grass at the edge of the orchard, and Elizabeth flopped down on the nearest blanket, leaning her back against the rough, sun-warmed stone wall and stretching her legs full length in front of her. "Oh, can you believe that smell?" The apples had been harvested, but their rich aroma still hung in the air to mingle with the spicy scent of autumn. "And the sky—such a clear, bright blue." Susan had been right—it was easy enough to forget dark clouds hanging over one's head in these surroundings. "Who would have thought when we met three years ago at that family reunion in Illinois that we'd be picnicking together in an apple orchard now?"

Susan took a bean salad out of the hamper and set it on the plaid picnic cloth. "I've never worked it out whether we're actually related or not. Have you?"

"I think it's one of those 'my uncle married your aunt' things. But we're kindred spirits. That's what counts."

"And Tommy is convinced you're his aunt."

"I'd be honored to be his aunt. My sister Tori is so determined to become a world-class costume designer there's little chance of my becoming a real auntie."

"Good. Good you don't mind Tommy, that is. I want to have him with me as much as possible until Julia has her baby. It's been seven years between pregnancies, and this one's really hard for her, so I like to give her all the time to rest I can."

Elizabeth surveyed the landscape as Sue spoke. A stately red brick house on the gentle green hillside above and to the left of the orchard caught her eye. The elliptical fanlight over the door sparkled in the sunlight. "What wonderful architecture. It's pure Federalist, isn't it? Is it really eighteenth century?"

Susan looked up from her unpacking. "I guess so. Architecture isn't really my line, but it's been featured in some magazines as being a very good example of whatever it is. It's really more of a Massachusetts style than Vermont—which probably indicates that the family moved here from Boston and brought their ideas with them."

"Do you know who lives there?"

"Sure. That's the Spenser family home—been handed down through I don't know how many generations. You know—the man you saw in church this morning."

Indeed, Elizabeth did know. "Well, so much for my hopes of getting an interview there. I can hardly picture myself banging down that stately door on some kind of long-shot search for first-hand information."

"Speaking of that, now that we have a quiet moment before Tommy and the terrors return, fill me in on your project."

"Love to, but it'll take me more than a moment once I get going," Elizabeth warned as she scrabbled in the depths of the large canvas bag she wore slung over her shoulder, perpetually carrying no fewer than three books. "My security blankets." She held up two paperback novels and a hardbound history. "You never know when there'll be a bridge out and you'll have to wait. Being able to read keeps the blood pressure under control."

She dug deeper. "Ah, here they are. I brought these to show you how it all started." She started to hand two slightly rumpled Xeroxed copies of letters to her companion, then hesitated. Would they make sense to Susan? Or just sound soppy? After all, even though they were practically neighbors Sue hadn't read Elswyth Thane's novels—or hardly any novels at all; she'd had her nose stuck in law books for years. And, for all that the women shared so many preferences, Susan wasn't the ardent Anglophile that Elizabeth was.

She started to snatch the letters back. "Never mind. Bad idea."

But it was too late; Susan had taken the top page and was already reading. "This was written more than five years ago?"

Elizabeth nodded. "Right. I'd just finished my junior year. Starry-eyed, very intellectual, bursting with literary theories—all of which Miss Thane listened to very kindly."

"You're implying that you've changed?"

"Two years of lecturing freshmen can take the stars out of your eyes fast. That's why I'm so anxious to get my Ph.D. and move to upper-division seminars. But really," she reached out her hand again, "you don't have to read all that..."

Susan shifted to move the paper out of Elizabeth's reach. "No, this is amazing. I never knew you felt like this. Just from reading a *novel*?"

Elizabeth nodded and withdrew her hand. She was into it now. But she dreaded her friend's derision. Susan let the first sheet fall, and Elizabeth picked it up, remembering just how she had felt as she typed the words in her small dorm room:

Dear Miss Thane,

I am having a dreadful time reading England Was an Island Once—I keep crying. I thought you would like to know that 40 years later your experiences are still alive and meaningful. Don't mourn the unwritten pages on Glastonbury. "Holiest Earth in England" says it all. I have read all your fiction (except Bound to Happen, which our interlibrary loan service has as yet failed to locate).

Whenever a book comes in I just throw up my hands and bury myself with it, no use trying to put it down.

The Lost General, Riders of the Wind, and From This Day Forward are my favorites. But I love them all. You reach an emotional depth I have encountered nowhere else. But I have learned not to trust you—it took me days to forgive you for Cabot's death. I'm not sure I've forgiven you yet. How did you have the courage?

I long to be able to visit with you. I would ask you about the Kipling influences on your writing (Riders on the Wind —The Man Who Would Be King? From This Day Forward

—<u>The Light That Failed</u>?) And, of course, <u>Tryst</u> and dear
<u>Puck</u>. I ran right out and unearthed the Kipling. I would
tell you that you have done more to heighten (or do I mean
deepen?) my love of England than I can ever thank you
enough for...

Thank you, Elswyth Thane.

Sincerely,
Elizabeth Allerton

Elizabeth let the page flutter to the blanket. Had she really written
that? Had she ever been so gushy? And still the memory made her
eyes sting. All those years longing to visit in person. And now it
was too late.

She held her breath for Sue's reaction. But her friend didn't
laugh. "She must have loved getting that!"

Still shy about having shared her inmost emotions, Elizabeth
didn't meet Susan's gaze. "I'd been wanting to write to her
through all the months that I was having a love affair with her
books, but I didn't know what I wanted to say until I read *England
Was an Island Once*; then it just spilled out."

But Sue's interest wasn't on her emotions; it was on the
process. "How did you get her address?"

"I looked her up in *Contemporary Authors*, then called the
Wilmington Chamber of Commerce for her address."

"And they gave it to you. Just like that?"

"They did. So I sent my letter, then held my breath for days,
hoping I might get some sort of acknowledgment. Then, just in
time to prevent my turning blue, I got that lovely reply."

Susan turned to the second letter and read it out loud to the
accompaniment of bees buzzing around fallen apples, birds

chirping in the trees, and the babbling of a stream at the bottom of the orchard.

Elswyth Thane Beebe
Wilmington, Vermont 05363
July 18, 1979

Dear Miss Allerton —

I have seldom loved a letter about my books more than I love yours! And I am afraid I would cry too, if I read England Was an Island Once again. I was fortunate in that few of my dearest friends there died in the war, but time has robbed me of some of them since, and I could never go back there now; it would break my heart! Another letter reminded me of something in This Was Tomorrow the other day, and I started to look that part of it up again, and that almost made me cry! I can still see that drear little school where we fitted the gas-masks, and the headlights of cars turned on at midnight so they could see to go on digging trenches in the parks all night—and there were funny things too, that you couldn't write about—like the time all the sirens went off down around Cheltenham where I was, and nothing happened, and the next morning a rather shame-faced BBC news man reported that a large green caterpillar had crawled into the mechanism somehow and caused a "short" that set everything off, and its incinerated body was found next day at the scene of the crime!

I am afraid Bound to Happen is gone forever—there is nothing so gone as a book that has been let to go out of print, and I hadn't enough sense at the time to buy a dozen

19

extra copies myself! They are supposed to give the author a chance to acquire a dozen of the last copies, but they never remember to tell you in time! Then everything went into paperback, with wild modern cover-drawings, and they sold out before I could gather in some extras, and the paperback market is so crowded now they never reprint!

I should tell you, however, that because I never passed my scripts around before they were in print, nor asked advice, nor wanted any, my husband had never seen Ever After till the printer's typescript was ready to go. He always sat down and read it straight through, and when I gave him Ever After he was sitting in the next room while I worked at my desk nearby, and suddenly this reproachful voice floated out to me—"You've killed Cabot!" It was the only way to bring Bracken to his feet, I thought.

Kipling was a darling, and I think he is in England Was—or maybe it was—yes, it was! I always have to count up on my fingers now, to know which of some 32 books has what in it. Did you find Reluctant Farmer, which has been reprinted as The Strength of the Hills—not my idea to change the title! I'm not sure he isn't somewhere in that, too, as he came to Bermuda when we were there and we all lunched at Government House, and it was pretty memorable. His wife was exceedingly tiresome. And have you found my Mount Vernon books, of which I am really proudest, as that was a unique experience in many ways— living inside the gates for weeks, going back again and again—it grows on you and holds you fast, just as it did Washington. Have you tried the nonfiction?

Some of that is fun too—at least, it was fun for me.

Do write again. I am permanently in Vermont now, but I love to get mail! Who are you, to know so well what I <u>meant</u>? And what do you do in Idaho?!

Sincerely,
Elswyth Thane Beebe

An injury to my right hand has spoiled my signature, I hope not forever!

"So that's how it all began?" Sue shook her head as she looked up from the last lines of the letter.

"Yes, unless you start counting from the day I stumbled across a copy of *Yankee Stranger* that had been mis-shelved at the library. But her line 'Who are you, to know so well what I *meant*?' is one I will carry in my heart forever."

"I can see that. She sounds like an amazing person."

"I think she was. I only hope I can do her justice in my dissertation. I feel so awful that I didn't get here in time to meet her in person. She just died in July, you know."

The women sat in silence, and a few yellow-brown leaves drifted down on them. At last Susan spoke. "So, what's the focus of your dissertation?"

"The committee has accepted my proposal to put our correspondence in publishable form, but it has to be shored up with tons of original research on her personal background—can't just be a compilation of old letters."

"Sounds like a fascinating project. Did she have any family?"

"No, so I have to rely on interviews with friends, neighbors— that sort of thing."

"But how…" The peaceful conversation was interrupted abruptly by a little boy's shrieks, frantic doggie barks and splashing water from the wooded brook at the bottom of the hill.

Both women jumped to their feet, shouting, "We're coming, Tommy!"

"I didn't think about water," Sue gasped as she raced toward the sounds of alarm. "If anything happens to Tommy Julia'll kill me. If I don't kill myself first."

Before they reached the bottom of the hill an ominous silence replaced the shouts. "No!" Sue cried.

"We can't be too late." Fearing what she would find, Elizabeth slacked her pace slightly. She had just put on a new burst of speed when the bushes before her parted and Richard Spenser stood there bearing a drenched and dripping Tommy under his right arm while two wet dachshunds fell about turning somersaults over their rescuer's feet.

The embarrassed-looking youngster struggled to get to his feet.

"Tommy!" Sue rushed to her nephew with open arms. After a soggy embrace she ushered him toward the sun-warmed picnic blankets, leaving Elizabeth to thank the hero of the hour.

He regarded her with a thunderous glare and opened his mouth to deliver what she was sure would be a lecture on dereliction of duty.

She rushed into her apology breathlessly, "Thank you so much, Mr. Spenser. I'm afraid we were rather negligent—we got involved in conversation and…"

The threatening look changed to confusion. "You know my name?"

"Yes, I saw you in church this morning." Elizabeth held out her hand and introduced herself. "Sue and I are really so grateful. I am so sorry about the soaking you took." She glanced at his still-dripping pants. "Won't you join us in our picnic to make reparations?"

"I'll dry just fine. No reparations are necessary." He started to turn away.

Elizabeth couldn't let him go. No matter how inauspicious the circumstances, she might not get another chance to talk to him. "Wait. Er—Please. Tommy and Sue will want to thank you properly, too." She was afraid she sounded rather desperate, but at least he inclined his head slightly and followed her when she turned.

By the time they reached the picnic group Tommy was happily playing Indian on the warpath with the blanket clutched around his shoulders while Jessie and Joey tumbled behind.

Susan introduced herself and repeated Elizabeth's gratitude. "Please, won't you join us?" She held out a plate of roast beef sandwiches on fresh whole wheat bread. "The beef's still warm from the roasting pan."

At that their guest succumbed and took a seat on one of the travel rugs just as Tommy raced back. Elizabeth was grateful for the brief hassle that ensued while Sue put the dogs in the car to keep them out of the food, as it covered the awkwardness she felt in this man's presence. Tommy, however, remembered his manners and thanked his rescuer with a demeanor that would have gratified his mother, then went on to describe in considerable detail the frog he had been chasing that had led him to fall headlong into the stream.

By the time Tommy licked the last of the chocolate frosting from the brownies off his fingers he was ready to take off again. "Just a minute, young man." Susan pushed herself to her feet. "Aunt Susan will chaperone you this time. We've had more than enough excitement for today."

Now was Elizabeth's chance for her interview. But how to jump in? She was struggling to form her first question when a breeze rose, blowing a swirl of leaves down on them. It made her glance at her companion. And what she saw there took her breath away. His rugged features bore a look that that she could only interpret as pain. Until she blinked and her second look revealed an air of cruelty.

Then the light shifted, and she realized it must have been nothing more than the play of shadows.

Still, the moment left her shaken. She rushed into conversation, blurting out the first thing that came to her mind. "I hope we're not trespassing on your property?"

He shrugged. "I'm not sure where the boundaries are, but we've never had any trouble with picnickers or hikers, so we don't worry about it much. School boys stealing Macs is about all."

"Macs?"

"Mackintosh apples." He inclined his head toward the orchard. "I suppose one of the stone walls marks the property lines, but I've never bothered to find out which one."

"I never see a stone wall without thinking of Robert Frost," Elizabeth mused.

"'Something there is that doesn't love a wall...'" As Richard quoted he leaned back on his elbows and stretched out his extraordinary length.

Elizabeth relaxed as his former harshness disappeared. "'...We do not need the wall; He is all pine and I am apple-orchard,'" she topped his quotation.

Her companion accepted the challenge. "'My apple trees will never get across and eat the cones under his pines, I tell him.'"

She thought for a moment, then smiled as she recalled the next line. "'He only says, "Good fences make good neighbors."' Your turn."

Richard nodded. "'*Why* do they make good neighbors? Isn't it where there are cows? But there are no cows.'"

Elizabeth was ready for him. "'Before I built a wall I'd ask to know what I was walling in or walling out...'"

Richard thought for a moment, then shook his head. "You won. It's something about elves, but I can't get it."

"I'm afraid it's really a tie," Elizabeth admitted. "It ends with the unimaginative neighbor saying again, 'Good fences make good neighbors.' But I've forgotten what goes in between too."

"That's very honest of you to confess."

"Yes. And I don't cheat at solitaire, either."

"Now that's positively noble." He got to his feet and broke a small branch of orange and red leaves from a nearby tree. "Prize for the victor."

She had the impression she held a flaming torch when he placed it in her hand.

"I take it you're a house guest of our new village attorney. Is this a pleasure trip?"

Ah, perfect. Here was her opportunity to get to her purpose. "Well, it's pleasurable at the moment, but I'm here to do research —" Further explanations were cut short as twin missiles of squirming brown dog hair and long, cold black noses landed themselves in Elizabeth's lap. And that was as far as Elizabeth got on her interview.

All the way home her mind turned a carousel of images from the afternoon: The light breeze showering them with leaves; the darkness of Richard's features; the delight of shared quotations; the coldness he emanated at times. And above all, her sense of failure as she berated herself for the lost opportunity.

What was the matter with her? She was hardly a blushing maiden who became tongue-tied in the presence of a single male. She was normally one who would rush into any situation and take charge.

The carousel turned again, and even her thoughts were struck wordless as she remembered the severity of his look. Once more she was left berating herself for a lost opportunity.

CHAPTER 3

The next morning the remembrance of her turning images was made even heavier by the weight in Elizabeth's chest. "Whoever said things would look better in the morning never spent a night like that one." She glared at her mug of coffee and pushed her hair back with unsteady hands.

"Are you worrying about this accident charge again? I thought we laid that specter to rest yesterday."

"I guess we forgot to tell my subconscious. I've got a headache, backache and upset stomach that makes flu look like a garden of delights."

"For a traffic ticket?"

Elizabeth shook her head. "This is much more serious. It's practically hit and run. I've never been hauled in front of a judge before."

"Maybe it is flu?"

"No such luck. Nerves. I think I'll just plead guilty. I don't want a hassle."

"You'll do no such thing. You're not to plead guilty if you aren't guilty. And I've already explained to you..."

"I know, I know. But I just want to get it over with. Of all things I hate a fuss the most."

Sue took the coffee cup out of Elizabeth's hand and dumped it in the sink.

"What are you doing?"

"Replacing it with Ovaltine. If there's anything you don't need at the moment it's a shot of caffeine in your nervous system."

"Are all lawyers nurses, too?"

"Yeah, and psychiatrists. At least it helps." A minute later she stuck a hot mug of Ovaltine in Elizabeth's hand and went into her room to finish dressing. "Elizabeth, did you borrow my—? Oh, never mind. Here it is."

"Whatever it is, I'm sure I did it. I'll plead guilty to anything." It was meant as a joke, but the solemn timbre in her voice showed she wasn't laughing.

Susan stuck her head back around the corner. "I just can't believe you're taking this so hard. It's not a federal offense."

"Maybe not, but having to go to court makes me feel like a criminal."

Sue came out and put her arm around her friend. "If anyone ever had any doubts, the fact that you're so upset over this is proof you're not a hardened criminal." She picked up her briefcase. "You'll be all right while I'm at the office?"

"Of course. If you trust me to borrow your car again I might run over to Wilmington this afternoon, but I've got to set up my files and organize some notes this morning—either way, I'll stay out of parking lots."

"And jails." Sue left with a wave.

As it turned out, Elizabeth became so engrossed marking circles on a large map of Vermont to correspond with items her notes told her she wanted to see, and then marking file folders with matching numbers, that the jaunt to Wilmington would have to wait another day—or rather, two days, since her court appearance would be tomorrow.

As soon as she had her files numbered she decided she needed to reread Elswyth Thane's autobiography, *Reluctant Farmer*, which she had in the 1950 original. That was just one of the many things she had meant to do before leaving home but hadn't gotten around to.

Soon the time simply fell away as she became absorbed in the story of the New York author and her world-famous naturalist husband who bought and remodeled a ramshackle farm (except "We couldn't rightly call it a farm because we had no animals") in southern Vermont. Only once did the vague unrest that "something was wrong" settle over Elizabeth. She set her book aside and thought a moment until she came back to the reality of the court appearance facing her the next day. *Susan will take care of it*, she told herself firmly and returned to her work.

More curiously, though, her concentration was interrupted several times by a strange feeling that almost seemed like happiness. The first time she merely passed it off as delight at actually being in Vermont and at last able to dig into her research. But that didn't seem a totally satisfactory answer, so she returned to Thane's description of the farm she and her husband bought: "old sugar and wood roads, much overgrown, ran up the hill and branched out and lost themselves in the neglected woods..."

The next tingle of elation came accompanied with a vision of piercing eyes and a memory of drifting autumn leaves with a sharp scent of overripe apples. "Enough!" She said out loud and turned to dig in her purse. She was certain she had a picture of Gerald in here somewhere. Dear, stalwart Gerald. She pulled the plastic-encased photo from her bag and propped it against a stack of books on the table that served as her desk. There now. That would keep her grounded.

She forced her mind back to her book: "Canned food was now rationed, which made stocking up the pantry impossible. Nobody in the family drove a car, so we didn't own one, relying on the village taxi service for meeting trains and doing errands..."

An hour or so later Sue came in, tossed her jacket in one chair and plopped herself into another. "I stopped by the courthouse and got a copy of the accident report, but I haven't had time to look at it." She pulled a paper out of her briefcase and scanned the sheet.

Elizabeth held her breath. She had been able to bury herself in her work sufficiently to put the specter of her court appearance out of her mind for most of the day. Now it returned with its full grip. A gasp from Susan chilled Elizabeth and stopped her breath. "I don't believe it!" Sue stared at the document, as if reading it again could change the words written there.

"Tell me." Elizabeth's voice was so tight she could hardly get the words out.

"The complaining witness." She held the paper out for Elizabeth to see the signature at the bottom of the page.

Elizabeth looked. And blinked. And looked again. It couldn't be. But it was. Richard Cabot Bracken Spenser was the complaining witness.

CHAPTER 4

*B*y the next morning, after another restless night, Elizabeth was still no closer to coming to terms with the fact that Richard Spenser was the "concerned citizen" who had blown the whistle on her. Of course, he wouldn't have any idea it was she since it was unlikely he had had more than a glimpse of the offending driver—of her, that was. She paced the small kitchen while Susan drank her coffee. "I'm sure he was just doing the good citizenship bit and all that. And I don't wish him ill or anything. But if he ever does anything stupid I just hope it's highly visible."

The phone interrupted her monologue, and Sue went to the other room to answer it as Elizabeth continued, "But it's so hard to understand. He just doesn't seem the type to be hanging around grocery store parking lots stirring up trouble..."

Realizing her listener had left the room, Elizabeth sank into silence. In the quiet she had to admit what her words had been walling out—that it wasn't her reaction to Richard's being the complaining witness that mattered most. Her real worry was what he would think of her when he learned she was the errant driver. The thought of appearing careless or stupid in his penetrating eyes was more than she could bear.

She sank into a chair and dropped her head into her hands. She only looked up when Sue spoke her name. "Elizabeth, I'm sorry, but that was Maxwell Barton on the phone. He's a Boston attorney, and I'm working with him for a client of his who moved to Vermont. Anyway, he's coming in this morning, and I have to meet with him."

Elizabeth gulped. "But the hearing..."

"I know. But it's only a pretrial. All you have to do is stand up when the clerk calls your name; say 'Not guilty,' when they ask you how you plead; and say, 'Court,' when the judge asks if you want a court or jury trial."

"You're sure that's all? No fingerprinting or third-degreeing or swearing on the Bible or anything like that?"

"Absolutely nothing like that."

"And if they lock me up you'll come get me?"

"I sure will. Now you can cope, can't you? I'm so sorry about this. Maybe someone else from our office could go with you?"

"No, no. I'll be fine." But she didn't sound the least bit confident to her own ears.

When Sue left for the office Elizabeth thought briefly of trying to ring Gerald. How comforting his imperturbable voice would be. She looked at her watch and counted two hours back to Mountain Time. No, Gerald wouldn't even be awake yet. Or he might be in the shower—but too early either way. She picked up a book but made no progress on her reading.

The sound of the ringing phone gave her a start. She almost didn't answer it. Anyone who needed to reach Susan could call her office. But even taking a message for her friend would be better than sitting here moping. She lifted the receiver. "Gerald! What a surprise. I didn't think you'd be up yet."

"Hey, what is this? I just finished a two mile run."

She shook her head. "I should have known."

"Right. I'm not the slug-a-bed some people I know like to be."

She didn't reply.

"I thought that as your department head I should find out how your research is coming along."

"Well, I'm just getting settled in..." She told him about organizing her files, planning her sites on a map, "and I've made contact with a possible subject for an interview."

Gerald was hearty in his encouragement, especially about the interview subject. "We're all missing you around here, you know." In spite of the fact that they had been an item for almost two years now, that was as personal as he was likely to get.

She thanked him for calling and hung up more depressed than she had been earlier, but she forced herself to return to her work. By noon apprehension and adrenaline combined to make any more work impossible, however, so with a sigh she threw her pen down and went to her room to put on her most sedate dress—a muted glen plaid, which she usually brightened with a silk scarf. The scarf seemed inappropriate today, though. *Like wearing red to a funeral*. She tossed the offending item on her dresser.

Her face hot with nerves, Elizabeth walked to the picturesque courthouse on the green—right across from the church where she had first seen Richard Spenser. But unfortunately, *not* where he had first seen her.

Elizabeth never arrived any place early. It was almost a matter of principle, because it wasted time. But today she arrived nearly thirty minutes early. She found her name posted on the list of cases set for hearing. Taking a deep breath, she yanked on the door handle and walked into the courtroom. The room was nearly empty. The black-robed judge looked over his glasses severely. "The courtroom is closed."

Feeling like an idiot, she backed out and heard the clerk lock the door behind her. So much for any idea of making a good initial impression. She paced the hall beyond the door until an attorney wielding a briefcase walked out followed closely by a uniformed officer. "May I go in now?" Her voice came out in a tone that none of her students would ever credit as having been hers. She was always the one so completely in control—known for running classroom, committees, her life like a very tight ship and no nonsense about it.

A few others entered the room behind her. She took a seat just in time to hear the judge announce that court would be in recess for ten minutes. As she stood for the black-robed figure to exit, she noted that he looked grim. Was he what they called a hanging judge? There were other people in the room, but Elizabeth didn't look to the right or to the left. She didn't want to be impaled on the penetrating gaze of Richard Cabot Bracken Spenser. Susan had assured her nothing dramatic would happen—no witnesses would be called. But she was taking no chances.

"All rise." Everyone stood at the bailiff's instruction. *Behold the Lord High Executioner.* Elizabeth grimaced.

All in the courtroom sat and the judge advised the defendants of their rights: Presumption of innocence, right to counsel, right to bail, right to subpoena witnesses in their behalf, right to appeal... Then he read a list of five names.

"Present." When her name was called Elizabeth replied in a voice that couldn't have been her own.

There were two cases before hers. The first woman, only a few years younger than Elizabeth, pleaded guilty but said she'd like to offer an explanation.

"I'm listening." He didn't sound like a hanging judge.

Elizabeth couldn't hear the woman, whom she thought of as the prisoner, but the judge replied, "Well, you're probably right to some extent. But you didn't fulfill your responsibility, did you? What have you learned from this experience?"

Elizabeth recalled Susan saying it was important that the smallest offense be dealt with fairly and clearly, because the magistrate court is the level at which most people have their experience with justice. They have to see that the system works. It seemed to be working for these people. The judge set a fine that the woman seemed to accept as reasonable.

A teenage boy was next. "Are your parents here?" The judge asked.

"My dad is."

Dad, obviously just in from the woods, in a red-and-gray plaid flannel shirt, his long hair held neatly back in a band, stood by his son. "I hope you appreciate your dad being here with you. I'm sure he'd rather be somewhere else right now."

Dad gave a slight nod. The boy explained he was riding his motorcycle on the street, because he just got it fixed and was testing it.

"Well, you can't test it on a public road until you're old enough to get a driver's license. Do you understand?"

"Yes, sir."

"Okay. I'm going to suspend the fine this time, but don't let it happen again."

"Thank you, sir!" The boy stepped down. It was Elizabeth's turn.

"Elizabeth Allerton." She stepped forward when the judge called her name. "Good afternoon."

She tried to say, "Hello," but it stuck in her throat, and no sound came out. Nothing could have made her feel like more of an idiot than being unable to return a simple greeting.

"You are charged with leaving the scene of an accident. Do you understand the charge?"

Already it was more complicated than Susan had said it would be. "I understand that in order to plead guilty I need to have realized at the time that an accident occurred?" It should have been a statement, but it came out unsteady.

"Not necessarily." The judge's reply threw her. Now she felt lost. The judge said something incomprehensible about mitigating circumstances that just added to her confusion.

"Well, I came in planning to plead not guilty..."

"Then that's what you'd better do."

"Okay." Her reply was inaudible.

"Not guilty?" The judge looked over the top of his horn-rimmed glasses.

She wanted to yell, "I don't know!" But instead she merely nodded.

"Court trial?"

Again she nodded.

The judge made some marks on a form in front of him. "Take this to the clerk, and she'll set it for trial."

Her stomach knotting so tightly she could hardly move, Elizabeth walked across the old oak floor, worn smooth by generations of feet. She wondered if all those feet had borne knees trembling as badly as hers.

The female clerk in the bright purple slacks that were the fashion of the moment took Elizabeth's citation and handed her a trial date notice. Three more days of waiting.

CHAPTER 5

"*T*his is impossible!" Elizabeth cried to the chintz-patterned wallpaper the next evening. "I came here to work, and so far I've accomplished nothing. I've been so hung up on this stupid trial business I can't concentrate on anything." The hearing had been such a simple thing. It didn't take half an hour. And yet it had been worse to her than she could have imagined. And now she had a real trial coming up.

"Phone for you," Sue's voice came from the next room.

Elizabeth frowned. Who could it be? Surely it wouldn't be Gerald again. He would never ring her two days in a row—didn't approve of "living in one another's pockets," as he put it. She had also given Sue's number to Tori, of course. Oh, no. Was something wrong with her baby sister? Since their parents' death Elizabeth had been more a mother than a sister to her. "Hello. Tori? Is anything wrong?"

"Sorry, were you expecting a call?"

The deep male voice with its slight New England accent chilled her. "Richard." Calling about the trial? Her impulse was to slam the phone down.

"I'm afraid I caught you at a bad time." She was silent, and he

37

hesitated as if deciding whether or not to end the call. "Perhaps this wasn't such a good idea, but the humanities department at Blessington College is offering a soiree in a Victorian parlour tomorrow evening. High tea with music and diversions—whatever that means. I thought it might be a good introduction to the area."

She was still silent.

"And a return on your picnic."

"It was really Susan's picnic."

"Yes, of course, Susan is included, too."

This was crazy. He was asking her—them—to some party thing on the evening before the trial?

"I can see I called at a bad time." His voice became very formal. "Perhaps some other time."

Elizabeth opened her mouth to agree when she realized this was her last chance. If she were ever to talk to Richard Cabot Bracken Spenser about his connection with Elswyth Thane it had to be before the trial. Before he knew she was the driver of that white car. When he knew, he wouldn't be inviting her to an entertainment in a Victorian parlour. Or anywhere else—except maybe sixty days in the county jail. "Um, no. That's all right. I'll check with Susan. I expect she's free."

"Good." He sounded hesitant after her ungracious reply but ploughed ahead. "I'll pick you up at six o'clock, if that's convenient."

Elizabeth agreed and replaced the phone with numb fingers. Then the insanity of what she had done hit her. She reached for the phone to call him back, but realized she didn't have his number. Predictably the Newfane phone book was no help. The Spensers were unlisted.

"Sue," she wailed.

Susan appeared at the doorway in record time. "What? What's wrong?"

"I've just done the dumbest thing. I've accepted an invitation for us to go to some event at some college. With Richard Spenser."

Susan looked as surprised as Elizabeth felt. "Good grief. Why? When?"

"So I could interview him. Tomorrow evening."

Susan shook her head. "Sorry. Bar Association meeting in Brattleboro."

Elizabeth groaned. "Oh, I knew I should have hung up on him." She thought fleetingly of having Susan meet him at the door and explain that Elizabeth had just come down with violent flu. But Susan would probably be on her way to her meeting. And he would see her the next day in court.

Court. She couldn't begin to imagine how angry he would be when he realized she had used him—accepted his invitation to get the information she needed. Or worse, might he think she had done it to try to influence his testimony? Would he color his story for the judge all the darker now?

But she had agreed. It seemed that for better or for worse—and she was certain it would be much worse—Elizabeth was stuck.

Elizabeth spent the next day buried in her research—as much to keep her mind off the evening before her as to make progress on her dissertation. When the time came to get ready she decided there was nothing for it but to make the best job of it she could. At least she had brought her ecru Victorian-style blouse with her so she could blend in with the theme. She even had her grandmother's cameo brooch to pin at the throat. Fortunately she hadn't had time to get her thick, dark hair cut before her trip, as wild as it tended to be in New England's more humid climate. It was just long enough to arrange in a turn-of-the-century upsweep.

Sue stuck her head in Elizabeth's door to say good-bye before leaving for her meeting. "Oh, you look great."

"Thanks. I'll have to admit that if the prisoner is to be granted a last meal I can't think of anything I'd rather have than a Victorian high tea."

Sue shook her head at her, but the doorbell rang before she could reply. Elizabeth heard Susan greet Richard and explain that she wouldn't be able to join them. A bang of the door told Elizabeth she could no longer cower in her room. For one wild moment she thought of charging into the front room and confronting Richard with his meddling. As she turned to pick up her stole, however, she glanced at the dissertation outline on her desk. The sight brought a return to sanity and gave her a burst of energy that carried her forward.

"Good evening." They spoke in unison—she coldly and he with an almost Victorian formality that matched his dark three-piece suit and white shirt.

Once settled in the car Elizabeth apologized for Susan being unable to join them, and an uneasy quiet filled the space until the white buildings of Newfane Common were well behind them and they were swallowed in a canopy of red and orange leaves overarching the road. Looking for a conversation opener that could lead to her subject, Elizabeth said, "Do you enjoy the publishing business?"

"There are parts I like—working with the authors. I don't like the business end. I never planned to take that on, but then..." He paused.

"What happened?"

He shrugged. "Life. No, really death. Dad was grooming my older brother James to step into his shoes. Then James was killed in a plane wreck. I was doing an internship with *Caudex* while I finished my doctorate."

"*Caudex.*" Latin for "bound book," she translated. "That's your publishing house?" She was impressed. It was well known—a small house with a big reputation for publishing literary works.

He nodded. "Dad just couldn't seem to get a grip after James was gone, and Drew, my younger brother, is in med school. So that left me to carry on."

She blinked at the finality of his words. Not so much the words themselves, but the flat, lifeless tone with which he spoke them. As if his life were over.

"So what did you want to do?"

He gave her a sidelong glance with the shadow of a grin that transformed his harsh features. "What you're doing."

"You wanted to be a college professor?" She was flabbergasted that her quiet, mundane world held attraction for this sophisticated man. But then, why not? It was a perfectly legitimate choice. "And you couldn't do that and keep the publishing house open? It seems ideal—you'd never have to worry about getting stuck in the 'publish or perish' syndrome."

"*Caudex* would hardly be interested in publishing my work on Elizabethan figurative language in 'The Faerie Queen.' Even if I had finished it."

Edmund Spenser, impressive. She nodded. "Who else do you like?"

"The usual." This time his grin was full blown. Apparently he had put darker memories behind him. At least for now. "Shakespeare, Milton, Alexander Pope, Jane Austen, Dickens…"

"No Americans?"

"The New England poets, of course: Bryant, Emerson, Thoreau—no surprise there." He glanced over at her. "But you're the English teacher. Who are your favorites?"

Wonderful, here was her opening to get him talking about Elswyth Thane. Why hadn't she brought a notebook with her? "Thank you for asking. Actually, I've been longing to ask—" but just at that moment they turned into the rolling, tree-lined campus of Blessington College and pulled up in front of the old President's House, where the event was to be held. A valet, obviously a Blessington student, dressed in livery a bit too snug for him, opened Elizabeth's door and helped her out of the car.

The house was a large Victorian structure surrounded by pine and maple trees and banks of bright red bushes. A butler opened the wide front door with a flourish. Richard signed the guest book while a white-capped maid took Elizabeth's stole before the waiting quartet of costumed singers gave them a musical greeting from the stairway curving upward to their left. "Pleasure awaits us —an evening of gladness. / May love and joy come to all who are here." A charming musical entrance, but Elizabeth doubted such a felicitous outcome as she allowed Richard to escort her to their seats at a small, round table draped with white linen.

A faculty member, playing the part of an early president of the college, welcomed them all to his home on this October evening in 1901 and set the scene by referring to a few notes of current events, such as the publication of some new poems by "that farmer over New Hampshire way named Robert Frost" and President Teddy Roosevelt's new treaty with Britain which would allow us to build a canal across Central America. "Although those fellows down in Washington haven't decided whether it should cut across Panama or Nicaragua yet. And, just this morning I read another article about that rich Mr. Carnegie, who's giving all his money to set up public libraries. Free libraries—open to all. Now that's quite an idea."

The ensemble sang again as little dishes of raspberry ice were replaced with chicken soufflé. The combination of music and dining made the evening flow, and Elizabeth found herself relaxing with the witty music hall tunes, but it made serious conversation impossible. Finally she settled for casual remarks on the entertainment. "Herman and the Hermits! I had no idea 'Henry the Eighth I am' was an old music hall number."

And she took the opportunity to study her enigmatic companion. The long face, the strong bone structure, the determined set of the mouth seemed so at odds with the air of loss he seemed to carry. Perhaps he was still grieving his brother.

The last bites of Victoria Sponge had just left Elizabeth's plate when President Fitchurst rose to thank them for coming and bid them good night, closing with the appropriate lines from Shakespeare: "Our revels now are ended... We are such stuff as dreams are made on..." Then the ensemble led them in singing "Auld Lang Syne." Elizabeth thought of her correspondence friendship with Elswyth Thane, and her throat tightened at the renewed disappointment that she would never get to meet her.

Then she thought how what could have been a friendship with Richard would be snuffed in its infancy tomorrow in that picturesque old courthouse on the village green in Newfane. All the more reason to plunge into her interview once they were back in the car. He had barely started the engine when she drew breath to begin.

But he was first. "Now, why don't you tell me about the professor that's pursuing you back home?"

Elizabeth's mouth fell open. She didn't know whether to be amused or offended. Mostly she was astounded. "How did you know? Did Sue say something?"

"No, no one told me anything. It's the obvious guess. Don't tell me. Let me tell you. He's head of the English department—or soon will be. He has a beard. And kind gray eyes that get dreamy when he's talking about Milton."

Elizabeth gasped at the accuracy. "They're brown," was all she could muster.

"And his name is Geoffrey. With a 'G.'"

"Close. Actually, it's Gerald."

"But no one ever calls him Jerry."

Elizabeth giggled at the very thought of it.

"Are you going to marry him?"

"I—" Was she? It had always been assumed—ever since she had worked as his student assistant her senior year at Rocky Mountain. Then she went off to UCLA for graduate school, and they corresponded—mostly sending one another rather snarky book reviews of their current reading. Except when that reading involved the classics, of course. And then she went back to Rocky Mountain to teach freshman English and finish up her dissertation, and… "There's nothing definite." That was the best answer she could give him.

Richard shook his head. "He let you come all the way back here without a commitment? He's not already married or anything, is he?"

"Certainly not."

"Of course not. I apologize. I just couldn't imagine any possible explanation for such irresponsible behavior."

Elizabeth frowned. "But how did you know all that?"

He smiled. "I don't know a thing. Except there's one of that type on every campus. And, of course, he'd be in love with you. I just haven't figured out yet whether you're in love with him."

Her muttered, "Neither have I" was inaudible.

Now was her chance to return the question. But why bother? After tomorrow it wouldn't matter anyway.

"You're too polite to turn the question around, aren't you?"

"You're a mind reader. It's scary."

"Not at all. Simple logic. You're either shy or just not interested."

"I'll admit to curiosity. If that can find a place in logic."

He shook his head, and a cutting edge crept into his voice. "There's nothing logical about the answer. My wife was very beautiful, and she died in a very senseless airplane crash with my older brother three years ago."

"Do you want to talk about it?"

"Oddly enough, it seems I do. Three years is quite long enough to keep something bottled up, don't you think?"

She nodded silently. If he needed to talk she was happy to oblige. It was supposed to be easier to tell something to a stranger, after all.

"James was a superb pilot and always kept the plane in topnotch order. It was a great help for living here and running a business in Philadelphia. No one seems to have any idea why Mary Ilona was with him that day. Anyway, the engines went out over the Green Mountains.

"I was in England, negotiating a contract with an author. By the time I got back it was all over—funerals and all."

"They didn't wait for you?"

"My father insisted, and her family agreed. Dad has always been very buttoned up. Especially about something like a funeral. 'Just get it over with and get on with life,' is his theory." Richard shrugged. "He might be right. I don't know."

"I can't think so. It left you without a sense of closure."

He nodded. "Drew showed me a stone in a cemetery in Boston with her name on it. Just Mary Ilona Walters Spenser and the dates. 1953–1981. That was it. I find myself still expecting her to walk into a room some evening in a rose floral dress with her platinum hair shining around her face."

Elizabeth nodded. "People who decry funerals as barbaric really don't understand how psychologically important it is to tell loved ones good-bye. Had you been married long?"

He shook his head. "Less than a year, and a great deal of that time I'd been in Europe. I'd known her for three years before that. We met at a big charity fundraiser in Boston—the sort of thing I abhor—but someone had to represent the family..." He gave himself a shake. "Well, it's all over now."

The empty finality of it all left Elizabeth silent the rest of the way home. When the door closed behind her she realized she had failed to ask him for help on her research.

CHAPTER 6

The next morning Elizabeth awoke with a heavy weight on her chest that erased all memory of the pleasant evening. It was all she could do to get dressed. She certainly couldn't eat any breakfast. She sat in front of her cooling coffee cup, a paralyzed lump.

Sue breezed into the kitchen and gave her a frowning scrutiny. "Buck up. It's not that big a deal."

"To me it is. Some people are terrified of snakes; some people are terrified of flying. I'm terrified of courtrooms."

Sue dropped a piece of bread in the toaster. "A white-knuckle defendant."

"My whole body's white. Circulation stopped hours ago."

She still felt stiff and cold a short time later when, dressed in the tailored suit Susan had recommended and with her hair battled into submission, they entered the courthouse. The moment Elizabeth had been dreading for days was upon her. Richard stood just ahead of her, leaning easily against the wall, talking to someone.

She half-turned to flee. Susan gripped her arm. "Steady on."

Something in her cousin's voice reached a distant memory.

She could have been ten years old, walking beside her tall, thin grandmother, the most stable influence in her childhood. She could almost taste a dollop of strawberry ice cream on her tongue. *Trust in Providence.* Nana would say. It was her theme, her mantra. *There is a Power whose care teaches thy way...*

Whether it was the warming thought of her nan, the comfort of the familiar lines from William Cullen Bryant, or possibly even Providence, Elizabeth felt herself relax imperceptibly. She could breathe.

And from somewhere deep inside she found the courage to walk up to Richard and wait quietly for him to conclude his conversation.

He turned with a broad smile. "Why, good morning. What a surprise. Seeing the local action with your cousin, are you?"

"Not exactly." She took a deep breath. She had to do this. "Richard, I was too much of a coward to tell you sooner, but—" She swallowed. "I'm the defendant in the accident you witnessed."

"It was your car that idiot bashed into?"

"No. I was the idiot. I said I'm the defendant. I was driving the white car."

His heavy dark brows met in a furrow over his flashing eyes. "*You* hit that car and then just drove off?"

Susan tugged at her arm. "It's time to go in." Susan steered Elizabeth toward the oak double doors. "You realize the other side will call you, don't you?"

"Mmm, the persecution."

"That's prosecution. Now, don't say anything more than you're asked. Don't volunteer anything. Do you understand?"

Understand? That was the whole problem—she didn't understand anything. It was a totally alien world. In her own sphere of academia nothing could have thrown her. But here, she felt as if she had landed on a hostile planet where different rules, even different laws of nature prevailed.

The courtroom with its northern exposure was cold and dim.

And silent. Elizabeth listened to a clock ticking—or was that her heart pounding?

Susan scribbled a note on the long yellow legal pad on her lap and handed it to Elizabeth. *Relax. They abolished capital punishment years ago.*

Elizabeth managed a weak smile, then stood as the judge entered. The gavel pounded, and everyone sat. "The court will hear the State of Vermont versus Jones Renovations."

"Rats! I was hoping he'd take us first," Susan whispered. "I'm going to go make some phone calls. I'll be back soon."

Elizabeth tried to concentrate on the proceedings in front of her as if she were watching TV, but it dragged on endlessly. The defendant, Simon Jones, had found a valuable antique in an abandoned house. When he advertised it for sale the prosecutor charged him with theft. If Simon Jones' attorney had given him the advice Sue had given her about not volunteering anything, the building contractor wasn't following it. He rambled on and on until his counsel cut him off.

Then expert witnesses were called on both sides. The lawyers argued and read long, legalese passages from heavy tomes. Elizabeth's nervous tension grew. If they didn't hurry up there wouldn't be time for her case. She *had* to get it over. Whatever the outcome, she just wanted to be done.

Finally the lawyers sat down. All was silent as the judge scrutinized the papers before him. Then he looked up. "I see no reason to detour from the letter of the law in this case. Under Section 15 of the unclaimed property statute the disputed property must be held for two years before the title can be cleared." A sharp rap of his gavel made Elizabeth jump.

There was a general shuffling as those involved in the Jones case left the courtroom and several others entered, including Susan. Elizabeth looked around the nearly empty room. Only the two lawyers and court officials, herself and Richard.

"The court will now hear the case of The State of Vermont

versus Elizabeth Allerton. Is Miss Allerton represented by counsel?"

Susan stood. "Yes, your honor."

There was a pause in the proceedings as the clerk stepped forward and handed the judge some papers. Elizabeth was certain everyone in the silent room could hear her heart pounding as the judge read.

Finally, the judge peered over the rim of his glasses. Elizabeth felt he was glowering straight at her. Had a new complaint been filed? She held her breath.

"Inasmuch as the owner of the other vehicle has failed to appear the prosecutor has moved that the case be dismissed." It took a moment for the meaning of his words to sink in. Dismissed? It was over? Just like that?

The judge turned to Susan. "Do you have any objections?"

"None, your honor," Susan replied.

The ringing of the gavel wasn't the death knell Elizabeth had expected but rather a joyous peal of release. Elizabeth felt weak with relief as Susan led her out into the suddenly glorious autumn sunshine.

"I didn't get a chance to be impressive." Susan grinned at her.

"*I* was impressed—you opened your mouth, and sounds came out. I was comatose. But why did the prosecutor move to dismiss? Wasn't that your line?"

"Yes, unusual, that. It was also unusual that the plaintiff wasn't there."

"Richard was there."

"The person who owned the car wasn't—Richard was just a witness. Odd. I think that's why the prosecutor moved to dismiss. If the judge had thrown the whole case out your insurance might have reneged on repairs."

Elizabeth took another deep breath. Then almost choked on it. Richard was waiting at the end of the hall. Blocking the exit. Elizabeth looked around for another door, but Susan approached him. "Just for the record, Mr. Spenser, my client *was* innocent."

Elizabeth found her voice. "I had no idea I hit that other car."

Richard regarded her with a straight gaze. "I believe you."

"You do? How can you without even hearing our case? I'm not even sure what I believe. It's the most confusing thing that's ever happened to me. I've been so worried…"

"That's why I believe you. You aren't the kind of person who would behave irresponsibly." He dropped his gaze. "And to tell you the truth, I'm rather worried now over how much I actually did see and how much was colored by my own fury a few weeks ago over coming out of a meeting in Philadelphia and finding my whole left rear fender crumpled. There was absolutely no way anyone could have done *that* and not known it. When I saw you nudge that other car in the parking lot I think I was reliving my own experience.

"I was raised to accept responsibility for my own actions and to do the right thing no matter what. I just can't understand someone who could run off from an accident—and yet it seemingly happens all the time."

Elizabeth nodded wordlessly.

"Oh, sorry." Richard grinned. "I got on my soapbox, didn't I? Well, you can see how strongly I feel."

Elizabeth nodded again, but suddenly the relief of being out from under the weight she had been carrying for days and the fact that she had eaten no breakfast caught up with her, and she felt her knees start to buckle. Susan grabbed her for support. "I told you you should have eaten breakfast."

Richard turned to her with concern. "I think I need to apologize for putting you through all that. Let me take you to lunch as a small reparation. There's a lovely inn just down the road in Wilmington. Both of you." He looked at Susan.

"Thanks, but I've got a conference." She jerked her head toward a man in a three-piece suit with his arms wrapped around a briefcase, apparently waiting for her. "Max Barton," she explained to Elizabeth, "the Boston attorney I told you about. I think we're fairly close to settling a case. It's always so much better for everybody if we can do that rather than go to trial."

She walked away, leaving Elizabeth and Richard alone. Elizabeth looked at the floor and bit her lip, trying to think of an excuse. Richard extended his arm. "No excuses." The shock of having him read her mind once again made her laugh.

"I've been so anxious to get to Wilmington," Elizabeth said a few minutes later in Richard's car. She snapped her seat belt on, feeling the need of something to hold her down, as she was weightless with excitement and relief. Now that she was free of the onus of the trial she could talk to Richard—really talk to him and tell him about her research. She let her imagination run rampant for a moment. Maybe he would have letters, anecdotes, manuscripts. Maybe he could give her a list of local people to interview and let her use his name as an introduction. Maybe he would even offer to help...

"Yes, it's a lovely little village," he cut into her reverie. "And I think you'll like the Heritage Inn. It's on a beautiful green hillside with woods behind it."

Elizabeth laughed. "Isn't everything around here?"

"Well, some things are down in valleys with woods around them." She loved the way his forehead crinkled when he smiled at her. "The inn is a favorite of skiers in the winter, but this time of year we should more or less have it all to ourselves."

The road from Newfane to Wilmington was a constant enchantment: Red, orange and gold maples and beeches interspersed with evergreens; then a bend in the road and a green pasture of grazing cows bordered with a stone wall; then across a brook and back again into a blaze of autumn foliage. And every fiery maple tree brought alive again the picnic with Richard—the experience she thought could never come again. And yet here he was beside her. The worst had happened. And he was still here.

The white inn with its black shutters and glassed-in sun porch welcomed them as graciously as it had been welcoming guests for almost a century and a half. Even in the autumn there was a low fire in the hearth at one end of the long dining room, and, just as they had for three quarters of a century before electric lights were invented, mirror-backed sconces lined the walls waiting to be lit as soon as twilight fell.

They crossed the well-scrubbed, wide-planked oak floor and took a seat at a white-clothed table on the porch where Elizabeth could feed on the colorful scenery as well as on the regional cuisine. Elizabeth would normally have looked for a salad or light soup for lunch, but in this setting only the traditional biscuit-topped Vermont chicken pie would do. She even succumbed to maple sugar ice cream for dessert.

"Oh, Richard, that was wonderful. Thank you so much." Elizabeth took a final sip of her tea and set the cup down with a satisfied clatter. "Now, let me get to what I've been dying to talk to you about ever since I first heard your name in church Sunday."

"My name?" He raised one eyebrow in a gesture of rather remote inquiry.

"Yes. I couldn't believe it when I heard it—it seemed just too good to be true. You see, that's what I'm here for—to do research on Elswyth Thane, and there you were, bearing two of her characters' names, so I knew—hoped, anyway—that there must be some family connection. Or at least your mother must have been a great fan and might have known her in person.

"I couldn't seem to get to it until this trial business was over, but now I'm really ready to get down and dig—"

"No!" He hit the table so hard the china rattled. His features turned to stone. "There is no way in the world I'd be a party to such a thing." His low tones were more alarming than if he had shouted at her.

CHAPTER 7

"$\mathcal{I}$ will not have her memory cheapened." He spoke each word with emphasis.

"And what makes you think my writing an academic paper would do that?" In spite of her shock at his reaction Elizabeth kept her voice as steady as she could manage.

"No one ever stops with academic papers. They snoop and scratch, and what they can't document they guess at and sensationalize. Generosity, honesty, niceness—they don't sell books. So someone must dream up a thick juicy case of *flagrante delicto* with the handyman at the very least. Although, I doubt very much that anything that mild would sell many books today. Not without alarming details."

"Not less than an hour ago you said you believed me. I'm still the lady who doesn't cheat at solitaire. Remember?" But she wrinkled her brow, puzzling. His reaction had been so alarming that for a moment she wondered if it could be possible he was covering something up—that there *was* something sordid to uncover. Then she dismissed the thought. She knew Elswyth Thane and her works far too well for that. Thane's sensible level-headedness came through in every letter. The woman reveled in her happy marriage to an older man, loved her research and would have nothing to do with writers dramatizing themselves. Besides, Elizabeth couldn't help smiling a bit... what would Gerald say if she turned in a racy story for her dissertation?

"I believed you when I thought I knew the whole truth. Before I learned what you're *really* doing here. Why did you keep it a secret so long? What were you doing? Trying to win me over so completely to your side you didn't think I'd be able to refuse you?"

This really was too much. Elizabeth barely restrained herself from hitting the table as he had done. "I told you. I was so upset over the trial I couldn't function. But even before I knew you were the complaining witness, I didn't want to gatecrash... Seem pushy..."

"Playing your cards very cleverly, huh?"

"That's unfair. I thought we could be friends now. That you might even help me. That perhaps your grandmother..."

"Listen, publishing is my world. I *know* what goes on. I've seen what's happened to memories of more illustrious careers than that of my honorary godmother." Elizabeth caught her breath. "Yes. The connection you suspected is there. Not blood, just a very, very special friendship. But as I was saying, I've seen memories besmirched posthumously by 'admiring' researchers who poked and poked until they came up with some discarded manuscript—usually unfinished so said researcher could conveniently complete it herself and then publish the whole botched affair with her name gloriously linked to the famous. I *told Mary Ilona*—" His words stopped dead.

He concluded in a tone of flat determination: "I'll do anything I can to stop this project."

As much as she would have liked to know what he told his wife, Elizabeth placed her napkin on the table with an air that matched his note of finality. "Then perhaps you would be so kind as to take me back to Susan's. I don't promise to get my suitcase out immediately, but I certainly can't pack here."

And with what he undoubtedly took for her capitulation, he escorted her to the car. Elizabeth sat as close to the door as she could without appearing ridiculous. There was nothing to be gained by telling him what an arrogant, haughty, self-important tyrant she thought he was. But she took full pleasure in rolling the terms around in her mind.

When the gratification of that exercise began to pall she asked herself, just how practical were his threats? *Could* he stop her research dead cold? Susan could undoubtedly call forth any number of freedom-of-inquiry cases, academic freedom principles and freedom of speech and press arguments, but in a real, rubber-hits-the-road sense, what could he do?

And to her unspeakable frustration, the answer was that he could do plenty. This was a small, close-knit community where his family had lived longer than the stone walls—Susan's description "came over with William the Conqueror and been conquering everything in sight ever since" came back to her with sinister application. One word from him would be enough to silence completely the already reticent Vermont tongue. She could walk around Wilmington, of course, and drive down the public road near the Beebe home, but without some kind of "open sesame" sanction for interviews and inside tours, there was very little she could accomplish. Certainly nothing of a high academic standard that would make her thesis the piece of scholarly excellence she dreamed of its being.

Richard's reaction really seemed to be all out of proportion. *Was* there something of a blockbuster nature to be found? Something he wanted for his publishing house? Nothing unsavory, she was certain of that, but something of real literary value he wanted to publish? Well, she really couldn't worry about second-guessing his motives. At the moment she had to decide what she was going to do. He would probably ask her for some kind of assurance before he left her, and Newfane was around the next curve in the road.

As they pulled up at Susan's house she knew what to do—how to test his motives and possibly break through his opposition.

If he was really looking out for Elswyth Thane's good, nothing else would bear so much weight with him as the author's own words. Richard got out of the car, came around to open Elizabeth's door and extended his hand to help her out. She stood to her full height, as nearly eye level with him as possible, and issued her challenge. "Would you be willing to read just two of her letters and try to assess what *she* might think before you resign this whole business to the closed files drawer?"

He looked slightly taken aback. "Letters? What letters?"

"Elswyth Thane's letters to me. We carried on a lengthy correspondence that I think might have meant as much to her as it did to me. I know those letters and her books had a great deal to do with promoting my love of literature and choosing to teach it as a career." He opened his mouth, but she held up a hand. "And before you accuse me of suppressing evidence, let me hasten to tell you that I had every intention of telling you all about it before you started banging on the table and shouting at me."

"I did not shout."

She ignored that. "The fact of the matter is that your godmother and I corresponded for more than a year and because of my admiration—yes—love, even—for her and her works I chose to do my dissertation on her." Elizabeth turned on her heel and walked into the house, hoping he would follow.

He did.

She went into her bedroom, rummaged briefly through the cardboard boxes that served as makeshift files, and selected the second and third letters she had received, still remembering the warm excitement she had felt when she found them in the mailbox, and the catch in her throat many of the paragraphs had produced. How this arrogant man could ever suppose she would... Never mind, she didn't want to go over that ground again.

She held the pages out to him. "You'd better sit down." She sounded purposely ungracious, taking the nearest armchair herself. She watched him closely for his reactions, the light from the window falling over his shoulder as he read:

> Elswyth Thane Beebe
> Wilmington, Vermont 05363
> July 30, 1979

Dear Miss Allerton,

It is a Saturday afternoon, and I have a house-guest, so this may be broken off any minute so that tea can go in. But we are waiting for Elmer to come back from his camp, where he went for a TV program that doesn't come in here, and we suspect that he has fallen asleep or has got company there—his buddies foregather there in hopes of finding him on weekends.

Richard looked up at the end of the first paragraph.

"I'm sure you met Elmer, the handyman." Elizabeth hoped her challenge sounded just a tiny bit nasty. "I had the pleasure only in the letters and in her book, but I think *I* can assure *you* there's nothing *flagrante* there."

Richard, however, didn't look quite as chagrined as she would have wished as he returned to the author's reminiscences of English teas:

Earl Grey tea should be drunk just as it comes with nothing in it! And not too strong. But by real English tea-drinkers it

59

is considered mostly for invalids who can't take it strong as the "kitchen tea" most of them drink! I miss the brown Hovis, sliced thin, which you can—or could, before the war —get even in the teashops, lightly buttered. Cakes they went wild on—you never saw such icing and rainbow effects! Strawberries whole in a glass bowl, washed (I hope!) but still wearing their hulls and taken in the fingers and dipped in granulated sugar, also in a glass bowl. But that was old-fashioned, even before Hitler. I hadn't thought of "white coffee" since I left there! I haven't been back to England since I left there in December 1939.

And did you ever visit the Longfellow House in Cambridge, Mass.—which to me is more important than the George Washington house where he had his headquarters the first year of the war, and where Martha joined him in time to hear the bombardment and the wounded coming back from Dorchester. I was lucky enough to know the curator there, or whatever they called him, and was allowed to work upstairs in Miss Longfellow's sitting-room—"grave Alice"—who was the Vice-regent for Massachusetts at Mount Vernon, when the Association took it over in the 1800s. Her correspondence, which was made available to me there, had remarkably little about Mount Vernon and a great deal (including pressed flowers) about her trips abroad. But it is an adorable house, and Longfellow's lilacs, which he so treasured, still bloom.

Our golden cocker is named Jody and is getting old, which we can hardly bear. But she is still beautiful and full of accomplishments, gravely performed for visitors.

For a moment Elizabeth almost thought Richard's eyes were misty as he murmured, "I remember Jody. Beautiful animal." He read on a line, then spoke without looking up. "You must have asked her which of her heroines she was most like—silly sort of question, but probably typical of starry-eyed fan letters."

"Yes, I imagine so," Elizabeth replied equably, but it was lost on her companion, as he was back into the letter:

> I was neither Liz nor Sandy—perhaps nearer to the always bumble-footed Phoebe than any other of my ladies, though I never wrote autobiographically nor used a live person I had known. Sometimes I "typed" a character on an actor as he might have played the part—Jimmy Stewart as Rodney, for instance. Fred Astaire as Stephen the dancer. It formed a mental image as I worked. They asked—my agent—asked for a script for Jimmy Stewart, who was then at his peak, but by the time I got it ready he was in the Air Force, and when he came out he had outgrown it.
>
> So you've been reading my Beebe. I went to Haiti with the expedition...

"What expedition?" Richard demanded so sharply Elizabeth jumped. She looked through some papers she had brought into the room with her but not offered to him—copies of her own letters to the author.

In answer to his demand, she read from her letter, "'I am reading *Exploring with Beebe.*'" she looked up. "Do you remember Rodney, the naturalist hero of *From This Day Forward?*" She threw it out as a challenge, then continued reading: "'Rodney's books may have been dull, but not William Beebe's!' That's what I said."

"She would have loved that." Richard said it almost grudgingly, but Elizabeth ignored him and continued reading.

"'Not that one would ever suspect that Elswyth Thane's husband could have been dull! His literary allusions are delightful in a scientific work—*The Three Musketeer* crabs, "The Ancient Mariner" albatross, the first reading of Alice (Rodney remembered his, too). The use of first person voice and sharing of his emotions are unexpectedly fresh from a scientist (Rodney would also have liked his game for annihilating time and space). And I enjoyed his endowment of inanimate objects with animate qualities—"The gun's backyard," reminiscent of your own reference to the park in 1939 London "where the guns lived."

"'Did you accompany any of these expeditions?—I guess I'm asking whether you're a Liz or a Sandy.'" She looked up. "Oh, there it is—the silly, starry-eyed fan mail question. I wondered what I'd asked."

He looked down impatiently at the letter in his hand.

"You're near the end, aren't you? Read it aloud," she urged.

Elizabeth thought he might refuse, but he complied:

I went to Haiti with the expedition—or rather joined it towards the end. I told him I wasn't an outdoors girl! But we had a house in Bermuda for a few divine years, tho I went to England while they did the bathysphere—they didn't want me around having a nervous breakdown while he did it!

There's the car. How we would gossip if it was you coming in. One of the dearest and closest friends I have in the world began with a letter—came to tea—and is now in D.C. And often drives up for a week! Made in heaven, that girl. It couldn't happen <u>again</u>!

He cleared his throat and reread the last paragraph silently, then nodded slowly and turned to the next letter:

Elswyth Thane Beebe
Wilmington, Vermont 05363
August 6, 1979

Dear Elizabeth,

I am enclosing a couple of extras. The photographs you may keep, so you won't have any more trouble with Will's characteristic modesty on Cheops—the other one, need I say, is our Jody-dog, looking rather cross about being made to sit still for his picture beside a bunch of silly violets! Will, sitting beside me, is wearing the expression he fell back on when I said, "Behave!" He took an instant dislike to the poor photographer who was sent up to photograph <u>me</u> in our apartment, for the new book (I think about the time of <u>Tryst</u>) and then was <u>caught</u> and had to have his picture made too! The poor unfortunate little photographer was very nervous and for some reason was wearing a violently <u>pink</u> shirt with a navy blue suit, in the days when "people" wore <u>white</u> shirts in NYC! Will took one look and instantly had no time to have pictures taken—but we got one anyway! Will is "behaving"—and very nicely too! (My London char paused to contemplate this picture of us, which always travelled with me, and said, "He's got a <u>thinking</u> sort of face." I liked that!)

"She sent you pictures?"

Elizabeth could have gloated at the almost crestfallen tone in his voice.

"Quite a few, and I later sent her some, too. Lest you suspect me of wheedling, would you like to hear what prompted her generosity?"

"Very much." And this time he actually looked at her while she read.

"'Of course I'm reading your Beebe—I want to get to know you both. Only a woman who has experienced cherishing could write of it so beautifully. And on the other hand, it is the woman who has mentally "put his slippers to warm before the fire and set a lighted candle in the window" who is cherished—not very popular opinions today, are they?

"'But I must say it does take a bit of dedication to find a picture of Dr. Beebe more revealing that the "close-up on top of Cheops" or those taken while wearing a diving helmet. (One of those does show wonderful eyes, though.)'"

"Hmm," Richard grunted and returned to the reading in his hand:

The other enclosure is the thing I wrote at the request of the new encyclopedia of writers being got out by some firm I never heard of, who wrote asking me for an account of how I wrote books, for the benefit of their readers, who they hope will be young people wanting to write. They sent me a horrific "coy" sample by somebody else I never heard of, which, to me, struck entirely the wrong note, which I endeavored to avoid! That should come back to me, as I had a copy made which I thought might be useful, and I hope it will be, to you, anyway! You may copy it, if you like, before returning it.

I don't believe in books about How to Write a Book, any

more than I believe in "courses" on the same. But as you can see by the enclosed, I am hardly entitled to an opinion! When I wrote this rather flippant piece for the encyclopedia I had just finished reading Borg's life of Maxwell Perkins, the editor at Scribner's in the 1930s, when I was starting—and was so thrown by the cry-baby performance of Wolfe, Fitzgerald, Hemingway, Rawlins, Davenport, Taylor et al. that I was just in the mood to step on the whole thing. It's all true, believe me, but I would never have written it down probably if it hadn't been for Borg's straight-faced account of how those "best sellers" were manufactured! They all drank like fishes and cried on Perkins' shoulder, and he pulled them together and got a book somehow. It's a recent book. Get it and read it and learn! I never heard a "click," either. And the line was originally that, "Genius is an infinite capacity for taking pains." Braine stole it from, I think, Carlyle, but if I stop to look it up I won't get this finished before dinner: Edna Ferber wrote a funny book about writing books—called Peculiar Treasure.

Now, about Kipling. He was heartbreaking, we knew him well enough to know that. (He's somewhere in something I wrote—Farmer or England Was...) They tried to make a silent film of The Light and couldn't—tho they had my good friend Percy Marmont playing it. The girl was all wrong, for one thing. I suspect that Kipling never knew a kind and loving woman in his life—at least not after he left India; there might have been somebody there, but I doubt it. He wasn't a romantic-looking figure, and he was a quiet man, and nobody ever found him.

His wife was impossible, but he bore with her infinitely and allowed himself to be bullied. She placed herself between him and any other lady, if possible—I remember being maneuvered into a chair beside her at a tea table while "the men" (on a sofa across the room) sat crying with laughter over the funny stories they were exchanging—all true, of course!—from mostly their East Indian days, no doubt, which were almost simultaneous; tho Will was a little late on the scene, some of Kipling's acquaintances were still there. So I think The Light was all the kind of romance Kipling could handle.

"What was that Kipling business all about?" Richard asked when he lowered the letter.

"I asked her to talk to me about *The Light That Failed*, because it puzzled me so. The heroine is particularly incoherent, since she is supposed to have been modeled on a friend of Kipling's sister with whom he was in love." Elizabeth picked up the copy she had kept of her own letter. "'It seemed so pointless. Not a classical tragedy, because the hero didn't fall from a flaw in his own character, unless his love for Maisie was a character flaw. Surely Maisie is the most despicable heroine since Scarlett O'Hara. Scarlett wins only because her book is longer, even though the results of her selfishness are less shattering. What was Kipling saying?'

"Shall I go on a bit? I think these next parts make her answers clearer, too."

Richard gave a nod, which Elizabeth thought rather in a manner of *noblesse oblige*, but she suppressed her impulse to chuckle.

"'In *Farmer* you mentioned doing research for a book on Charles II. WHAT BOOK??? He's a favorite of mine. I just close my eyes to the parts I don't like, as Catherine learned to do. One author I read waxed Freudian and said his promiscuity was a seeking for the security he had been denied as a child of preoccupied parents. If that was the case, seems to me poor Charles had it rather backward—he missed the real security of a happy marriage. Anyway, I think he ruled extremely well...'

"Oh, never mind," she scanned ahead a bit. "I didn't mean to bore you with my opinions. Here's the next part I think she responds to: 'I have often wondered where you found the courage to make some of your characters wait *years* to get together when life is so short. I wonder if your own long separations from your husband helped you there.

"'You didn't get back to England after '39? So that's why the Williamsburg series ended with the Battle of Britain rather than the end of the war. I wondered.'"

She was quiet then to allow him to go on with his reading:

Charles II never got written. When the war came I could no longer get to the British Museum reading room, and tho I had brought back a lot of books, I let them go with my Tudor Wench and Disraeli sources when I cleared out the NY apartment after Will's death. Charles II was a lovely character in the TV Marlborough series a few years back. I meant to do his European exile before he came to the throne, and the battle of Worcester, as per Queen's Folly. Never got to it.

Speaking of waiting—have you had my Melody? It was a fun book to write, and Adrian was a combination of the actor A. E. Matthews and the painter F. O. Salisbury—both of them heavenly clowns and delightful to know! The nearest I ever came to using anybody I knew in a book, and that was only for their style. Salisbury had been happily married for years, Matthews never—or not for long!

To continue the Williamsburg series past Homing would

have meant getting into either the Invasion or the South Pacific—too much, too big, too difficult. Besides, the story was told, with Mab's arrival in Williamsburg.

Dorothy Sayers and Ngaio Marsh and Manning Coles and Oppenheim for mysteries, not to mention Christie. (Get her autobiography!) And John Buchan. Angela Thirkell, Elizabeth of the German Garden, and lots more for pre-war England.

Elizabeth smiled with satisfaction when Richard's eyebrows rose. She knew he had come to the last paragraph. She had the letters so nearly memorized she could follow the reading almost line for line.

I hope it won't spook you when I say that the most precious friend I have acquired in recent years began with fan letters sort of like yours—she came to tea, driving a beat-up Volkswagon with a Hawaiian number-plate—she had been to Williamsburg—my fault!—and I have never liked anyone so much so soon. Since then, she has been back several times and recently been hit with multiple sclerosis, which prevents her driving at all, tho it is a light case, they say, and she is now able to work half-days. But heaven knows when she will be able to travel back here again, and I am feeling sort of bereft, which makes your letters singularly welcome. I can't quite say why, but you sound like the same sort of person!

Now I must go, it's dinner time!

Elswyth Thane Beebe

Richard dropped the letter with a sigh and ran his long fingers through his thick black hair. "You've made a very telling point. I can see that your relationship did mean a lot to her."

"And to me," Elizabeth said softly.

"The letters are really marvelous. Her voice is so strong. I feel as if I've been sitting in one of the overstuffed chairs by her fireplace-turned-wood-stove drinking Earl Grey with her and listening to her reminisce." He shook his head. "But that's all the more reason to guard against exploitation."

His pig-headed mistrust of her motives made Elizabeth want to grind her teeth, but instead she said as sweetly as she could manage, "How about a second opinion. These are photocopies; would you like to show them to your aunt or grandmother?"

"Aunt Frances isn't very literary; her talents are in the line of keeping the house running smoothly from the background. But my grandmother would love them. Don't think, though, that she'll be easier to get around than I am. Grandmere always was the toughest nut in the family."

"You've made your opinion of my motives very clear, so I won't even bother arguing the fact that I had no intention of wheedling your grandmother. As an act of goodwill, I'll even throw in an extra." She went to her files and returned in a moment with a four-page letter dated August 17, 1979. Richard started to peruse it, but Elizabeth placed her hand over the page.

"Ah, ah, ah—reading other people's mail, Mr. Spenser? This one's for your grandmother. She can decide whether it should be subjected to the dangers of being read by a publisher. Or, more to the point, by an academic committee."

For the first time since the topic had risen between them Richard smiled his slow smile at her, even letting it make his eyes twinkle. "Right. Can't be too careful."

She held the door open wide for him and closed it crisply on his departure. "Well!" She fumed to the empty room, "have you ever witnessed such unmitigated arrogance? Ohh!" She twisted her fingers in a gesture of wringing his neck.

Susan had to work late that night, so Elizabeth readily agreed to fill in for her friend and babysit Tommy so Julia and Stuart could have a much-needed night out. The first part of the evening went just fine as Elizabeth and her young charge shared hot dogs and Oreos in Julia's comfortable kitchen and then Tommy went out to play for an hour. Bedtime, however, was another story.

As a matter of fact, if she hadn't hit on the idea of reading him a story, Elizabeth would likely have made medical history by being the first subject on record to succumb to a fatal case of babysitting. The third time she fled up the stairs to see what the commotion in his room could possibly be, she found him crouched on top of a bookcase sailing model airplanes and UFOs around the room.

"Look out, Auntie Liz, the aliens almost got you!"

She ducked just in time to avoid being hit in the head by a well-aimed missile. "Come down from there right now, Tommy! Be careful—" Her voice rose in a shriek, and she turned her face to the wall, unable to look on the certain disaster, as Tommy, rather than climbing down the bookcase, obeyed her order by taking a flying leap into the center of his bed.

"Tommy!"

"Yeah?" He grinned at her. "You didn't watch. Wanna see me do it again?"

"No! I most certainly do not. How you or your bed or your

mother have survived this long is proof positive of guardian angels."

"Yeah, that's what my mom says, too. And then she usually says she hopes the next one's a girl." Tommy was flinging the planes and spacecraft off his bed. "But I don't think a girl could do that nearly as good, do you?"

"No, Tommy, but a girl might be better at other things."

"Like what?"

"Oh, I don't know. Tea parties, maybe. Or playing Strawberry Shortcake."

"Yuck! I hope it's a boy."

Elizabeth thought of praying for a girl for Julia's sake but then decided that at this advanced stage of pregnancy it might be a little late, so she just decided to petition heaven for strength for Julia instead. "Now, I want you in bed and quiet, and I will read to you." She turned to the bookcase, which was miraculously still standing. "What do you want to hear?"

"*Pirates of the Galapagos*, the blue one on the second shelf."

The book was well illustrated with cutlass-wielding pirates, overflowing treasure chests, and exotic settings including the giant turtles of the Galapagos. The fast-paced adventure story kept Tommy's vivid imagination occupied, and Elizabeth was impressed by the unusual amount of exotic background detail included in a children's book. She hoped it was accurate, because she was interested in the area—Dr. William Beebe had been one of the first to explore the islands early in the twentieth century and had written a couple of books about his expeditions there, including one for children. Maybe she could find a copy in a used bookstore for Tommy.

Tommy yawned, his eyes drooped, and he curled into a ball and went sound asleep. Elizabeth heaved a sigh of relief and looked around at the desolation of his room. She'd really had no idea what she'd volunteered for. Closing the book, she started to return it to the shelf when she stopped mid-motion.

The author's name was Ilona Walters. Why did that ring a bell? She thought for a moment, then heard Richard's clipped voice as he pronounced the name on his wife's headstone. But if this was Richard's wife, shouldn't the last name be Spenser? Could this be the same woman? The Ilona was unusual enough to warrant a second look. She turned to the back fly leaf. There she met a beautiful smiling face surrounded by a halo of platinum hair. The brief biographical sketch added the information that the author made her home in Boston.

Surely there couldn't have been two Ilona Walters, even in a city the size of Boston. Still looking at the picture, Elizabeth groped at a very fuzzy memory that seemed to be playing peek-a-boo with her brain: Richard saying, "I *told* Mary Ilona ..." What did this have to do with Richard's obvious overreaction to her desire to do research on Elswyth Thane? It was true, as he asserted, that most posthumous "finds" of manuscripts that authors had abandoned would have been best left to the oblivion to which the authors themselves had assigned them, but few, if any, artistic reputations had been severely damaged by such disrespect or lack of judgment on the part of a publisher. His point about scandal and innuendo was probably more valid, but surely he didn't really believe she was about to launch into anything like that. No, somehow, there must be some connection between Richard's dead wife's work in this field and his reaction to Elizabeth's project. But whatever it was, it was beyond her to guess at the missing link.

She snapped off the bedside light and, moving cautiously to avoid disaster with the toys on the floor, went out to the blessed peace and quiet of the living room.

"How'd you get along with Tommy the Terror?" Susan asked when Elizabeth got home, wreathed in glowing gratitude from Tommy's parents.

Elizabeth laughed. "Pretty smart aren't you? I think *I'll* have to work late next time." Elizabeth started to go on into her own room when she paused. "Was Richard's wife the writer Ilona Walters?"

"Yes, that's it. That's how I remembered the Ilona bit. Did you see Tommy's books by her?"

"*Pirates of the Galapagos.* Are there others?"

"I think she did three—all set in remote places like that. She must have been a pretty good writer; Tommy sure likes the books."

"Yes, I thought it was well written. I'd like to see the others."

"Sure, next time you babysit."

"I had something less dangerous in mind—like the public library. I don't know, I *had* hoped for children of my own some-day..." She laughed.

"Julia must think it's worth it, since she's having another one."

CHAPTER 8

*B*ut the next morning Elizabeth's idea of finding the nearest library was thoroughly overshadowed by an unexpected phone call. "Miss Allerton? This is Alexandra Spenser. I believe my grandson Richard has mentioned me to you. I have thoroughly enjoyed reading the letters my grandson showed me. Would you like to come up to tea this afternoon?"

"I'd love to. Thank you, Mrs. Spenser," she paused, not certain how to proceed. "But would Richard—er, does he—"

Alexandra Spenser gave a little laugh that sounded surprisingly young. "My grandson is not my social secretary. I know he seems to have taken some kind of maggot into his head about these letters and some research you want to do. That, however, has no influence on whom I choose to invite to tea. Shall we say three o'clock?"

Elizabeth was thrilled to be going to the beautiful house she had seen only from a distance. The old red brick was warm and mellow in its green and red-gold setting, the two-story-high black-shuttered windows sparkled in the afternoon sun, and Elizabeth was enchanted with the creativity of the architect who, instead of merely putting the usual Federalist sunburst window over the door, had ordered one over each of the first-floor windows as well.

Alexandra Spenser opened the door herself and led Elizabeth into a perfect colonial parlor complete with a Williamsburg blue-paneled fireplace, Chippendale furniture and Chinese wallpaper above the wainscoting. The tea table was set near the window, which looked out over the back lawn running to the woods ablaze with autumn color. "How charming! Autumn crocus growing right in your grass."

"The Dutch call it naturalizing. In the spring the lawn is a sunburst of daffodils. The only drawback is not being able to cut the grass until the daffodil leaves turn brown. I always think the beauty of it in April is worth a few shaggy weeks in June, though. And, of course, in the autumn the fallen leaves cover it all."

"That has to be the ultimate in naturalizing," Elizabeth commented as a maid entered quietly, bearing a tray of tea and cakes. Feeling like the guest of royalty, Elizabeth sat in the rose damask chair near the window her hostess indicated.

Alexandra Spenser had silver hair done in a classic French roll, finely lined porcelain skin, aristocratic features and perfect posture. Elizabeth thought she looked at least fifteen years younger than what must have been her late-seventies age. The Spenser matriarch took her place at the tea table looking as if she had been born with a china tea pot in her hand. "Thank you, Annie. That will be all."

She turned to Elizabeth as the maid departed. "How do you take your tea, my dear? I believe I shall call you Elizabeth; it's such a pretty name. Not fluffy, like the Mimis and Yvettes mothers seem to name their daughters these days. People never think ahead to how a name will look on a diploma or something serious."

"I'd love to have you call me Elizabeth. And I take my tea with milk."

"I could have guessed. I knew you were my kind of person." Mrs. Spenser poured the steaming liquid through a silver tea strainer. "This is Boston Harbour Tea—the same blend of Indian, Ceylon and Darjeeling and packed by the same company that supplied tea for the colonists in 1776. I only serve it to people that I feel fairly certain will be able to restrain themselves from saying, 'That's strange, it doesn't taste salty,' after the first drink."

Elizabeth laughed and took a sip. "It's delicious!"

"And not a bit salty?" Mrs. Spenser's eyes danced.

"Oh, I see, you want to say it yourself!"

"Well, it seems someone has to." She passed a tray of small cakes to Elizabeth. "The sponges are called Queen's Cakes; they're my favorite."

"Oh, how lovely! I've read of Queen's Cakes all my life, but I never saw one in captivity before."

Mrs. Spenser took a cake, then got down to business. "My grandson seemed most anxious that I not talk to you about Elswyth Thane. So, of course, that's what I'm dying to do. Tell me about your interest in her."

Elizabeth explained briefly how she had read all of Miss Thane's books, except the one she couldn't find, and had felt such an affinity for the author and her works that she had been compelled to write to her. "The letters Richard showed you are a part of that marvelous experience. Did Richard tell you I want to find unpublished information to round out the picture for my doctoral thesis?"

"It seems an excellent idea to me. I can't imagine why Richard would try to block such a thing. Of course I'll be delighted to tell you all I know."

Elizabeth was so thrilled she almost held her breath for fear the lady might change her mind. "Did you know her well?"

"Very well, indeed. The publishing industry was very close,

almost cliquish, back in the '30s when my husband ran *Caudex*. Even though we didn't publish Elswyth Thane's works, we got acquainted at parties and various literary gatherings. Then, of course, when she moved here in the '50s we were practically neighbors."

"I envy you."

"Yes, she was always one of my favorite people as well as a favorite author—which doesn't always happen, you know. But she was very down to earth, outspoken, and yet with a wonderfully whimsical sense of humor. Not many people can see things as they really are and yet not let it get them down. I think that was a rarer gift than her writing ability."

"Do you mean in her personal life?"

"Oh, no, as far as anyone can ever judge from the outside, I think she was very happy. Of course, her marriage was rather unconventional for that day, but she was a fiercely independent woman and William Beebe an incredibly adventurous man—I'm sure any other arrangement would have driven them both crazy.

"She told me she simply wrote whenever she could find a chance to sit at a desk, often late at night and sometimes still wearing the evening dress in which she had returned from theaters or dances with Will. She never allowed her work to interfere with their crowded social calendar.

"And then they would be separated for months at a time—he at his jungle field stations or oceanographic work, she at the British Museum or somewhere like Mount Vernon on her own. She once told me these separations never did their thirty-some years' marriage any harm, because they always had plenty to talk about. They never got stale or bored, I know for a fact. Their household was based at a duplex apartment in the West Sixties in New York. Later, when they got the place in Wilmington, Will would come here, or she would go to New York, whenever either of them got lonesome."

Elizabeth longed for a tape recorder or at least pen and

notepad, but she made do with accepting a refill on her cup of tea. "Do you know anything about how she wrote? I always suspected the process she described for Jamie in *Remember Today* must have been a bit autobiographical."

"She was very no-nonsense about it. She couldn't abide the agony and ecstasy a lot of writers liked to brag about at parties. I remember sitting by her at a party where the bestseller of the moment, some entirely forgotten fellow now, was holding forth on his 'calling'; she told me in her very dry voice, but with her eyes sparkling, 'I never made an outline before beginning a book. If you lock yourself into a pattern before you begin, you just create a handicap. Things just develop as I go along. But I never write myself into a corner and have to throw away chunks of superfluities as *some* do.' I think we both had a terrible time to keep from bursting out laughing, because right after she said that to me the fellow who was being lionized told his spellbound audience how he had thrown a hundred pages of freshly typed manuscript into the fireplace: 'just like burning my very own flesh.'

"I also know that no manuscript of hers was ever worked on by any but her own hand until it was sent to the publisher. She always wrote the first draft longhand in ruled notebooks from Woolworth's and then typed and retyped every page herself through the final copy. Even at her busiest she never had a researcher or secretary."

"That's really incredible, when you realize she produced more than thirty books and they were so thoroughly researched." Elizabeth paused. "But I'm keeping you talking so much you haven't had a chance to eat one of these wonderful cakes." Elizabeth apologized, then went right on to ask her next question. "Do you know how she got started?"

"I know she simply never wanted to do anything else. I think she mentioned serving a brief apprenticeship on a newspaper reviewing books and films. I believe she worked for a time at a film studio just as the silents were turning into talkies. She said once the scenario problems taught her something about economy of words and not over-writing. But I doubt if she would ever have been guilty of that anyway. She wrote a few short stories, but I don't believe any of them were ever published. I'm sure you know *Riders of the Wind* was her first book. It was accepted by the first publisher who saw it and was printed straight from the original script with almost no alterations. That must be a hallmark in the publishing world. I know my husband used to pull his hair at the poor quality of manuscripts they received, and Richard says it's even worse now. Editors deserve far more credit than they receive."

"Do you know if she went to India to research her setting for that first book?"

"I asked her that myself once. She said she never went there and had no desire to go. She had just been reading a lot of Kipling and Talbot Mundy. She also said there was nothing she wanted less for herself than adventure like her heroine had in that story. But my husband had been to India several times and said there were absolutely no mistakes in the settings or atmosphere—just some sort of writer's sixth sense or something, I suppose."

Elizabeth laughed. "I hope she wouldn't think you were ascribing 'airs' to her by that."

"I'm sure she wouldn't. Remember when Sally began writing in *Yankee Stranger* and someone—was it Cabot?—asked her, 'How do you *know* that the street goes up in that part of London, or how a man's arm aches after a duel?'"

"Yes, I remember. Sally didn't have an answer for it either."

"But Elswyth Thane's career really flowered when her inherent, she called it atavistic, love of England took over and she began to write books laid there. She finally got to London in the '20s and Dr. Beebe, who already knew England, and even Kipling, very well, opened all kinds of impressive doors for her. But even then, Will once said she had an astonishingly instinctive knowledge of what to see and where it was."

Elizabeth nodded. "I've always wondered if there could be something like genetic memory. We inherit other characteristics from our ancestors, why not the grooves in our brain or something?" She paused to sip her tea. "Of course, much of that could have been developed through early reading—but then, why did she choose *those* books? Do you know if she had any formal training as a writer?"

"I don't think she held much with that—too independent. But she always enjoyed reading other author's autobiographies, or biographies if they were carefully researched from letters or diaries after the author's death. Still, she told me once that reading about other and more famous writers always made her wonder if she hadn't done it all wrong."

"But surely, if she felt that way about reading others' biographies, she wouldn't object to having a dissertation written about herself!" For the first time that afternoon, Elizabeth's utter frustration crept into her voice.

"I very much doubt that she would object at all as long as the writer didn't get silly and give her 'airs.' I also know, though, that she never kept a diary. As to what goes on in the head of my stubborn grandson, however, I would never attempt to hazard a guess."

"And very wise of you, too!" Both women started as Richard strode into the room and bent to kiss his grandmother.

Alexandra patted him as if he were a schoolboy. "I'm afraid the tea is cold. Shall I ring Annie for some more?"

Elizabeth's gaze jerked up in surprise to see a tapestry bellpull by the fireplace.

Richard laughed—a short, brittle sound that Elizabeth found chilling. "Yes, antediluvian, isn't it? We still pull bells in this house for fresh pots of tea, just like something out of a Victorian novel. But no bell-pulling today, thank you. Now that you've undoubtedly told Elizabeth even more than she needs for her paper, I'm taking her for a walk."

Even though he treated his grandmother with an air of amused indulgence that spoke of his real fondness for her, there was a stony abruptness in Richard's manner that told Elizabeth he was seething inside. She had no desire to have the full force of his fury unleashed on her, but when he held out his hand to her, wordlessly commanding her to join him, she had no option but to place her hand in his and accompany him through the French doors into the garden.

CHAPTER 9

or several minutes they walked in silence, the warmth of the sun on the bright leaves only serving to sharpen the effect of the chill from Richard. He still gripped Elizabeth's hand so fiercely that if it weren't for his obvious anger she would think he held it desperately as a drowning man might. But that was silly. If anyone were being taken out to be drowned, it was Elizabeth. She shivered involuntarily, making him turn to her with a startled look, almost as if he had been momentarily unaware of her presence.

Elizabeth felt great relief when she saw the wooden bench Richard was apparently headed for at the edge of the woods. Even having him lash at her in anger would be better than his awful silence and the piercing vibrations that seemed to emanate from him. When they sank onto the bench and he let go of her, however, her relief at having her hand released from his vice-like grip was overshadowed by her amazement as he dropped his head in his hands and his shoulders shook.

For a terrible moment she thought he was crying, but when he raised his head he was completely dry-eyed, and nothing could have shocked her more than his first words. "I dreamt of Mary last night. It was more than a dream. Almost a vision. Or a—a haunting." Elizabeth sat absolutely still; only the widening of her eyes evidenced her shock at his words. He hit a fist hard into the palm of his other hand, then ran his fingers through his hair. "Why won't she leave me alone? Haven't I suffered enough? Why must she plague me? What do I have to do to be free of her?"

Elizabeth shivered, as if a chill passed over the lawn. "Do you dream about her often?" She kept her voice soft, hoping it would be soothing to his ragged nerves.

"I did at first—every night until I got to the point that I dreaded going to bed. Finally it got less and less. I thought I had come to terms with it until you turned up and opened the whole thing again."

"*Me?*"

"It was the most incredible sense of déjà vu—more like a recurring nightmare—when you told me you'd come here to research Elswyth Thane. Mary Ilona was consumed with her passion for researching William Beebe. Sometimes I'd tease her about being more in love with him than she was with me. I was never sure it was entirely a joke. She wanted to do a 'life of Beebe'—even though his will specifically forbade it."

"I know. Elswyth Thane told me there was to be no 'Life of Beebe.' Well, mentioned it in a letter. I asked because I wanted to read it if there was one."

"But Mary Ilona was really irrational about it. She'd go on and on about how her research would make her rich and famous—or both of us if *Caudex* published her story. I tried to laugh it off, asking her how rich and famous she thought a scholarly biographical work would make her. And then she'd get very enigmatic about the leads she'd discovered in her research."

"Did she ever hint what it was?"

"Only once, and you could hardly call it a hint—the last letter I received from her when I was in England. She said she'd found something really exciting, something she'd long suspected was there, and she was sure it would change my mind about a joint venture. She sounded so happy and excited—that was her greatest charm and why her children's books were such a success. She could be almost magically lighthearted and take everyone around her into the mood with her." He paused, and Elizabeth sat there feeling heavy-handed and lumpish. "But I wasn't convinced. As a matter of fact, I fired a scathing letter back telling her just what I thought of her violating Dr. Beebe's express request that no biography be done.

"When the telegram came I thought it was her reply. Instead it was from Aunt Frances..." In the long pause Elizabeth sought in vain for words, but then Richard continued, "I'm sure she was leaving—running away—in response to my letter. And she ran straight to her death. She must have felt she had to get away in order to be truly herself. I killed her. "

"Ridiculous. You're a gentleman. You would have given her space."

Elizabeth could feel him relax. "Thank you. You don't know what that vote of confidence means to me. But I have to ask myself if she knew that. What had I done to demonstrate it? On the contrary, I applied so much pressure I drove her to her death."

"Richard! That's nonsense. You did no such thing any more than you sabotaged the airplane." Elizabeth sturdily ignored niggling thoughts of the pressure he was putting on *her*.

"I wrote the letter that put her on the plane in order to escape me. It comes to the same thing."

"It does not. And besides, you don't know anything for sure—you're just guessing at her motives."

"Well, whatever anyone's motives were, that's what happened..."

The sentence hung unfinished. Elizabeth put her hand lightly on his arm, trying to imagine what it must have been like when that telegram arrived. "And then the lights went out." She said it softly as a simple statement and was rewarded with a look of real gratitude from her companion.

"And you really don't have any idea what she had found?" Elizabeth ventured after several more moments of silence.

He shook his head. "That's just another one of the things that's so haunting." For the first time he turned on the bench so he was facing her directly. "And then you turned up, the first woman I've been attracted to since Mary—and *you're* doing research on the Beebe household, too. It's just too much." It seemed that he started to drop his head back into his hands, but then, somehow—perhaps because her hand was already on his arm—Elizabeth was holding him with his head against her shoulder.

It was the most extraordinary moment she'd ever experienced as a jumble of emotions battled for supremacy. She felt awed and humbled that this strong, brilliant man had turned to her for comfort. She felt a flood of understanding for his irrational objections to her research. And she felt the most wonderful, singing desire to turn cartwheels and dance on the grass. He had said he was attracted to her.

As her emotions deepened, her arms tightened around him and she dropped her cheek to the top of his head. After a few moments—which she would have been perfectly content to have extended to hours—he sat up. "I didn't know I could be so emotional." His tone was apologetic.

"Have you been this troubled for three years?"

He gave a wry laugh. "You must think I'm pretty well around the bend by now." She felt his hesitation. "I thought I was doing fine until you came along. Once you get the technique down it's not too hard just to bottle some things up and wall others out. But three years is a long time to live in a vacuum."

"Well, then, it's time to break out." With a flash of inspiration Elizabeth jumped to her feet. "Race you to the stone wall!" She pointed to the bottom of the long green lawn, kicked off her high-heeled shoes, and with a shout of laughter that was quite unlike her, took off across the grass, jumping occasionally to avoid a clump of autumn crocus. She heard Richard's rich, deep laugh behind her, and in a moment his long legs carried him a stride ahead of her. She cried a breathless, "Oh!" But there was nothing she could do to achieve any more speed. So he slowed to what was practically a jog for him, and together they ran across the flower-strewn, sloping lawn. At the very end he put on a burst of speed and arrived at the wall ahead of her just in time to turn and catch her in his open arms. She ran right into them and clung to him, panting and laughing and gasping for breath. His heart was pounding, and he was breathing heavily as his arms came around her.

"I haven't felt so light for three years. Thank you for this beautiful gift of—of freedom." For an instant he held her to him even more tightly, then released her just enough so that she could lift her face. His full-throated head-thrown-back laugh that followed his kiss spoke most clearly of all of the release and elation this moment had brought him.

Finally they pulled apart and leaned against the low stone wall. For the first time Elizabeth glanced down at their feet and realized they were almost standing in a bank of purple asters growing along the wall. With a cry of delight she sank to her knees and gathered them into her hands. Richard knelt beside her and picked a handful for her. She held them to her face for a moment, then looked up at him.

"I didn't realize you had violet eyes," he said. "How could I not have noticed before?"

"Because they weren't violet before." She laughed. "They're hazel—they change with whatever is around them."

He took her hand, and they turned to sit with their backs against the sun-warmed wall. "I knew you were an enchantress. Do you realize that only a few minutes ago I thought I'd never laugh again?"

She leaned over and gave his cheek a peck of a kiss. "I'm a very ordinary woman, and you're a very wonderful man who's being incredibly charming, if a little melodramatic, at the moment. You'd probably have sent a very cold rejection slip to anyone submitting a novel with characters that talk like that."

Again he lifted his head and gave his wonderful, irrepressible laugh. It was as if he couldn't get enough of the experience. "On the contrary. Our rejection slips are very warmly worded."

"As in, 'We advise you to burn this manuscript'?"

And then they were laughing together again. After a time, though, the mood grew more somber, and they sat on in silence, drawing fractionally apart until Elizabeth wondered if that moment of closeness had been a dream. With a little shiver she recalled that their whole time of transported timelessness had begun with him telling her of his dream. A dream that had not ended happily but left him haunted.

"It must have been awful for you—losing your brother and your wife so suddenly. How did you deal with it?"

He shrugged imperceptibly. "I just got on with it. I told you I was abroad and the services were all over by the time I got back."

"Did that strike you as strange? Surely they could have waited for your return? Planes fly across the Atlantic every day."

"I think I mentioned how stiff upper lip my father is about such things. And Mary Ilona's family—such as they are—mostly a distant cousin, I think, wanted to get on with the arrangements more quickly, too. They were never a close family. Only an aunt and uncle came to our wedding, I got the feeling they were just as happy to have me out of the way for the funeral." He paused as if trying to remember. "It was all so crushing—the weight of the publishing house dumped in my lap alongside the deaths. I know that sounds strange, but the business was more immediate. And it was something I could *do*."

"You were in shock."

"I suppose so. Anyway, I didn't raise any objections. It was easier that way. I could block out the loss with constant activity.

And when I got back I continued with the fiction: the whole thing just didn't happen. It was as if James was off in Philadelphia seeing to business and Mary was off on a research trip. My heart wouldn't accept anything more, even though my rational brain kept arguing with it. It felt as if they would be back—just walk in someday.

"Then when I did admit what had happened I got angry. Angry with myself because I should have somehow prevented it, angry with everyone around me because they couldn't tell me what caused the crash..."

"Angry with God," Elizabeth finished.

"Oh, God. Yes." It came out as a cross between a prayer and an oath. "And then, probably as much from fatigue as anything else, depression followed. It's simply too much work—being angry all the time. Depression is a sort of empty anger that's drained of its emotion. I was left with a great hollow void that looked like the rest of my life."

"And then?" She prompted.

"And then you came into my life with crashing cars and a drowning boy and your blasted research project." There was almost a shadow of a smile behind his eyes.

"But there's more." She sounded insistent.

"More what?"

"Depression is not the final stage in bereavement. Acceptance is."

He shrugged. "Well, I suppose I have accepted it. What else is there?"

"No, that's not it at all. Not passive acceptance; simply putting up with things as they are. Active acceptance is more like willing commitment.

"I was heart-broken when Nana died. My parents helped me through it all. Then they were killed in a car crash..." She took a deep breath. "You don't have to stay in depression." She wanted to go on, but her voice broke and tears welled up in her eyes. She started to dab at her eyes with her sleeve, but Richard whipped a white linen handkerchief from his pocket and caught the tears just as they spilled.

"Thank you," he said as if he were still very deep in thought.

She nodded, wishing she could leave it there. How lovely it would be to end the day with the memory of his kiss, of their lighthearted dash down the lawn, of her helping him to what was hopefully a new understanding. But she needed the complete truth. So she pressed on. "You're still in love with her."

His silence was her answer.

CHAPTER 10

"Surprise!" Susan greeted Elizabeth the next morning. "Omelets and fresh honeydew."

"What are we celebrating?"

"The fact that I'm taking the day off. There's a limit to just how jealous a master one can let the law become." The ringing of bells from the steeple of the church across the green filled the air. "Afraid I'm even skipping church."

Elizabeth stretched and looked at her watch. "Goodness, I am being prodigal. I had no idea I'd slept so late." She refused to give a thought to what her grandmother would have said about such behavior on the Lord's Day.

"The sun's getting around to the back garden. Shall we carry this out there?" In answer to her own question Susan turned to the kitchen and began stacking things on a tray. "I wasn't in the mood for coffee this morning, so I put the tea kettle on. Do you want English Breakfast or Earl Grey?"

"English Breakfast at this time of day. But Earl Grey was one of Elswyth Thane's favorite blends."

"Aha—you can work your favorite topic into any conversation, can't you?"

"Guilty. But you opened the door. Actually, I just looked at those letters again last night—taking tea at Mrs. Spenser's reminded me of what Thane wrote about tea." As Elizabeth spoke she walked out into the back garden and was met with the heady, smoky scent of autumn leaves.

Susan set their breakfast on the glass-topped table. "Well, let's hear that letter, then." She sounded amusedly resigned.

"I'll get it. It just happens to be on the top of my desk."

When they were comfortably settled in the morning sunshine at a table in the grass near a bed of marigolds and Michaelmas daisies and enjoying Sue's delicate omelet, Elizabeth picked up one of the pages she had brought out and read:

Earl Grey is getting hard to find around here, and now Altman's in NY writes me that they won't have another shipment till autumn! Will of course knew Grey himself— the 1914 one—during the war. And the Morgan blend is also good, and I have had that at the Morgan house under the kindly eye of the last J. P., whose sister Louisa supplied much of the detail of the Presentation of Virginia in Ever After. She had gone thru it as a girl when father J. P. lived for a time in England as a country squire, and she acted as his only hostess while still in her teens. Lovely people and lovely days, gone forever! She also taught me the almost forgotten basket-weave stitch for needle-point chair covers, and the Chippendale chairs in the library of the Administration Building at Mount Vernon are now covered with needlework seats in Chippendale patterns that I worked for them in return for their hospitality while I was doing my research there. I get homesick for the place, but most of my friends on the staff there have either retired or died. In the '60s it was an enchanted spot. Have you had all my MV books? There are 5 or 6. Herb teas in England are "tisanes" for invalids! But I like them, too! Not chamomile!

"And they say the art of letter writing is dead!" Susan held a pale green scoop of melon poised above her plate. "It was like having a leisurely conversation with her, wasn't it?"

"Precisely, that's what good letter-writing is. Very stream-of-consciousness." Elizabeth put the letters aside.

"No, go on. I'm fascinated."

"My omelet's getting cold," Elizabeth protested, but she picked up the sheet of paper. "I think I had said something to her about my love for English literature having started with an early reading of *Wuthering Heights*, and she replied:

My childhood reading <u>began</u> with <u>The Virginian</u> and the Wolfville books. Then Alcott and whatever and F. H. Burnett, of course. Bronte's too grim, compared to Jane! Have just finished a rather sycophantic life of Laurence Olivier and his playing <u>Wuthering Heights</u>. He used to pronounce the r, when I knew him; now he has become so grand it is pronounced as tho it was a French name. Actually, it has been English for generations, and like the Himal<u>ay</u>—as they pronounced it <u>their</u> way! He is by no means the greatest actor in the world today, and I don't know <u>where</u> he got that going! But he is indestructible and has survived several illnesses enough to kill most men, to say nothing of that dreadful business with Vivian Leigh, who in spite of their Great Romance became manic-depressive and put him through hell.

My first airplane ride was when one of the Vanderbilts,

with a place on Long Island, had us down for a weekend so he could satisfy a whimsical ambition to take Will <u>up</u> as high as he had been <u>down</u> in the bathysphere. Vanderbilt's private sea-plane, with two resident pilots, was moored at his landing, and at half a mile <u>high</u> he came back beaming from the pilot's cabin to where Will and I sat looking down on Long Island and said, "You are now 3,028 feet <u>up</u>!" It delighted them both.

Susan was leaning back in her chair, a faraway look on her face. "Can you believe the *people* she knew? It's like glimpsing another world!"

"She said that herself several times—that before Hitler it *was* a different world." Elizabeth skimmed the letter silently, sipping her tea for a moment. "Oh, here's a good part—I had written something about always disagreeing with J. B. Priestley—when I taught high school seniors in Boise before going back to lecture at Rocky Mountain, I used an English lit textbook Priestley edited, and we had a running battle all year. I'm sure my students must have been convinced their teacher was suffering from delusions of grandeur —her first year out of college and arguing with the editor of the book."

"Such as?"

"Oh, saying that in a few hundred miles England's terrain varied more than thousands of miles in the United States. The lucky man had undoubtedly never seen sagebrush. More beautiful, or at least *greener* I would grant him, but not more varied."

"What did Thane say about him?" Susan nodded at the stack of papers as she refilled her tea cup.

Elizabeth shuffled through her papers. "'Priestley did some wonderful broadcasts on the BBC during the war, which we got somehow on a big radio set in NY.'"

"Goodness," Sue interrupted. "It's rather like watching an old black-and-white war movie, isn't it?"

Elizabeth nodded. "Yes, a lot of her letters have the same sense of nostalgia. She goes on about the radio and ends with a bit of personal advice: 'It was one of the things Will brought in as a surprise, and I didn't really appreciate it at the time. He did so many things I didn't know enough to appreciate at the time! Keep up with things. Don't let things *go by*—you will think of it later!'"

"Mmm, yes. Good advice."

Elizabeth didn't want to dwell on that, so she continued reading. "'Priestley's novels are good reading—"The Good Companions" made him,' she says. And they give 'a true picture of the concert-party life—which was a sort of vaudeville. He was not educated as an historian. But then, neither was I!'

"Oh, and then listen to this—I had asked her about her experiences doing research at the British Museum:

My British museum experience arose out of Tudor Wench —and Young Mr. Disraeli. John Buchan assisted, by getting me into the House to hear Baldwin speak. A darling. We dramatized Disraeli, and the boy who was to play it went with me to the House for a debate and adopted Baldwin's stance while speaking—both hands grasping his coat lapels either side. Tea on the terrace overlooking the Thames— strawberries. Buchan you should read—The Thirty-Nine Steps—Greenmantle—they can't write adventure like that these days. Robert Donat played Thirty-Nine Steps— tormented by asthma, which he died of, during the war. I didn't know asthma could kill people! Another of Buchan's we loved was The Path of the King—in the same school as Kipling. They must have been friends, but I never thought to ask—only, thanks to Caroline, Kipling had very few friends!

Elizabeth lowered the sheet of paper and looked up. "Thane mentioned that several times—she *really* didn't like Kipling's wife —but I read that Caroline did a great job protecting the privacy Kipling himself so much wanted. She was an American, the sister of Kipling's agent. Balestier was the family name. And Kipling bought the property for his Vermont house from one of her other brothers. Anyway, I can't wait to get to his house. And Elswyth Thane's house, too, of course. And—oh, I've *got* to get organized or you'll have me on your hands forever. I've made so little progress. This really isn't like me to dither around so."

Susan laughed. "Number one, I'd love to have you on my hands for ages and ages. Number two, stop feeling guilty. How long has it been since you've had a vacation? And number three, several unforeseen and considerably more interesting and potentially more important things than research have been happening. So relax!"

"More important than my Ph.D.?"

"Speaking as one who put her career ahead of everything else, it's just possible," Susan paused.

"Wanna tell Auntie Liz about it?" She pushed her hair out of her face and leaned back in her chair.

Susan took off her glasses and closed her eyes. "There isn't much to tell. His name was Donald: tall, blond... We were madly in love, but unofficially attached. We wrote for a while when I went off to George Washington to law school, but the pressures of studying were so heavy that something had to give. So my letters got fewer and fewer and finally stopped." She shoved her glasses back on and sat up. "I suppose it was always in the back of my mind that he'd be here waiting when I came back..."

"But?"

"But he wasn't."

"Where is he? Married?"

Sue shrugged. "Just gone. Left. Without a forwarding address." The two women sat in silence for some time before Sue asked, "Is there any more to that letter?"

Elizabeth was surprised to see that she was still holding a sheet of paper in her hand. "Oh, yes, another page. She always gave me the most wonderful advice on authors—guided my reading for a whole year. I told her it was like taking a directed study course or a master class." Elizabeth dropped her eyes to the letter and read again:

Angela Thirkell, who wrote delicious English countryside was related to three giants—Baldwin, Burne-Jones, and Kipling. So I suppose they were related to each other, but I don't know how. You should get going on her—start with Before Lunch; then she goes into the war, with her sense of humor—Cheerfulness Breaks In—Northbridge Rectory —Marling Hall—like very fragile china teacups.

"I took her advice, of course. Read every one of Thirkell's books. Thirty some, written one a year from the early '30s to the early '60s. And I loved every minute of it. Angela Thirkell carried on where Trollope left off—the books are all set in his Barsetshire, and the Pallisers are still there. But she was also a chronicler of her times. If England was having a cold summer that year, Barsetshire had a cold summer. And, of course, the way those charming people dug in and weathered the war." She paused and swallowed. "Well, back to the letter." She read:

Elmer is back and off again with a load to the dump, Jody sitting very straight on the seat of the jeep beside him. Jody

97

is like a small boy with a favorite uncle—he longs to go wherever Elmer goes and is downcast if left behind. The ride to the dump is a nice one, way across town to an enclosed fill near an abandoned farm—very sanitary, and takes all morning to get there and back! There is a truck that will call for your stuff and take it away—but Jody and I like to go for the ride, and you always meet somebody there that you know! People come up to the jeep and want to buy Jody right out of the front seat! Elmer says, "One million dollars, cash."

Now I must clean up breakfast and think about lunch. I have an elderly once-a-week lady, cheerful and efficient, but this isn't her day! Everybody around here either has several small children, one of which is always sick with something contagious, or else they have a cranky husband who doesn't want them to do anything but feed him, clean for him, and always be there, in case he wants something more! And the wives seem to acquiesce! There is a new women's lib book out about women flyers, the first chapter of course on Amelia Earhart, who would have been a women's libber if it had been invented then! They all seem to be as unhappy and unadjusted as she was! I would sit beside her at horse shows, etc. And could never think of anything to say! Neither could she! I suppose I bored her. She certainly bored me! But the man she married was a friend, and for a time our publisher, and that was supposed to be something in common, I suppose! I was sorry for him! Not even Will could shake her up! He had flown before she was born, in World War I! You couldn't talk to Lindberg either. I suppose they never came down to earth. But Will did! As you saw, he had a sense of humor! They didn't. As I wrote somewhere—"He doesn't know anything is funny!" So many people don't. And so many people, especially nowadays, are always giving themselves a performance, of being Tragic or Inspired or Sick-unto-death, or Misunderstood! See P. 319, Kissing Kin. (I looked it up! And I did write that!)

If I don't get this into the envelope before the dump-people get back they will think I am writing a book.

Elswyth Thane Beebe

"Like I said—the *people* she knew! The world must have been smaller then." Susan shook her head.

Before Elizabeth could reply the phone rang in the kitchen. While Susan answered it, Elizabeth finished the last bits of her omelet and melon and sat half daydreaming in the autumn sun. She opened her eyes when Susan returned. "It's tall, dark and troubled for you."

Elizabeth blinked. "Richard? Why do you call him that?"

"I don't know. I didn't even think about it. It just came out that way."

"He is, you know. You must have sensed it without realizing it. I so wish—"

"Well, whatever he is, he's waiting at the moment."

"Oh, of course." Elizabeth jumped up and ran to the phone. "Hello, Richard." Her voice was light and breathless from her sprint across the grass. "Isn't it a gorgeous day!"

She could hear the smile in his voice. "It must be where you are. But then, how could it help it?"

"Ooh, that's charming. Thank you." Elizabeth felt as if she should curtsey and hold out her hand to be kissed.

"Would you like to go out to lunch?"

"Oh, dear, I just finished an enormous breakfast, and Susan has taken the day off so we could spend some time together. I'm sorry, but I'm afraid I really can't today."

The line was silent for a fraction of a moment. "Oh. All right, then."

"If you won't think I'm terribly brazen I'll suggest an alternative. Not five minutes ago I was telling Sue how anxious I am to get over to see Kipling's house. Would you like to go with me tomorrow?"

"That's just over near Brattleboro, isn't it? I'll be busy all morning, but we could go early afternoon."

"Great. I'll go through my notes and be all read up on it."

Elizabeth and Susan decided to spend the afternoon gardening. But first, a country drive to select some plants. "I usually have pots of mums on my doorstep from the first of September, but I couldn't seem to get at it this year. Just too busy," Sue explained as she drove down a winding, unpaved country lane. "I always get my plants from this man who grows seeds in his basement all winter as a hobby and nurtures them all summer, then sells them for next to nothing in the fall just for the pure joy of the enterprise. His plants are at least six times bigger and healthier than anything from a commercial nursery."

Susan pulled up beside a roadside stand at the foot of a sloping green lawn where a man in jeans and a plaid flannel shirt sat on a folding chair beside a mound of enormous orange pumpkins and pots of copper, garnet and amethyst chrysanthemums. Two little girls, apparently his granddaughters, manned a stand of jams and jellies. "Did you make these?" Elizabeth asked.

"Our mother and Grammy did." The older girl with pigtails replied.

"But we helped pick the crabapples." Her sister held out a jar of shimmering red jelly.

Elizabeth laughed and reached for her purse. "Oh, I remember picking crabapples. What a nuisance. They're so small. It takes forever to fill a basket. But the jelly is definitely worth the effort."

She looked at their other offerings. "Mmm, apple butter. My favorite. I'll have two jars of that, too."

While Elizabeth was busy Susan selected pots of deep red, amber and purple chrysanthemums. And their biggest pumpkin to set by her front door. Feeling smug with their purchases, they drove home with golden afternoon sun filtering through the autumn foliage and scarlet and orange leaves drifting down on them.

They spent the rest of the afternoon digging happily and muddily, trimming back the perennials that were finished and cleaning out weeds. Elizabeth offered to rake the scattering of leaves on the lawn, but Susan explained her philosophy. "I won't rake the grass until the leaves are through falling. One big clear-out will do it. The important thing now is to get all the beds cleaned before the leaves get serious about falling; then I let them collect to serve as mulch all winter."

A couple of hours later an evening chill drove them indoors and Susan lit the fireplace. They sat on the floor and ate toasted cheese sandwiches with cocoa for supper. It had been a perfect day of rest: relaxation, sunshine and physical work that both women much needed, and Elizabeth felt blessedly refreshed after the emotional heights and depths of the day before. Later, back in her room, however, she turned her thoughts to Sue's intuitive analysis of Richard. Her own sense was that he was groping in an emotional darkness like a blind man. She wanted to turn the lights on for him.

CHAPTER 11

*T*he next day the contrast between her confident, amusing host and the shattered man she had attempted to comfort two days before was so sharp that Elizabeth almost wondered if she had dreamed the whole thing. It was not surprising he had simply held his grief behind closed doors and carried on with life, if he was this skilled at masking his feelings.

As they drove south from Newfane along the winding, rushing West River, Richard chatted engagingly about the manuscripts he had been reading and some new marketing plans his sales department was working on. "The big thing in toys is collecting, and everything has to have a collector's carrying case for keeping it all together and toting it all over to friends' houses. So we're going to come out with collectible lines of books for children—complete with carrying cases. Then we're going to launch a book club for young men—high school and early twenties—adventure oriented, but factually based. Enough action for good escape but quality writing to appeal to college men for leisure reading. It's quite a departure from the more academic and literary things we're known for, but I think we can fill a real market need here."

Elizabeth was surprised. For someone who had said he didn't

really want to be a publisher he certainly sounded like he was making a good job of it. "If I plug them with my freshman English classes will I get a commission?" she asked. The conversation flowed as between two old friends. Not as between two who had recently been antagonists. And more recently something beyond friendship. Or had they?

Best not to attempt definitions, Elizabeth told herself. *Accept the moment, and let the future take care of itself.* She was searching for another topic that would keep them on neutral ground when the weathered planks of a long, double-span covered bridge came into view. "Oh, just like Sleepy Hollow!" Elizabeth cried.

"Yes, the Dummerston Bridge is the longest working covered bridge in Vermont," Richard said with some pride. "We have about a hundred of them." He turned to enter the long, wooden tunnel but had to pull to the side, as another car was already coming toward them through the narrow enclosure.

"Why?" Elizabeth wrinkled her forehead. "Why build covered bridges?"

"To protect the wooden trusses from our harsh winter weather. Especially to keep snow off and to keep ice from forming on the bridge."

"Hmm. That makes sense." She paused. "It's really a genius of engineering, isn't it? And beautiful, too."

"Yes, that's another reason for building covered bridges in the first place—to allow the builder to show off his craftsmanship."

The approaching car passed, its driver giving a wave of thanks to Richard, and they entered the cavern, their tires rumbling on the wooden planks. They emerged onto a winding, dirt road lined with tall black tree trunks topped with a canopy of gold and orange leaves. Beside the road the mirrored surface of a small pond reflected the emblazoned images punctuated with leaves floating on the surface.

Elizabeth felt she couldn't look hard enough at each new scene. She wanted to print it on her memory. Knowing winter snows would soon swallow such breathtaking glory made the ephemeral beauty almost painful.

"If you read up on this last night you'd better fill me in; it's been a long time since I've thought about Kipling's having been practically a neighbor of my grandparents." Richard broke in on her reverie.

Elizabeth opened her mouth to reply when he asked, "This is part of your research?" The words froze in her mouth. Was he going to open that battle again? But, no, his question was entirely neutral without the least hint of animosity in his tone. So, did that mean he had capitulated in his objections to her project? It would mean so much to her to have Richard as an ally rather than an adversary.

"Well, of course I went to my primary source," she said cautiously.

"You mean your letters?"

"Mhmm."

"Right. Let's hear what my refreshingly candid godmother had to say. I assume you brought the letters with you?"

She was never far away from her precious letters, but still she hesitated. "Richard, are you sure?" She wanted to communicate that, even though she had no intention of abandoning her subject, she did care about his feelings in the matter. The last thing she wanted to do was to infect his festering wounds even further now that she understood the reasons for his objections.

He raised one heavy black brow quizzically. "Academic freedom, right to inquiry—where would the world be without researchers? I can't let my personal feelings interfere with such great issues as all that."

The idea of telling him that to her, his personal feelings were more important than he knew flitted through her mind, but instead she gave a jerk of a nod and began reading:

Kipling's house. It has become just a tourist-trap, with special weekend affairs, and he would not be happy about it, with his passion for privacy. And <u>she</u> would make everyone feel most unwelcome! The famous row with the Balestiers which drove him away from Vermont stemmed from a brother-sister feud between his wife and her brother—whose first name was Bailey Balestier. I can't remember the family name offhand—it <u>was</u> Balestier, pronounced <u>Bal</u>-ester, come to think of it! Brother Charles wrote <u>Naulahka</u> with Kipling, and another brother, who lived on the family place here, waged a war with Caroline over a boundary line, which Kipling got drawn into—of course on Caroline's side. A famous roadside brawl took place, in which somebody knocked somebody down, and to avoid a lawsuit, which he would have lost, Kipling left Vermont forever. His House in Sussex was—especially by Caroline's taste—so painfully "period" in furniture and general lack of comfort that it must have been awful to live in. Big authentic places like the famous Salisbury house, Hatfield, has modern overstuffed furniture set around the fireplaces and in corners, with the Restoration and Queen Anne furniture pushed back and not required to be sat on in discomfort.

Richard grinned and shook his head. "That's my godmother to a tee. She was so wonderfully practical. Sensible comfort. Always. She didn't get the name quite right, though. The warring brother-in-law was Beatty Balestier, and the co-author was Wolcott. The house is named Naulakha, like the book, although I don't know why the two are spelled slightly differently."

"Sounds like an Indian word."

"Yes, Kipling was said to have admired the Mughal architecture of the Naulakha Temple, which he visited in Deoghar. Although the architecture of his house looks nothing like a Hindu temple."

"What does it mean?"

"'Nine hundred thousand rupees.' Now, the next question is, why? Only I don't know."

"Maybe how much the house cost?" Elizabeth suggested.

"Or perhaps the cost of the shrine for which it was named? As good a guess as any." Richard gave her a quick, sidelong grin. "Actually, I've forgotten more about the whole thing than I ever knew, but I did do a bit of research myself." He gestured toward the back seat with his head. "At least, I dug through some old magazines and pulled that out for you. I didn't get the article read, though."

Elizabeth turned to the back seat and gave a cry of delight when she saw an old issue of the English magazine *Country Life* with an article about "Rudyard Kipling in Vermont" featured on the cover. She hugged it to herself momentarily and felt inexplicably warmed. Far from blocking her research, Richard had actually done some for her.

She turned to the article. "Oh, listen to this: Kipling recorded in his journal that the night they arrived in Vermont it was thirty degrees below freezing and Beatty met their train looking like 'a walrus sitting on a woolpack.' Mmm, great imagery—and this: 'The night was as keen as the edge of a newly ground sword... But for the jingle of the sleigh-bells the ride might have taken place in a dream, for there was no sound of hoofs upon the snow; the runners sighed a little now and again as they glided over an inequality, and all the sheeted hills round about were as dumb as death.'"

Richard signed. "I wish we got manuscripts like that over the transom every day. It's not only beautiful; it's accurate. I've seen nights just like that in a Vermont winter."

Elizabeth was still scanning the article. "He wrote *The Jungle*

Book, The Second Jungle Book, most of the stories in *The Day's Work,* and *Captains Courageous* here. Goodness, I had no idea *The Jungle Book* was written in America."

"That's an impressive output for fewer than four years."

"Probably largely due to his nine-to-five writing routine that Caroline protected, 'sitting and knitting watchfully at the one entrance to his study,' as it says here. Everything Elswyth Thane says about Caroline's watchdogging seems to be accurate, but this writer says Kipling was undoubtedly happy. I hope so; I can't stand to think of people being perennially unhappy."

"Little Miss Sunshine." His voice wasn't quite mocking.

"Oh, I hope not. That sounds as abhorrent as Pollyanna. But the world is so beautiful, it just seems an awful waste when people have to be unhappy in it. Especially in such a beautiful place as this."

The way marked Kipling Road by an inconspicuous sign wound uphill through clumps of trees, and Richard stopped beside the road across from a clearing that broke through to a sweeping expanse of green valley and blue sky. Richard got out and, ever the gentleman, went around the car to open her door. "Careful, these damp leaves are slick under foot."

Elizabeth took his offered hand and emerged from the car. Even before she turned to the house on the hillside above them, though, her attention was caught by the view. Framed by the nearer branches of deep red foliage, the aspect across the road revealed a sweep of vibrant green pasture running down the valley to thick pine woods interspersed with clumps of gold. "No wonder Kipling loved it—just think of seeing that from your study window every day!"

Richard pointed eastward across the valley. "Over there is the Connecticut River—on the other side is New Hampshire."

Elizabeth forced herself to turn from the wide vista of pastoral green and showy autumn color, but before she could take a step toward the house she jerked back toward the woods. What was that gleam of light? Was someone flashing a lantern in the daytime? More likely the sun striking a metal object. Or binoculars. That must be it. Perhaps a birdwatcher.

A low stone wall bordered the property. Stepping carefully through the weeds and tall grasses matted with fallen leaves, Elizabeth led the way to a cut in the wall where a chain across the driveway kept out cars, but not pedestrians. She walked on toward the two-story green shingled house. Had it been resting on water rather than its high stone foundation she might have thought it an eccentric houseboat. No wonder the author himself had described it as "a ship a-sail on a hillside."

"That doesn't look like a Vermont house. Is it like something he might have seen in India?" Elizabeth asked.

"The low-sloping roof and double verandahs do give that feeling, don't they? But I think it was designed by a New York architect who was influenced by fashionable seaside cottages of the day —therefore the hand-split shingle exterior."

They walked across the stretch of overgrown wooded meadow dividing the house from the road. Part of the meadow showed signs under its covering of fallen leaves of having once been an ornamental garden. "Oh, this must be the garden that the lawsuit was about. Beatty claimed he had reserved the mowing of the meadow when he sold the land to Kipling, and here was Caroline planting the thing in flowers. What a shame, that patch of ground couldn't possibly have produced enough grass to bother quarreling over—especially between brother and sister—in *court*." She shivered as she emphasized the last word, remembering her own terrors of a court proceeding.

Richard took her hand. "You know I am sorry about that."

"Well, I lived through it. And I'm sure the owner of the car who got their fender fixed isn't sorry." She forced a smile that she hoped looked more reassuring than she felt. "Is there any chance of our getting inside the house?"

Richard pulled a large, old-fashioned key from his pocket.

"Assuming they gave me the right key, I'd say there's every chance."

"How did you manage that?"

"What good are family connections if you don't trade on them occasionally?" The key fit perfectly, and smiling conspiratorially they crossed the same threshold that Rudyard and Caroline Kipling crossed many times to the main entrance of the house.

"Were those Kipling's clubs?" Elizabeth pointed to a wooden rack of golf clubs by the door.

"Probably. The Kiplings left most of their furnishings behind when they went back to England. Although there's an even more interesting possibility. Arthur Conan Doyle visited Kipling here and brought his golf clubs with him. He gave Kipling an extended lesson, which Kipling apparently enjoyed so much he continued the pastime. He was supposed to have been fond of hitting red-painted balls around in winter over the thickly crusted snow."

"So they could have been Arthur Conan Doyle's clubs?"

"Or at least ones he played with." Richard nodded.

Elizabeth looked around. "It has such a wonderfully airy feeling for an old house—it must be the big windows." She examined the dustily faded India print curtains at the dining room windows.

"Big windows are very impractical in a Vermont winter—as Kipling undoubtedly learned, to his grief."

Elizabeth laughed. "You do sound like a practical New Englander. But with a view like this, anything other than big windows would be impractical." She walked to the picture window and stood for a moment, gazing out. *Oh, that flash of light again.* There must be something nesting at the edge of the woods if a bird-watcher was still focusing on it.

Elizabeth followed Richard into the author's study. Looking out yet another wide expanse of window, she thought about her imagined birdwatcher lurking just at the edge of the wide lawn. Wasn't it the wrong time of year for nesting? She opened her mouth to ask Richard, but he called her attention to the wall behind her. "Beautiful paneling, isn't it?" He ran his hand over the rich, dark red wood. "It's cherry. And the trim is chestnut—very rare now. Kipling's father, John Lockwood Kipling, did the carving on the mantelpiece when he visited them from England. He was an art teacher and curator of an art museum in Lahore, India. He illustrated many of his son's books."

Elizabeth read the beautifully hand-carved letters. "'Night cometh when no man can work.' That would keep you at it, wouldn't it?"

"Now we know the key to Kipling's productivity."

"Guarded by his wife and goaded by the scripture."

Richard smiled. "No man could fail with a combination like that."

Elizabeth looked at her notes. "It seems that their first daughter was born in Vermont before they built this house. The second daughter was born while they lived here. Their only son, John, whom they called Jack, was born shortly after they returned to England. He was only eighteen when he was killed in World War I."

"'If any question why we died, Tell them, because our fathers lied.'"

"What?" She frowned at his odd quotation.

"Kipling's lines. Most interpret it to mean he felt guilt for his son's death because he had pulled strings to get him a commission in the Irish regiment. Jack's eyesight was so bad he couldn't have passed the physical otherwise."

On that melancholy note they left the house. "Did they ever come back?" Elizabeth asked.

Richard shook his head. "Not to Naulakha. They made another trip to America about three years later. I suppose they might have had it in mind to come here, but Kipling and their older daughter, Josephine, got terribly sick on the crossing. Josephine died, so the family returned to England. They sold the house to the American family who still own it."

What a sad tale. Elizabeth walked in silence back across the disputed meadow, contemplating all the loss the famous writer's life had encompassed. Little wonder that an air of desolation hung around the house, in spite of the beauty of its setting. They were almost to the car when Elizabeth stopped and turned sharply. She hadn't so much heard something as felt it. Felt a prickling at the back of her neck as if someone were watching her. But she could see no one. If the birdwatcher had momentarily trained his field glasses on her, he seemed to be gone now. She walked on to the car, picking her way carefully through encroaching brambles, ferns and fallen leaves.

When they were again on the road Elizabeth turned to her host. "Richard, thank you so much for bringing me here. It wouldn't have meant half so much without... I mean, you know so much about it, and you were able to get the key so we could go inside..." She realized she was babbling. "This will make marvelous background for my paper." She pulled a notebook out of her handbag. "I think I'd better jot a few notes before I forget."

"You're determined to go ahead, then?"

She was aghast at the grim note. She thought they had settled all that. "Of course I am. I thought that was understood. Why did you bring me here if you didn't acquiesce?"

"I'm not sure myself. I thought I did—brave words about academic freedom and all that. But then it all comes flooding back." As he spoke she could feel the darkness of the past months and years settling around him.

"Richard, I—" Not knowing what to say, she reached out to him. He took one hand from the wheel and held hers. "Can't you trust me?"

"I don't know. I want to. Desperately. But Mary and I fought over that so often. I just couldn't take having the whole thing go wrong again."

She wanted to yell at him that she wasn't Mary Ilona Walters, but instead she forced herself to speak quietly. "Don't you think that learning what she found might help to lay the ghost?"

"No!" His face was ashen, and the lines in his features deepened alarmingly.

And then Elizabeth had an illuminating flash of understanding. *That's what he's afraid of—whatever it is. He's afraid that if I find out I'll become obsessed by it like Mary Ilona was.* Now it was time to say it. "Richard, I'm not Ilona."

He shook his head. "When the Bible said the love of money was the root of all evil it wasn't talking about just Ilona. No one is immune. I don't have any idea what she was getting at, but she was convinced it was worth a fortune, and that obsession overtook her beyond all reason." He pulled to the side of the road and stopped the car. "Don't you see, Elizabeth? I don't want it to happen again."

There was so much more they needed to talk about, so much she wanted to say to him—must say sometime—but at that moment his look of anguish silenced her. Wordlessly, she snuggled into the curve of his arm.

They sat there in silence for some time until at last Richard gently pushed her upright. Perhaps he had received the essence of the comfort she wanted to communicate, because his dark mood seemed to have passed. "Canoodling in broad daylight like teenagers. Right in the heart of Vermont. It's enough to bring Mount Wantastiquet down on our heads."

"Well, luckily no cars came along." She spoke lightly, but then she wondered. Had she heard a car whiz past while she had her eyes closed, relishing the comfort of resting on Richard's shoulder?

"Would you have cared if they had?"

"No." Of course not, what difference could it possibly make?

"Brazen hussy." He started the car.

"Well, I'm a westerner. We're much less inhibited out there."

"Must have something to do with your wide open spaces." He glanced at his watch. "Between Grandmere and my trips to England I've become thoroughly hooked on afternoon tea. Would you like to stop somewhere? Maybe the inn in Newfane?"

"That sounds perfect, but Julia had to go into the hospital in Brattleboro for some tests this afternoon, so Sue has Tommy. I know she really needs to work, so I feel like I ought to get back and relieve her."

"Let's collect Tommy and take him home to Grandmere for tea." Richard suggested with a perfectly straight face.

"Terrifying Tommy and Mrs. Spenser's bone china teacups?" Elizabeth was breathless with the images the very thought conjured up.

Richard threw back his head and laughed in the way Elizabeth loved but knew was all too rare. "Scared you, didn't I? We could entertain the terror on the lawn. Croquet, badminton, paper airplanes. I'm actually more worried about scaring off Annie, their daily help, than upsetting either Aunt Frances or Grandmere."

"If you really think you're up to it." The idea of a firm helping hand was too much to resist.

They stopped at the Newfane Market to lay in provisions for Tommy's tea—the same market where Elizabeth had so recently come to disaster in the tiny parking lot. "Beware of tight parking spaces." She grinned.

"Maybe they should post a sign: Warning: this parking lot can be hazardous to your fender."

"Or one on my car that this driver can be."

"Does it still trouble you?"

"It more puzzles me. But I take it as a healthy reminder to be cautious."

"Good." He parked without mishap.

In the market Elizabeth spotted a basket of bright red strawberries. "Oh, look! I thought it would be too late in the season for these. We can serve them the way Elswyth Thane described, with their stems still on and little bowls of sugar to dip them in."

Richard added a package of bright orange fresh cheese curd. "Ever had this? We call it squeaky cheese because it squeaks when you bite into it."

By the check stand Elizabeth made the find of the day. "Bubbles! I loved these when I was a child. Let's take some to Tommy."

"They've fancied it up since I was a kid." Richard observed the package. "Two kinds of bubble pipes, two sizes of rings. What's this world coming to?"

"Just because you still use wooden buckets for sugaring and horses for winter logging up here, don't think the rest of the world hasn't moved on."

"I know. Why do you think I live up here all I can? It's not a jungle out there; it's a plastic metropolis."

"Well, maybe fancy bubble-blowing equipment will help prepare Tommy for the real world."

Sue didn't even try to hide her relief when they stopped to collect Tommy and the ever-present puppies. "He really isn't naughty. He's just such a bulldozer. And he never thinks before he leaps. Are you sure you can manage?"

"We'll keep him outside," Elizabeth promised.

A short time later Tommy and the dachshunds were rolling head-over-tail and boy-over-dog down the long slope of the Spensers' lawn. Shrieks of laughter and excited barks greeted Elizabeth and Richard as they came around the side of the house bearing the tea things. They stood and watched for a moment, both grinning broadly at the uninhibited sight as Tommy and the dogs fetched up by the stone wall.

"Do you think they're having as much fun as we had there?" Richard asked.

Elizabeth replied more dreamily than she meant to, "Nothing

could possibly match that." She spread Aunt Frances' lace tea cloth on the round white metal table on the terrace and turned to pick a bowl of asters for the centerpiece while Richard unloaded the heavy tray he bore. When she called, "Tommy!" the youngster responded with a speed that could only mean he knew there was food about.

"Yum!" He started to reach for the plate piled high with country oatmeal cookies, but Elizabeth caught his wrist mid-grab.

"Uh, uh, uh. Go wash, young man."

Tommy opened his mouth to protest, but Richard jerked an authoritative thumb in the direction of the back door of the house. "Wash room's just inside."

In a minute Tommy returned with clean, but still wet-looking hands, and began contentedly munching away.

Elizabeth shook her head and laughed. "I know, I said wash; not wash *and dry.*"

Before Elizabeth could pour her second cup of tea Tommy had eaten his way through most of the goodies and was sitting like a coiled spring. "There's a brown paper bag on the bench." Elizabeth pointed. "It's for you." The spring uncoiled with a snap that propelled it halfway across the lawn and left its spectators breathless.

"Bubbles! All right! Look at this giant blower!"

"Now, don't spill it," Elizabeth cautioned as Tommy poured the clear liquid into a dipping pan. "Put the lid back on tight."

Amazingly enough, Tommy obeyed, and a moment later his six-inch red plastic ring was trailing a six-foot-long marbled rainbow that broke off into separate bubbles.

Elizabeth's own delight rose with the display. "Turn around slowly, Tommy. See if you can make a complete circle... Oh, it broke!"

"Look out, Auntie Liz!" A bubble made a bounding bomb drive for her head and burst, showering her with tiny drops.

"Your turn." Tommy held the ring out to her. The breeze

caught some of her bubbles, carrying them almost as high as the house. She laughed and dipped the ring again, then twirled with it, filling the garden with opalescent orbs. "'This life which seems so fair is like a bubble blown by sporting children's breath...'" She quoted a line from a once-memorized poem.

"'...But in that pomp it doth not long appear; / For when 'tis most admired, in a thought, / Because it erst was nought, it turns to nought.'" Richard finished the poem at the same moment a bubble hit her face and broke. She wasn't sure whether her shivers were in response to the cold drops, the somber turn of the poet, or Richard's grave tone.

Elizabeth thrust the bubble ring back to Tommy and turned to Richard, her earlier delight disintegrating with the bubbles. The shadows the late-afternoon sun cast on his sharp features highlighted the pain she knew he carried. She couldn't deny that she was becoming very fond of this difficult man. And there was no doubt in her mind that he cared for her—perhaps even loved her as far as he could. But *as far as he could* wasn't far enough. He had once referred to Mary Ilona as being possessed with her search. Now Elizabeth realized how appropriate that word was to the hold the deceased woman had on Richard. And until the phantom could be put to rest, the spirit exorcised—whatever it was that would break the hold his dead wife had on Richard—he would not be free to love anyone.

The more Elizabeth thought about it the more convinced she became that the only way to fight a ghost was to give it substance. In spite of Richard's resistance to her suggestion, she was determined. She would find out what Ilona had found. When she knew that, then she could dispel the apparition.

CHAPTER 12

$\mathscr{B}$ack in her room after delivering Tommy into the care of his grateful mother, Elizabeth went to her file and drew out her next letter from Elswyth Thane. She could only hope to find a clue to the mystery in one of her letters. It was the only thing she had to go on.

This one was a particularly long, gossipy letter, filled with reminiscences that once again made Elizabeth feel she was being transported back to the 1930s. She must have just read *Remember Today*, Thane's novel with a cowgirl heroine. She remembered sending a snapshot of herself riding her uncle's horse—a favorite teenage pastime, although the western rodeos she was familiar with were a far cry from the one at Madison Square Garden recounted in the novel.

She plumped the pillows on her bed and settled back for a good read.

Dear Elizabeth—
I love having these pictures, especially the Sierra one of you in your cowgirl outfit. I had such fun on the "research" for

<u>Remember Today</u>, which took me downstairs and behind the scenes at Madison Square Garden during the rodeo performance and into the hotel where they all stayed. I was convoyed into "the works" of the place by Foghorn Clancy, the 200-lb. cowboy who managed, or ran, or whatever, the famous King Ranch in Texas, and what a character <u>he</u> was! I particularly remember his showing off his longhorns, massed behind a frail barrier at the end of the druggeted aisle that ran between the pony stalls on the lower floor of the Garden. Everything there was as clean as the upstairs ring, and by some magic there was not even a Smell! People were coming back from the arena on stretchers while we were there, but nobody seemed to be very concerned about them! Fascinating.

Elizabeth smiled as she read the next lengthy paragraph. What a fresh view of Charles and Anne Morrow Lindberg. Her grandmother had adored Anne Morrow Lindberg's writing. What would she have said to all this?

The boxing world was one Elizabeth knew—or cared—nothing about, but her correspondent's word pictures gave her a sense of some of the people involved and the world Elswyth Thane moved in. Period-piece pictures aside, though, was there anything here that could be a clue to Ilona's fixation?

Lindberg. Yah. I didn't like him. Granted, he was shy and out of his depth at a Park Avenue dress-dinner soon after he returned from his flight and before he met the woman he married—but he was surrounded by the friendly supportive men who had backed him, and there were only two women at the dinner—myself and the hostess.

Granted, he didn't know straight up about how to behave in the surroundings—somebody had put him into a dinner-jacket—but there should have been some <u>instinctive</u> behavior pattern with which to meet the situation, which by then could not have been entirely new to him, some inborn <u>manners</u>, which he never showed a sign of! And his wife, who came later and <u>was</u> born to it, with a distinguished father and a money background, was apparently as introverted and odd as he was, and as for the stuff she <u>wrote</u>—!!!!

I met Gene Tunney at about the same time, on the crest of his own wave, and a more charming, self-possessed host I never encountered, dinner-jacketed in his own hotel suite to which we were taken by mutual friends, able to pay me a humorous compliment, able to get thru the evening without falling over his own feet. And his background was no more sophisticated than Lindberg's, and he, too, married a "society girl," who was warm and friendly and helpful to him, and look how he turned out! There must be something about boxers—(he didn't like the term prize-fighters)—because we got to know Eddie Eagan very well, and <u>he</u> had married a "society girl" who became one of my dearest friends, tho we don't see each other nowadays, because of distance. Eddie was Boxing Commissioner or some such title, and we attended the Golden Gloves matches at Madison Square Garden (they were sort of for the beginners, the hopefuls in the game) and sitting next to Eddie in seats, which were too small for him, I felt the muscles tighten in his arms in his instinctive, subconscious "punches" as he watched his protegees—he knew what they should be doing, tho he never joined in <u>helping</u> each boy in an unconscious reaction. I suppose flying is impersonal and self-centered—Amelia Earhart was impossible to know

121

too. She and Lindberg should have had each other to get along with, tho Anne Morrow was close!

Elizabeth pondered. Of course, there was that terrible business of kidnapping the Lindberg baby. But that must have been considerably after the time of Thane's reminiscences. Could there have been anything about that to catch Mary Ilona's interest? The ransom money? It was recovered, wasn't it? And the kidnapper caught and punished. All long before Elizabeth's time, but Nana had talked about that, too.

She gave only half of her attention to her reading about Thane's brush with a career writing for film and stage, but she couldn't see any leads to anything that might help her solve the puzzle.

My Disraeli play was brought to NYC with only the two leads from the London production—a mistake. The American Bulwer had no style, Old Isaac couldn't learn lines, and the critics couldn't remember anything but Arliss's performance of Disraeli, so the "young" part was incomprehensible to them—tho Arliss himself came to the first performance and enjoyed it. There was a darling man! With one of those dragonlady wives!

They bought Riders of the Wind film rights but never made it. Tudor Wench was wanted for Katherine Hepburn, but they couldn't get a script that wasn't laughable, so she made Anderson's Mary of Scotland, which was disastrous. My things are too simple to attract film or TV—you should have seen what they tried to do to Tryst for films—the script made it all a dream of Sabrina's, because they couldn't cope with the idea of Hilary's actually coming back!! So that fell thru! They can't see what is <u>there</u>; they have to try to make it <u>harder</u> and kill it.

Hm, she couldn't see a clue there, but the reference to *Tryst*, one of her favorite Thane novels, was certainly appropriate. A ghost story. But entirely different from the ghost she was dealing with. Hilary, the hero, dying in the African desert, had prayed, "God, give me England before death. No, give me England *instead* of death." And his prayer had been answered. He returned to his home, where the heroine, Sabrina, had already fallen in love with him from reading his journal. Charming. But hardly applicable. Unless Mary Ilona had prayed to become a ghost. Which Elizabeth found exceedingly unlikely.

The letter continued for two more pages: Thornton Wilder and Eugene O'Neill—whom Thane didn't like. Talbot Mundy's *King of the Kyber Rifles*, Agnes Strickland's *Lives of Queens of England*, and Carola Oman's *Crouchback*, which she did like. Oh, yes, and Josephine Tey's *Daughter of Time*. One of Elizabeth's favorites. Was it Elswyth Thane's recommendation that had led her to that book? She couldn't remember, but she was grateful for it if it was.

One final recommendation:

What else? I'll think of something, when I seal this. Oh, and there's a book by Violet Trefusis called <u>Don't Look Round</u>, which gives the most superb picture of Edwardian life before 1914—Trefusis is the friend of V. Sackville-West (of Knole) and the daughter of Alice Keppel, who was the friend of Edward VII—if you follow me. Anyway, Edward is mentioned only twice in the book, so there are no sidelights on that—but the life they lived is entrancing.

Time and money. Both so scarce nowadays!

Elizabeth sighed and let the page slip from her fingers. All fascinating memories and food for thought. But not much to the point of solving her problem. If only she could find one clue. Just one lead to spark her search...

Consciousness returned sometime in the middle of the night. Why was she sleeping on the top of her bed? Why was she still dressed? Why was the bedside lamp on? Elizabeth turned on her side and was met by a crunching sound as several sheets of paper crumpled under her. She pulled out the rumpled pages of the letter she was reading last night, and memory returned—a clue, a starting place—that was what she had been searching for. Something to exorcise the ghost of Richard's dead wife that was beginning to haunt her as well.

She flung her arm across her eyes and tried to think. The harder she tried, however, the more futile it seemed. Finally she realized she was just lying there listening to her head ache. In disgust, she rolled off her disheveled bed and made her way groggily to soak in a tub of hot water.

Such an interrupted night was not highly recommended to produce clear-headed thoughts the next morning, but Elizabeth did manage a cheerful, if bleary-eyed appearance over the skillet as she stirred the scrambled eggs when Susan emerged fresh from the shower and blow dryer. "I couldn't believe your light was still on when I came in from burning the midnight oil at the office." Elizabeth held the skillet out to her and Sue put a scoop of golden eggs on her plate. "I would have looked in to say goodnight, but all I could think about at that hour was getting to bed. Were you researching or reading a whodunit?"

"I'm not sure. Maybe both. Ghost story, I think."

"Wonderful! Vermont is full of creaky barns and covered bridges for headless horsemen and such. And we can always dump the body in the marble quarry at Barre."

Elizabeth grinned. "I wish it were that easy. Remember telling me about Richard's friend—wife, it turns out actually—who was killed in that plane crash with his brother? Well, strangest thing, but his wife was into some kind of research on Elswyth Thane, too—or, really, more on Dr. Beebe. Anyway, Richard says it was an obsession with her, and it's my theory she was onto something of value—monetary or literary or something."

"Like an unpublished manuscript, you mean?"

Elizabeth shrugged and buttered her second piece of toast. "Your guess is as good as mine."

"William Beebe was a really famous naturalist in his day, wasn't he? I can't remember much about him, but I was raised on stories of his exploits—my father was a great fan of his."

Elizabeth nodded. "Seems he was the Jacques Cousteau of his generation. He explored all over the globe, then wrote some apparently pretty terrific books about it all. Teddy Roosevelt said Beebe's *Jungle Peace* would stand on the shelves of cultivated people as long as readers of taste appreciated charm in writing."

"Wow. That's some recommendation. Have you read it?"

Elizabeth nodded. "Loved it. I suppose, though, his most famous achievement was going down in a diving device off some Bermudan island to observe deep-sea life. His record dive was over—or rather, under—3,000 feet of water. The record held for almost twenty years."

"Well, there you are."

"Where? Under 3,000 feet of water?"

"Precisely. Under 3,000 feet of water in the Bermuda Triangle. Deep-sea life there must include more than guppies—like Spanish galleons and buried treasure, maybe?"

Elizabeth laughed. "Do you always hallucinate after a late night at work?"

"Well, you're looking for something Ilona Walters could have been obsessing about. People do obsess over buried treasure."

"Yes, counselor. But I need something that will hold up in court, so-to-speak. *Treasure Island* I can get at the library."

"Okay, let me review the evidence. I always knew my legal training would come in useful for something more than traffic violations someday."

"You didn't tell me my case bored you," Elizabeth said over her shoulder as she crossed to her bedroom.

"Never bored, but you've got to admit, it didn't exactly make me F. Lee Bailey."

Elizabeth returned with her folders of letters. "I've been hoping I'd find a clue in here. Thane does write about her Will quite a bit, but I haven't seen anything helpful."

The paper Elizabeth had rumpled in her sleep was on top. Susan smoothed it out on the table. "Taking your aggression out on a defenseless piece of paper?"

"I slept on it."

"But didn't get any vibrations?"

"Just a headache." Elizabeth refilled their coffee mugs while Susan glanced through the file, pausing to read carefully wherever her eyes caught William Beebe's name.

"Oh, here she talks about the bath whatsis," Sue held out a letter dated November 23, 1979, and Elizabeth read aloud:

Dr. Beebe's courage, you mention, took years off my life, I can assure you! The bathysphere had a facial expression, I

always said—smug and secretive, with 3 eyes! I was glad to
see the last of it! It figures in my book <u>England Was an
Island Once</u>. Small wartime printing, now scattered. There
was no "device" for buoyancy, as you suggest—if the cable
broke, it was gone forever.

This is all I can manage for now. Love—

"I remember," Elizabeth said. "I had been visiting some new
neighbors; he was a retired Navy man—deep submergence was
his specialty—commander of the *Bathyscaph Trieste*. I asked him if
he was acquainted with the work of William Beebe, and he went
into raptures over Dr. Beebe's work and *courage*—told me how
terribly dangerous the bathysphere was, just a cable against the
whole weight of the sea. He was enormously impressed that I was
corresponding with Mrs. William Beebe and showed me a picture
of his own, more modern, bathyscaph—a little metal ball but with
a huge blimp-like thing above it to provide buoyancy." Elizabeth
paused a moment at the recollection before continuing. "But you
don't really think there *is* anything like buried treasure, do you?
We don't even know if Ilona was interested in the Bermuda stuff.
After all, Beebe worked all over the world: Mexico, Southeast
Asia, Trinidad, Venezuela, Brazil, British Guiana, the Galapagos
Islands, Baja California…"

"Peripatetic doesn't really cover it, does it? I see your problem…" Susan continued perusing the letter Elizabeth had fallen
asleep on, then abruptly she tossed it to the center of the table
with a triumphant cry. "There! I told you I'd find something."

Elizabeth looked blankly at the rumpled sheet.

"You wanted a place to start, right? Go to the Mugar."

Elizabeth frowned.

Sue sighed impatiently. "And you're the researcher—the

Mugar Memorial library at Boston University. Thane said she gave them the papers when she cleaned out the apartment after her husband's death. You appear to have read every word either of them published. So if there is anything, it has to be in something unpublished, right?"

"That's just it—I don't know if there *is* anything to look for." Then the image of Richard's haunted her eyes filled her mind, and she sat up straighter. "But I intend to find out. What's the best route to Boston?"

CHAPTER 13

The Mass Pike let Elizabeth, driving Sue's little Satellite, off right at the foot of the Harvard Stadium, and she drove along the broad green banks of the Charles River, where Harvard men and Radcliffe women, in various states of undress, were catching some of the last rays of sunshine before autumn gave over to winter snows.

When the gray cement towers of Boston University came into sight around a bend in the river, she crossed over the Charles to Commonwealth Avenue and turned into the campus. After considerable scrabbling and scrappling, like a small animal looking for a burrow, she finally found a parking spot.

The beehive atmosphere of the Mugar Library gave evidence to the settling in of the new school year, as students bent intently over their books. Elizabeth had an almost overwhelming desire to ask for Elswyth Thane's "adorable archivist who was at Oxford during the austerity years," but when a pale-faced young man in steel-rimmed glasses and a thin mustache offered to assist her, she simply asked where she could find their manuscript holdings in contemporary literature and was directed up the stairs, through the stacks, to a special glass-walled section. The door into this holy of holies was locked, so she was required to search out another librarian, an efficient lady in a navy blue skirt and sweater; surrender two pieces of identification; and follow a respectful two paces behind the key-bearing guardian.

"You may work only in this room, and no papers are to leave the room. The catalog is by the window." Giving her a parting glance of inspection the straight-haired librarian left the room. Elizabeth was relieved they hadn't required a security clearance.

But when she turned to the catalog her respect for the library holdings and the precautions taken to protect them increased. She found listings for original manuscripts of Robert Frost, H. G. Wells, Robert Browning, Walt Whitman, Pascal, Theodore Roosevelt... Being encompassed with so great a cloud of witnesses almost made her forget her mission. But then she found the listing she had come for: BEEBE, (CHARLES) WILLIAM (July 29, 1877–June 4, 1962), naturalist and oceanographer...

Elizabeth was soon lost in a world of exotic birds, giant Galapagos turtles, and strange sea creatures. The photographs fascinated her most. Many she had seen reproduced in his books, but some were new to her. The earliest ones, taken on a bird-watching expedition to Mexico at the beginning of the century, were as amazing for the Gibson Girl attire worn by his female companion in jungle exploration as for the flora and fauna. Imagine exploring the tropics in a tight-waisted, ankle-length skirt, a high-necked, mutton-chop-sleeved blouse, and a wide-brimmed hat with ribbons. Would that have been Beebe's first wife? Little wonder Elswyth Thane had been so insistent about not going on expeditions if that had been her predecessor.

She moved on and smiled again, as she first had when seeing it in a book, at the "Photograph of author atop Cheops." Her reference in a letter to that enigmatic speck on top of the great pyramid had resulted in Elswyth Thane sending her a beautiful glossy photograph of the two of them taken in the '30s. And then the pictures of the bathysphere, looking, as Elswyth Thane suggested, almost humanoid—or in today's terms, like something out of the *Star Wars* saga. Although Indiana Jones would perhaps be a better analogy.

Entranced in her work and lost to all sense of time or of the need to stop for lunch, Elizabeth pored over manuscripts, research notes, letters. She searched for some veiled reference to an ancient Inca statue, buried treasure, a lost civilization—Atlantis, maybe? Or maybe something outer-spacy. Had Carl Sagan been among those theorizing that space aliens had a base in the waters of the Bermuda Triangle? Some of her students were fanatical fans of his "Cosmos" show.

Beebe had explored the waters around Bermuda. She racked her brain for anything she had ever heard, no matter how far-out, about that mysterious place. She vaguely recalled a TV movie suggesting that the strange disappearances of ships and planes in the area were due to demonic activities...

She closed the file with a sigh. What a fascinating day, resulting in pages of notes for her dissertation. And plenty of fertile ideas should she ever want to write a fantasy novel. But how utterly, hopelessly futile for any scrap of evidence that would lead her closer to solving the Mary Ilona mystery. One last file: Résumés, curriculum vitae, and biographical listings from various Who's Who publications, *Contemporary Authors*, and Dr. Beebe's obituary from the New York Times. Well, there it was; the life of a great man had passed before her eyes—but without any hint of mystery or hidden riches. She doubted Dr. Beebe would have been particularly interested in a chest of treasure. His fascination was with the world of God's creation—or Darwin's evolution.

But then, perhaps that was the point—if Beebe had found something like that, he most likely would have left it unexploited while he went off to write a monograph on the pheasants of the world, study coral life in Haitian waters, or observe color changes in the water as surface light became diffused in diving descents, leaving something of mere monetary value for someone like Mary Ilona to profit from

Outside the library windows the sun had set, and the Greater Boston area came alive with millions of points of electric light. Several times during the day the librarian had looked in on Elizabeth and, apparently satisfied that her charge intended no harm to the precious documents, slipped out again quietly. The entrance of a different, younger, but no less earnest-looking, worker signaled the changing of the guard, and Elizabeth knew it was time to be on her way. She was taking one final perusal of the file in front of her, intent to gather the last crumbs from her efforts, when she noticed a footnote to one of the biographical listings: "Some of Beebe's letters are in the Alpheus Hyatt Correspondence at the Princeton University Library." With a listlessness born of fatigue and disappointment, she noted the information.

When she stopped at the reference desk to retrieve her driver's license Elizabeth expected to be frisked but then realized the doors of the library were guarded electronically, so the fact that she wasn't required to turn her pockets inside out represented no slacking in the security system. She asked for the address of the Princeton University library and got it, much in the spirit, however, of, "What could they have that we don't have?"

She stopped at the Howard Johnson's near the Harvard Stadium for an overflowing platter of tiny, crispy Ipswich clams with coleslaw and French bread to sustain her on the homeward drive, but, even hungry as she was, it was impossible to think about anything other than the day's investigations. If only she could talk it over with Richard.

It was well after midnight when a weary Elizabeth arrived back in Newfane. The village was long asleep, as was Susan, so Elizabeth made her way silently to her room without bothering to switch on any addition to the small night light Sue left burning for her. But the square whiteness of a sheet of notebook paper taped to her door halted her like a glaring red stoplight.

Sir Galahad called. He's off to slay a dragon in the publishing world in Philadelphia. He sounded sorry he missed you. Probably do him good!

Love, (I suspect he does, too)
S

Shaking her head at her friend's flippancy and regretting the long-lost days of knights in shining armor when all a maid had to do was wait—embroidering a tapestry and plaiting her hair in a high tower while her prince dispersed the fire-breathing barriers to their happily ever after—Elizabeth went to bed.

Her dreams, however, were not filled with images of a prince on a white charger and a castle in the sky but rather of a giant Galapagos turtle that morphed into a dinosaur that suddenly became a sea creature battling with Elizabeth in a diving ball, which it dispatched with the single swat of a fin, breaking her life-giving oxygen line and sending her to the bottom of the ocean.

Elizabeth flailed madly and awoke with her sheet tangled around her neck and her pillow over her face. She lay in the dark, gasping for breath. Thank goodness her window was open, letting in invigorating fresh air. She drew in deep lungfuls, trying to make sense of it all.

An owl screeched outside her window, jolting her upright. How did her window get open? She was sure it had been closed when she went to bed. She looked at her jumbled bedclothes and the pillow she had flung to the floor. Had she pulled that over her head herself in her nightmare? Or did her suffocating experience have a far more sinister explanation?

CHAPTER 14

"Yes, I opened your window," Susan replied blithely to her question the next morning. "You must have been having a terrible dream. I heard you call out. And no wonder, it was stifling in your room."

Elizabeth relaxed. Such a simple explanation. And, of course, it followed that the pillow over her face was equally innocent. Telling herself that, however, couldn't entirely suppress the shiver that shook her spine.

Elizabeth determined to focus entirely on her dissertation. Noble as her idea of helping Richard might have been, it would get her nowhere with her academic committee, and Richard wasn't even here. Who knew when he would return?

"It's weary days waiting." Julia patted her ripening belly as she and Elizabeth sat under a golden, but somewhat thinning, tree in Susan's back garden a few days later.

"I know what you mean." Elizabeth spoke with emphasis as she realized that the sun had made six weary trips across the sky since Richard had gone.

Julia gave her a startled look. Elizabeth laughed. "Don't be so egocentric. Unborn babies aren't the only events that fatigue one with delays."

"No, but I'll bet they're the heaviest." Julia shifted in her canvas lawn chair.

Elizabeth nodded. "When you're too tired you lose your sense of delight." Certainly she had managed to push herself forward with her research and writing, but much of the joy had gone out of it. And forcing herself to read late into every night until she fell asleep from exhaustion—always with her window firmly locked— had been of little help.

Fortunately, Julia didn't look for any darker meaning behind her words. "That's it, isn't it? All the wonderful projects that I'd love to get done are just sitting there—and I'm sitting here. If only one's energies could match one's enthusiasms."

"What does the doctor say?"

"Oh, the doctor's never felt better. And he has a wonderful facility for judging everyone by himself. He says any time now, but he won't commit himself. It seems 'anytime' could mean anything from twenty minutes to twenty days."

"Well, we're ready." Elizabeth put as much assurance in her voice as she could. "Any time night or day. Give us a call, and we'll come get Tommy. And we'll plan on Stuart for dinner while you're in the hospital."

Julia laughed and struggled out of her chair. "That will be such a help. I learned long ago that top billing on the list of life's meta-physical questions goes to, 'What's for dinner?'"

In a determined effort to shake her own lethargy—waiting for a grown man to call was considerably less sensible and would have far less to show for it in the end, than waiting for a baby to decide to be born—Elizabeth grabbed a notebook, asked Sue for the car keys, and headed down the road to Wilmington. It was strange that she hadn't been to Elswyth Thane's home yet, consid-ering that was one of her primary objectives in coming to

Vermont. But then, nothing about this whole trip had gone according to her preconceived schedule.

As she drove up a winding hillside overhung by colorful foliage Elizabeth tried to analyze her reluctance to make this pilgrimage, because that's what it was—a pilgrimage—the journey of a devotee to a shrine. How the no-nonsense Elswyth Thane would laugh at such a high-flown metaphor being used on her simple Vermont farm. Elizabeth recalled her description of the place written in a mid-August letter:

… this house is more than a hundred years old and in many ways inconvenient and not the way I would have built a house—the stairs are steep and narrow, the windows are shaded by porches—except where we have cut in picture windows—and there are not enough rooms for all that goes on here. Three maples, which have grown enormously since we have been living here, shade the front lawn and are convenient for Jody, who is not a "her"—he says just because he's blond people always think he's a girl, and boys can be blond too!

Elizabeth smiled. She had always enjoyed the moments of anthromorphism in Thane's writing. And she was so glad she was here in the autumn so she could see the maples in their glory. Good thing she was getting there before they dropped more leaves. The trees were all at a stage now that a good wind could strip most of them.

Today is clear and cold, and I am afraid the "turn of the year" has come, into autumn, after unusual heat and humidity. We have a little old-fashioned wood stove—they are now worth their weight in gold in this part of the country!—which Elmer had had tucked away in his "shop" in the barn, after picking it up at a shop with a broken foot—the stove, not Elmer. So several winters ago he welded the foot back and said could he set it into the fireplace, which is enormous and leaked heat in a shocking way, and created a draught to the stairs, etc.—open fires are <u>very</u> wasteful and extravagant to a New Englander! I said Sure, and he closed off the chimney except for its own stove-pipe, and the draught stopped, and the wood went farther—I do still miss the open flame, but the stove has developed a personality and is certainly the <u>coziest</u> thing in the house! I notice that now several of our rather fussy friends with handsome living rooms are installing <u>replicas</u> of the old wood stoves, at great expense, and cutting their wood a little shorter to fit them! It was lighted last evening, and of course it confuses the furnace thermostat, by keeping the living-room warm, so the upstairs doesn't get its share of furnace heat—but one can't have everything, and a couple of electric heaters, which can be snapped on and off, take care of my bedroom and the bathroom. And our Vermont winter is on the way!

Elizabeth choked as she realized she would never get to watch the "turn of the year" with her friend. How Elizabeth had dreamed of visiting and sitting around the "sensible" wood-burning stove with her. Must life always be so full of missed chances and might-have-beens?

That was undoubtedly the problem—the reason Elizabeth had delayed going to Wilmington—her reluctance to enter a dream that could never live up to itself in reality. All the times she had driven this road in daydreams to find the little white farmhouse with hollyhocks growing across the front, ivy on the chimney and three giant maples shading the porch at the end of her trip. And inside, her dear friend waiting with a steaming pot of Earl Grey and the petted and pampered, gravely golden Jody to welcome her.

Her friend had shared her fantasy as well: "There's the car. How we could gossip if it were you coming in to tea…" she had closed one of the letters. The author had never eaten the lemon poppyseed bread that was one of Elizabeth's favorite tea-time treats, so Elizabeth baked a loaf and entrusted it to Uncle Sam's men in blue, who apparently completed the mission successfully:

Aug. 23, 1979

Dear Elizabeth—

The lemon cake has arrived, and is delicious! We are enjoying it, tea after tea, as there are only two of us to eat it! How nice of you to make one and send it!

Things are humming here this morning, as my one-day-a-week girl is here bustling around with the vacuum. I had a daily char in London in the '30s for what this girl gets for one day a week!

I must now stop this and see what I can scare up for lunch —there must be something left over in the ice-box! Meals are still a problem here, as Elmer has been having tooth trouble and is still "eating soft."

Beautiful weather here today. Do you know D. E. Stevenson's books? Very nice bed-reading.

No, Elizabeth hadn't known D. E. Stevenson, but after that hint she lost no time in seeking the author out and reading all she could find—as she did all of Thane's suggestions.

Elizabeth had to admit that she now dreaded facing the scene of such fond imaginings to find it empty of the charm and warmth of the remarkable woman who lived there for nearly forty years. Why couldn't she have made the trip sooner? The answers were obvious: Time, money, distance, teaching commitments… but it did seem mean of life to make one wait until it was too late.

Or was it? If she had come sooner would Richard have needed her then? If she had come when he was in the first flush of his love for Mary Ilona? Or when his grief for her was too raw to seek any measure of recovery? And now? Was it too late? Or too early?

On an impulse she pulled up at a roadside stand and bought a pot of bright yellow chrysanthemums. She would certainly have taken Elswyth Thane flowers had she been calling on her for the imagined tea party. This was the least she could do.

The road now was paved but only slightly wider than the dirt road that had taken them to Kipling's home, the double yellow line in the middle a perfect match for the overhanging leaves. The way led through yet another covered bridge, then past small houses scattered alongside the route which followed a tumbling river. Elizabeth was amazed at the density of the trees and undergrowth. What must it have been like for the early settlers? Imagine clearing land for a farm, hacking out roads, cutting through all this untamed wilderness almost 200 years ago with only deer and raccoon for neighbors?

An out-cropping of rock—solid Vermont granite—told of the sturdiness of the land and its people. And now she was crossing yet another rushing river—or was it the same river, twisting through the landscape? Then the view opened out to a green pasture dotted with dun-colored cows.

At last she came to the tiny village of Wilmington strung alongside the swirling Deerfield River. Quaint wooden buildings lined the hilly street and white-steepled churches faced one another from each side. She stopped first at the red-brick library, its classic pillars and Federalist fanlight giving dignity to the small building.

The young librarian was welcoming and delighted to show Elizabeth the library holdings on their local celebrity, beginning with a heavy tome titled *Two Bird Lovers in Mexico* written in 1905 by William Beebe and Mary Blair Beebe. Elizabeth was fascinated. Especially by the black and white photographs, many showing Beebe's first wife toiling in the field. Elizabeth smiled, recalling his second wife's scorn at the idea that *she* might undertake an expedition: "I *told* him I wasn't an outdoors girl!"

Elswyth Thane refused to be hampered by the shadow of her husband's first wife. But Elizabeth staunchly brushed the thought aside. This was about Thane, not about Elizabeth's personal daydreams. Ironic, though, that Beebe's first wife's name was Mary, too—until she changed it to Blair Niles in honor of the man she married the day after she divorced William Beebe.

Next the librarian brought Elizabeth a loose-leaf binder containing letters from Barbara Streeter, the dear friend Thane had alluded to in her letters to Elizabeth. Elizabeth felt an immediate kinship with this woman whose friendship Thane had likened to her relationship with Elizabeth.

She took copious notes and put a star by her notation that Streeter was to get the books not taken by the Mugar. Would there perhaps be a clue in these volumes? Elizabeth shook her head. She had no idea how to begin tracing any such possibility. Hadn't Thane said her friend lived in Washington, D. C.? The letter from Streeter bore no return address.

But one clue she could follow. The librarian sent her to the town clerk to learn the exact location of the next stops on her pilgrimage.

Following the town clerk's directions, Elizabeth drove along Haystack Road beside the river under Haystack Mountain, the highest point in the neighborhood, until she spotted a mailbox standing sentinel at the turning into a secluded country lane. She started to drive in, then hesitated. No, she wanted to approach quietly, on foot, as became an ardent pilgrim. Besides, Elswyth Thane had walked this lane almost daily for many years—for a time to receive Elizabeth's own letters or mail ones to her. She pulled well off the road to park and carefully locked the car.

The lane was unpaved and thickly wooded on both sides, but a hayfield stretched off behind her while flaming maples and dark green pines covered the rising hillside ahead. At the top of the lane she stood stock still and surveyed the scene. It was perfect. In her imagination, informed by the drawings on the end papers in *Reluctant Farmer*, she had seen the scene many times: the white farm house with its long covered porch, the barn off to the side, and in front, the big tree where Elswyth Thane sometimes sat to write, if the artist's sketch told the truth.

Now Elizabeth stood under that same tree, leaves floating down on her, and recalled the owner's words: "We bought it early in the war as a summer home where my mother could grow some flowers and where Will and I could work peacefully on manuscripts and take walks and watch birds and have time to read aloud in front of a log fire."

Was there ever a better reason for buying a house? A life filled with flowers, birds, and books in front of a cozy fire.

Elizabeth walked slowly and unobtrusively along the driveway until she could see the small stone-flagged, covered stoop outside the back door of the kitchen that Elswyth Thane and her mother had so painstakingly sewn with wire netting as a giant aviary for Cheewee, the purple finch she had rescued from a storm, turned into a cherished family member, and then made the hero of her book *The Bird Who Made Good.*

The porch was now glassed in, rather than wire-netted, but several trees and bushes still bore some birdhouses and feeding stations, because Will, accustomed to lavish tropical life, had complained there weren't enough birds around the place.

Somewhat whimsically for so level-headed a woman, Elswyth Thane believed that houses were beings with personalities and auras and, like people, could choose their friends. She must have been right, because this house was obviously missing its friend. The family who lived with Elswyth Thane during the last months of her life had seen to many repairs and much-needed improvements and still lived here—although no one appeared to be about at the moment. One could almost imagine their busy, happy-family sounds filling the house. And yet there seemed to be a forlornness about the place. Or was Elizabeth just being fanciful, projecting her own feelings?

Elizabeth walked around the rebuilt barn, wondering if swallows still nested in the cupola. She noted the windows that had been added where former stall space had been converted into a room with a view for Will. She paused under the big window that looked eastward toward the rising sun and moon and across the hayfield where deer came to graze at twilight, as Thane recounted. She knew that inside was a window seat, framed by bookshelves. If only she believed in ghosts she was sure she could have conjured up William Beebe sitting at the window with his field glasses. A family of tree swallows still had a nest in the birdhouse in the cedar tree at the end of the porch, but the Beebes no longer took tea on the delightful spot of lawn below.

Although no one appeared to be home at the moment, Elizabeth was respectful of the strong sense of Vermont reserve, so she made no attempt to knock on doors or look in windows. Besides, she had seen it so often in the scrapbook of her mind that there was no need to: the living room with its landscape paper, comfortable stuffed furniture, antique red-brick fireplace set in plain ivory-painted paneling—now sealed off with Elmer's wood-burning stove in front of it; Will's room with bamboo wallpaper and scotch plaid bedspread; Elswyth Thane's own room with red rose wallpaper. It really would break her heart so see those changed—as they undoubtedly were now. The repairs that had so pleased the author during the last months of her life had no real bearing on Elizabeth's work.

She turned and walked slowly down the lane to her parked car, thinking long, but rather unproductive thoughts on the brevity of life. The lesson from church last Sunday flitted through her mind, along with her remembered desire for Richard to be there to read it as he had on her first Sunday in Newfane: "You have no idea what tomorrow will bring. Your life, what is it? You are no more than a mist, seen for a little while and then dispersing." And with her facility for mixing Shakespeare and scripture she added, "And our little life is rounded with a sleep."

Somehow all that should have made her feel melancholy, but instead, she was strangely warmed and comforted by the visit to her friend's home. Dr. Beebe was almost eighty-five when he died in the warmth of Trinidad, surrounded by the jungle and work that he loved; his wife lived an exciting life in America, England and Bermuda, ran a productive farm in Vermont and wrote thirty-two books of history, fiction, and biography. One could hardly wish for more.

But Elizabeth had one more visit to pay. Her final stop of the day was Riverview Cemetery. With a silent *Thank you* to the town clerk for her precise directions, Elizabeth drove back toward town, her mind whirling with memories of events long past and more recent. She allowed her fancy full range, mixing imaginings with reality, knowing full well she would have to keep a tight rein on herself, indeed, when she came to writing her dissertation. Facts only, there. But for the moment she could revel in conjecture.

Past Wilmington she followed Stowe Hill Road to the green and gold Riverview Cemetery atop a knoll that provided a panoramic view of the autumnal hills, if not actually of the river. Her foot barely pressing the gas pedal, Elizabeth crept along the network of narrow trails that wound among the tombstones. One section was distinctive for the small round markers bearing stars, which told her these were graves of Civil War veterans. On toward the newer area, she spotted the small green groundsman's shed, which the clerk said was near the grave Elizabeth sought.

Elizabeth parked her car, took the pot of chrysanthemums from the back seat, and walked toward her goal, reveling in the intense gold of the trees bordering the emerald grass. She took a deep breath, thinking how lovely it was to have this moment to herself. No sooner had the thought crossed her mind, however, than a movement at the side of the building gave her the feeling she was not alone. Why that should give her a chill, she couldn't understand. It was most likely the sexton, although of course, the cemetery was open to anyone.

Shaking off her slight shiver, she walked on across the grass. What she sought wasn't hard to find. The sod hadn't yet sealed into the established grass. A pot of bronze chrysanthemums and a bouquet of roses and asters, beginning to droop, marked the small, upright granite rectangle. She stooped and set her floral offering beside the others.

Elizabeth ran her hand over the stone, feeling its solidity, its roughness, the small valleys of the incised letters:

Elswyth Thane Beebe
Author
1900–1984
Wife of
William Beebe
Naturalist

She sat, gazing at the simple marker. The essence of a life captured in less than a dozen words. Feeling the autumn breeze in her hair, Elizabeth recalled the conversation she and Richard had shared. "Tell me about her death and funeral. Was she ill for a long time?"

He was quiet, remembering, then nodded as agreement with her request, not in answer to her question. "She had been very well all spring. She was so happy with the improvements being made on her house. The family that lived with her was marvelous.

"Elswyth was so happy to have people in her house—people and laughter. She showed me the repairs they had made to the back rooms, and she was just delighted. 'I never thought it could look like *that*,' she said." He paused again.

"Then she got sick in July. The doctor told us it was a fifty-fifty situation... She died the last day of the month."

"And her funeral?"

"She had planned it all out in detail, and we followed it to the letter: A graveside service, very simple and peaceful—the minister read three Psalms: One Hundred Twenty-one, Twenty-three and Eighty-four. Then he recited the words to 'All Things Bright and Beautiful.' We said the Lord's Prayer and left quietly. She was adamant that there be no eulogy, but the day gave her one—the kind she would really like. It *was* bright and beautiful with birds singing and flowers in bloom."

The remembered conversation faded. Elizabeth looked again at the peaceful grave at her feet. Swallowing hard, she dug in her shoulder bag for the New Testament with Psalms that lay buried under all her other books and papers. She had found it on Susan's shelf and brought it especially for this moment. She turned to Psalm Eighty-four. *How amiable are thy tabernacles, O Lord of hosts!... Yea, the sparrow hath found an house, and the swallow a nest for herself, where she may lay her young...*

Elizabeth found herself smiling. The words were so appropriate. *Blessed is the man whose strength is in the Lord... For the Lord God is a sun and shield; the Lord will give grace and glory: no good thing will he withhold from them that walk uprightly. O Lord of hosts, blessed is the man that trusteth in thee.*

A bird sang to her from a nearby tree, and her heart sang back. A sparrow or a swallow, perhaps? She wondered. Or maybe a purple finch like Cheewee? The Beebes would have known, but she was no birdwatcher.

She turned the pages to Psalm One Hundred Twenty-one: *I will lift up mine eyes unto the hills, from whence cometh my help. My help cometh from the Lord, which made heaven and earth... The Lord shall preserve thee from evil: He shall preserve thy soul. The Lord shall preserve thy going out and thy coming in from this time forth, and even forevermore.*

Elizabeth didn't need to look up the twenty-third Psalm. Her beloved nana had required a rather strenuous course of Bible verse memory from her. Elizabeth hadn't cared so much about the memory work, but she cared deeply for her grandmother and for the strawberry ice cream cones from the sweet shop Nan provided as reward. So she had acquiesced with good grace. She was comforted now with the thought that her friend could be dwelling "in the house of the Lord forever." Amen.

Wanting to continue the service the best she could she searched her mind for words to the English hymn that had been recited. She hadn't sung it for years, but snatches of it returned to her: *All things bright and beautiful, All creatures great and small, All things wise and wonderful, The Lord God made them all. Each little flower that opens, each little bird that sings... the purple-headed mountain...* Here she lost the words—something about tall trees and meadows and God has made all things well.

Elizabeth wasn't sure how much she believed. But the words were beautiful. And her grandmother, who did believe, would be

147

so happy to hear her reciting them. Maybe Nan did hear—and Elswyth, too—if Nana was right about the hereafter.

Or was there more to it than even Nana suspected, and ghosts were for real? As a reflex Elizabeth glanced at the caretaker's hut, where she had seen the stealthy figure earlier; then, giving herself a shake, she slammed the door on that thought.

Elizabeth turned in something of a daze of conflicting emotions and made her way slowly back to her car. It was only when she was fumbling for her key that she noticed the small red car parked at the back side of the cemetery. She tried to tell herself it probably belonged to the sexton, although it seemed more likely the caretaker would drive a pickup. And she couldn't help feeling the vehicle looked vaguely familiar. Had she seen it in her rearview mirror shortly after leaving Newfane?

Through the lengthening shadows of evening she drove slowly back. This had been a pilgrimage, and like all successful pilgrims, Elizabeth returned renewed. No matter how long Richard's business kept him away and too busy to call, she and her days would not drag their feet. She had come here to do a job, and with her research now well in hand, she could begin drafting her paper.

Her mind firmly set on her new determination, she pulled into Susan's street, vowing to eat only a quick, light supper, then get immediately to her typewriter. She would spend the evening refining her outline...

Her reverie ended abruptly when a small figure came hurling itself toward her car. She slammed on her brake so hard the tires squealed. She parked at the side of the road. "Tommy! What are you thinking? Never run at a car like that!" She jumped out and shoved him back onto the lawn.

"We're getting a baby tonight! Mom and Dad 'uv gone to the hospital to see about it!" .

Elizabeth grabbed his hand, and they raced for the house. "Sue! Julia's gone into labor?"

Susan was setting bowls of chicken noodle soup on the table.

"Sure has. About an hour ago. So it may be a long evening. Tommy, go wash. Stu promised he'd call *the minute* there was news, so we might as well relax."

Elizabeth accepted the theory of relaxing, but a few minutes later she realized she was sitting on the edge of her chair, barely aware of what she was eating. When the phone rang a short time later both women jumped for it so fast they slopped soup all over the table and reached the phone in a tie and a flutter of nervous giggles. "Go ahead," Elizabeth said. "She's your sister."

Susan answered but, after her initial hello, wordlessly held the receiver out to Elizabeth with a wink and turned to engage Tommy's attention in an endeavor to provide Elizabeth with some privacy, although that was hardly necessary. After Elizabeth's surprise at hearing Richard's voice and a pedestrian exchange of greetings, conversation ground to a halt.

"How's your business going?" Elizabeth attempted to move things on a bit.

"Fine. I'll be able to wrap it up here in a few days." His pause was so long she was wondering what to ask next when he continued, "Save Thursday for me, will you? Later afternoon or evening —not sure what time I'll get back."

"Well, you know what the social whirl is like in Newfane, but I'll try to squeeze you in."

He chuckled and relaxed, so she told him about her trip to Wilmington that day, and coming home to learn that Julia was in labor. The conversation ended leaving her in smiles.

Back at the table, however, Tommy was not smiling. "Cold soup is yucky. Can I have dessert?"

"Did you eat any cheese and apple?" Susan asked.

"Yeah. A slice of each."

When Susan set a piece of chocolate cake in front of her nephew Elizabeth was amazed at her easy compliance, but Susan laughed. "Julia said just to keep him happy. She'll worry about his nutrition and his immortal soul when she gets home."

149

"Ah, the wisdom of motherhood."

But later in her room Elizabeth felt devoid of any type of wisdom. It was her practice to put her research notes in a useful form as soon as she could, but none of the disjointed impressions she had jotted down during her time in Wilmington seemed to her to be of any academic use. The day's expedition had been important for personal fulfillment—perhaps closure was a good word—but it was hardly literary analysis.

She sat long at her desk, her eyes closed, watching the day again in her mind: the drive along the curving, hilly road, the rich autumn colors of the town forest—now beginning to fade on the higher slopes—walking the lane to Elswyth Thane's home, standing by her grave in the cemetery... And now, reliving it all in the quiet of her room, she saw what she hadn't consciously noted before. Woven in and out among the snapshots her mind had taken was a little red car. Surely not the car she hit? If the driver didn't care enough to show up in court they would hardly be stalking Elizabeth now.

Coincidence, surely. But the image and the slight tingle it produced would not go away. Had she seen it before? Had it been there when she and Richard visited Kipling's home? Had it been parked next to her at the market her first evening in Newfane?

She shook her head. Who could remember such detail that long ago? And why should she try? What possible importance could it have?

CHAPTER 15

The next morning Elizabeth was determined to make progress on her dissertation. She would certainly enjoy her Thursday date with Richard more if she could accomplish some work first.

She caught herself up at the thought. Date? No, she couldn't have a date. What about Gerald?

She scrabbled around in the pile of papers at the back of her desk and retrieved the photo she had set there. Goodness, had she really forgotten his existence? Or had he forgotten hers? How long had it been since he'd called? Well, she didn't have time to worry about that now. But it was definite she did not have a date with Richard. She had an appointment with a friend.

Gray streaks of rain were washing down her window in counterpoint to the clack of her typewriter keys when Sue stuck her head in the door. "News! It's official—I'm an auntie again. Six-pound, nine-ounce girl. I told Stu I'd bring Tommy up later, but I have to call in at the office first. Can you hold the fort here? Tommy's watching television, but I don't think the children's programming goes much longer. I'll try to get home early."

She waved Sue off with blithe assurances, but a short time

later when, indeed, *Sesame Street*, *The Electric Company* and *Mister Rogers' Neighborhood* gave over to a soap opera, and the bowl of potato chips was exhausted, she began to realize what she had taken on.

"Jesse and Joey want to blow bubbles."

"Sorry, Tommy, not today."

"Why?"

"Because it's raining—the raindrops would break the bubbles. Besides, bubbles need sunshine to make them beautiful."

"Then what *can* we do?"

Elizabeth looked desperately around the room. Reading a story or playing Candyland would require her full attention. He couldn't very well play ball in the house. She needed something Tommy could entertain himself with. Then she spotted a bundle of clipped notes labeled "emergency resources" that Julia had packed with her son's belongings. They had been pushed to the back of the counter, almost out of sight.

Elizabeth clutched at them like a drowning woman. Play dough, collage, banana pops, peanut butter chews—the life raft inflated in her hands. "Well, Tommy, let's make a batch of nice pink play dough, and you can design toys for your new little sister's room to surprise her when your parents bring her home to you in a couple of days."

"Pink? Are you sure she wouldn't like brown and purple better?"

"Babies like bright colors. Besides, I don't have brown and purple food coloring."

The logic worked, and Tommy happily stirred the pan while Elizabeth dumped in the ingredients of flour, water, salt, oil and—after an extended search through Sue's cupboards—two teaspoons of cream of tartar. Tommy was rather heavy-handed with the food coloring, so they achieved a somewhat turgid red rather than the delicate pink Elizabeth envisioned for a new baby girl; but, as

Tommy blissfully pointed out, "You *said* babies liked bright colors."

"I did, but is this the way it's supposed to look?" She surveyed the lumpy mass in the pan.

"Sure, when it all globs together you bread it."

"*Bread* it?" Elizabeth had visions of dipping it in beaten egg and then bread crumbs like a veal cutlet.

"You know, punch it around. Like when you make bread. I always help my mom."

"Oh, you mean *knead* it." And amazingly enough, the globs did knead out smooth and pliable in a few seconds.

The playdough was a huge success, and Tommy spent the rest of the morning rolling, cutting and shaping with only occasional interruptions of, "Auntie Liz, look!" Things went so well that by the time Sue called to check on them in the early afternoon Elizabeth was able to give a guardedly optimistic report. "I think I'll get this chapter done today—although it's only five pages and I consider ten standard in normal times."

Susan laughed. "No one ever accused Tommy and those dogs of anything so dull as normal times."

"I'm really having more of a problem with my own goals. Why is it that for the self-motivated the possible must always be the minimum?"

Before the counselor could give counsel, however, another "Auntie Liz, look!" rang out.

By the time Sue arrived home in the late afternoon a still-smiling but slightly frazzled Elizabeth was dipping frozen banana chunks into a mixture of melted chocolate chips and peanut butter, and Tommy was helpfully licking up all the drips. "No, Tommy. Don't practice your karate on the bananas," she said in a flat voice.

"Are you really that controlled, or are you past the point of vehemence?" Sue popped a chocolate-coated banana chunk in her mouth.

"Don't ask. I can't cope with hard questions."

"You're dismissed. I'll clean up here. Then if we can scrape an adequate amount of chocolate off Tommy I'm taking him to see baby Allison."

"Will they let me hold her?" Tommy asked.

"Not till she gets home. You'll just have to look at her through a big glass window tonight."

"Like in the snake house at the zoo?"

"Well, not *exactly* like that."

A short time later the door clicked shut behind Sue and her nephew, leaving the house echoing with blessed silence. Even though it was only late afternoon the black clouds made it as dark as evening. Elizabeth switched on her study lamp and settled in at her desk.

Perhaps an hour later she was completely absorbed in her work when Jesse and Joey startled her by setting up a din of yapping barks and growls. Was something in the garden? Perhaps a deer or another dog? She got up from her desk and turned toward the cacophony.

She had taken one step when a crash of breaking glass made her spin back toward her window.

Shards of glass covered her books and papers. A large granite stone occupied the chair she had been sitting in moments before.

If the dogs hadn't alerted her... She shivered.

Elizabeth ran to the back door and flung it open. The dachshunds raced out. They continued their barking, but now it was unfocused, and they ran around the garden enjoying their freedom, not chasing an intruder. Had she spotted a running figure beyond the fence? Or had it been her imagination?

She called the dogs back in and hunted out a paper bag to put the broken glass in. Then she realized she needed to call the police. This wasn't random vandalism. Whoever it was, for whatever incomprehensible reason, had been aiming at her.

CHAPTER 16

"*A*nd you have no idea who might wish to harm you?" This time Sheriff Norris's presence was a reason for comfort, not dismay.

"Absolutely not. I hardly even know anyone here. And everyone has been friendly."

The front door banged, and the dogs ran, yapping, to Tommy. Susan entered, shaking the rain from her short, blonde hair. "Elizabeth, is that the sheriff's car out front? Oh, hi, Ed. Not more trouble about that car, surely?"

Sheriff Norris started to explain that this time Elizabeth had called him, but Elizabeth wasn't listening. No, not quite everyone had been friendly, had they? What about the sense she had had of a watcher in the woods that day at Naulakha? And the car that seemed to be following her yesterday? *Could* that have been the same one involved in the accident? The world was full of little red cars, wasn't it?

The case had been dismissed and the insurance company agreed to pay. Surely the driver didn't bear a grudge? And when she mentioned it to the sheriff he didn't seem to think it any likelier than she did. Still, he did take a powerful flashlight and walk around outside her bedroom window. Any clues as to the identity of the intruder, however, had been well washed away by the rain.

"I'll just keep this rock for evidence, even though it doesn't tell us much. Can't get fingerprints off Vermont granite, and it's hardly distinctive. Do you ladies need help cleaning up?"

Elizabeth had already begun picking the shards off her desk and moving books and papers out of the way of any stray raindrops that might blow in. Susan answered. "Thanks, Ed, but I'll get my brother-in-law to come over and board up the hole for tonight. He owes me one, since we're keeping Tommy." Sue walked the sheriff to the door, telling him about her new niece.

Elizabeth's mind had moved on to a new thought when Susan returned with a broom and dustpan. "Sue, maybe we've got this all wrong. Whoever it was couldn't have seen very clearly in here. Maybe they thought it was you. Have you sent anyone to jail that's been released lately? Or someone still inside whose family might retaliate?"

"Hm," Susan pondered as she began sweeping. "I'm not a state's attorney. I don't prosecute. Can you move that chair so I can sweep under it?" She continued after a moment. "There was a shoplifting case a couple of months ago. I represented two teenagers. One of the fathers was really steamed when the boys were fined. I think he blamed me." She shrugged. "I did my best, but let's face it. His son was guilty."

Susan stopped sweeping and looked at Elizabeth. "I can't imagine anyone mistaking our silhouettes, no matter how rain-streaked the window was." She shook her short bob.

Elizabeth shivered as she ran her hands through her mane. No. If they were aiming at anyone, it was at her.

By the time Thursday afternoon rolled around, however, Elizabeth had put the incident behind her in her excitement at seeing Richard again. She was looking forward to her time with him more than she cared to admit. It had been a week of ups and downs. Stuart had installed a fresh pane of glass and put a screen on the outside, just in case the intruder should decide to repeat his attempt. With her room put to rights, the alarm of a granite missile shattering through her window had faded. Julia had gone home from the hospital with her tiny pink bundle, and Tommy, Jesse and Joey had joined their family. And, at last, Elizabeth had managed to make satisfying inroads on her dissertation.

It seemed the only area she hadn't made progress in was her goal of finding some explanation for Mary Ilona's strange behavior. But then, perhaps there wasn't an explanation, she told herself. Some people didn't need a reason to be obsessive.

Richard rang to say he would pick her up at four o'clock. They would have dinner, and he had a surprise for her. His usual enigmatic self, she mused as she eyed her wardrobe. Surprises were all very well, but how was she supposed to know what to wear? Not that she had all that many choices. "Do you have a warm jacket?" Susan asked. "Evenings are getting pretty cool now."

That made her decision. She had a black coat, so she would wear her black dress with pearls. Basic, but it was hard to go wrong with black. When Richard called for her wearing a black suit and dark tie she thought they looked like they could be going to a funeral—a thought she kept firmly to herself.

"What's the mystery? Where are we going?" she asked when she was settled in his car.

"Ever heard of the MacDowell Colony?" He asked.

"Afraid not. Should I have?"

"Well, it's world famous. At least in this part of the world."

"I am a westerner, you know."

While Richard explained they drove on through the late afternoon, across the green iron bridge that spanned the river between Vermont and New Hampshire. Around every corner another breathtaking vista opened before them. Elizabeth was torn between focusing on Richard's words and the scenes before her.

She wanted to drink it all in, to keep every snapshot forever—the deep reds, augmenting the brightness of the yellows, rusts and tangerines.

She smiled in amazement at a moose crossing sign, then turned her attention back to Richard, who was explaining that the MacDowell Colony was founded in Peterborough more than a hundred years ago by the composer Edward MacDowell and his wife.

"Oh, I'm with you there. I played 'To a Wild Rose' when I took piano lessons—years and years ago." She shook her head. How could time go so fast? Third grade at Sunny Ridge School. A lifetime away.

"That's the one." Richard's voice brought her back to the present. "Artists from all over the world are granted fellowships to live and work in complete freedom. Thornton Wilder wrote 'Our Town' there. Peterborough was his model for Grover's Corners."

Now Elizabeth was truly interested. "I love it! My first year of teaching—high school, before I went to Rocky Mountain—that was the senior play. I directed it."

"I knew you must have some New England blood in your veins." Richard smiled. "Aaron Copeland wrote 'Appalachian Spring' there, too. They claim to have sponsored more than sixty Pulitzer Prize winners. Not bad for a town of fewer than 5,000 people.

"The colony is normally all very secluded and private, but tonight they are doing a program for the community. Kamnachandra Uri, a poet we publish, is giving a reading."

Oh, that explained it. "Great." Elizabeth managed to sound enthusiastic even though modern poetry wasn't her favorite genre. She was hoping she hadn't misheard about the evening including dinner. They had been driving for more than an hour and a half, and she was hungry.

The sun was setting scarlet, peach and apricot when they passed the "Welcome to Peterborough" sign. Still deep in the woods, they drove down a long, wooded hill as if between two walls of fire, then into town. The hilly streets of Peterborough were lined with red brick buildings topped with white cupolas. Richard paused at the corner of Main and Grove streets and pointed to the street sign. "Oh!" Elizabeth clapped her hands when she read the street sign: "Grove Street at Grover's Corners. It is 'Our Town!'"

Elizabeth was just beginning to worry that hunger would take the edge off her delight when Richard pulled into a parking spot. An old mill along the rushing Contoocook River had been turned into a restaurant. Elizabeth smiled appreciatively when she saw the two stars it had been awarded—not many Michelin stars in these back woods. Their table was beside a wide window looking over the river, and her plate of seared sea scallops with homemade ravioli was well worth its stars. They chatted about their work to the accompaniment of the sound of the tumbling water.

Elizabeth was pondering whether or not to accept the offered lemon tart when Richard glanced at his watch. "No thank you," she told the waiter. Delicious though it sounded, she hated to be rushed.

Outside town they drove along the densely wooded MacDowell Road, Elizabeth glimpsing flickers of lights from cottages set back in the dense woods. Then Richard turned uphill to High Street, which, indeed, was high. He pulled into a small parking lot beside a large white building surrounded with a stone wall and a hedge of bushes dotted with lampposts and clearly marked with a large white sign: "Please do not enter Private Property."

But Richard led the way confidently. "This is the administrative center for the MacDowell Foundation. They own about 450 acres of woods." He swept the landscape with his arm as he ushered her into the building. "There are lots of studios dotted all through the land. Artists with fellowships work there in complete seclusion, then come together for dinner in the evenings."

Elizabeth, who had been struggling all week to get writing done on her dissertation, which was far less an artistic endeavor than she might have wished, could certainly appreciate the value of such cocooning. Of course, that's what the time at Susan's was supposed to have been for her. She smiled at the irony. Being charged with hit and run, Julia giving birth, helping care for Tommy—and most of all, meeting Richard... Her time in Newfane had been anything but cloistered.

They sat in comfy chairs in the pleasant parlor, and the colony administrator welcomed the guests, then explained that since the founding of the colony on the farm where Edward MacDowell loved to compose in 1908, they had given space to thousands of artists. Their host named a few including Leonard Bernstein, Aaron Copland and Alice Walker. "Our goal could be summed up in the words of Marian MacDowell: 'To prevent the non-writing of a poem.'"

Kamnachandra Uri was the first artist to perform, and in spite of her former misgivings, Elizabeth was enchanted with the sibilant, almost magical sounds his poetry produced in the flow of his soft voice.

The classical guitarist who followed was a perfect accompaniment to the words of the poetry still floating in her mind. A choreographer then explained and performed a scene from a dance she was creating, a novelist read a cutting from his new book, which sounded far too dark and violent for Elizabeth's taste. The evening concluded with coffee and lemon bars that more than made up for the dessert she had denied herself earlier.

Richard introduced her to his poet, who was as charming and gentle in person as he had been in his performance. She congratulated him on his superb presentation and told him she looked forward to introducing her students to his work. The two men discussed a few details of Uri's upcoming volume of poetry before another guest claimed the poet, and Richard and Elizabeth were able to make their escape.

They drove back slowly along the thickly wooded, two-lane road, the headlights of their car picking out trees crowding the verge and giving the impression of endless darkness beyond. Past Brattleboro the road followed the winding West River, and vegetation crowded closer, broken only by an occasional house.

"Might we see deer?" Elizabeth asked.

"Quite likely earlier in the evening, when they would have been going to the river to drink. Less this late, I should think, but still a good idea to keep our eyes peeled. Beautiful creatures, but not the brightest."

"Have you ever hit one?"

"No, I've been lucky. My father did once, though. Fortunately, it didn't go through his windshield. His shoulders ached for weeks, though, from tensing up so hard." Richard looked over and smiled at her. "Don't worry. I'll be careful."

And she didn't worry in the least. A lovely companionable silence filled the car, and Elizabeth leaned back in her seat, feeling no necessity to fill the space with talk. Letting the beauty of the evening play through her mind, she closed her eyes. Then opened them just in time to glimpse something walking by the side of the road. A deer? She barely had time to register that it was a young woman when Richard slammed on the brakes.

They both turned toward the lone pedestrian, but she had vanished like an apparition. Elizabeth turned toward Richard to speak, but the words caught in her throat as she saw him drop his head onto the steering wheel. "Richard!"

He looked up. Even in the pale light his ashen hue was alarming. "Did you see her?" His words came as if from a long distance.

"Yes, of course. But Richard, you didn't hit her or anything. What's the matter?" And then she knew. Before he could speak she remembered seeing that same moonspun hair on a book jacket. "Ilona?" She whispered the name. "But she's dead."

"At least if you saw her too I must not be completely crazy."

"Richard, it was just a glimpse from a moving car at night.

There must be thousands of women with Jean Harlow hair like that."

But she knew her words were falling on deaf ears. The closeness—oneness she might have said—she felt with Richard earlier had been shattered more thoroughly by that elusive vision than her bedroom window had been by a chunk of granite. She had thought—hoped—Richard had somehow come back from Philadelphia freed from his former haunting, but, no matter who or what they had seen in that fleeting moment, if such a mere suggestion could recall the intensity of pain she now saw in her companion, he was much further from recovery than she had hoped.

"I thought she was gone." Elizabeth straightened her position in her seat.

"I thought so, too." He gave a jerky nod. "I was determined. But I guess some things can't be accomplished by sheer willpower."

He restarted the engine, and they drove on. Over and over Elizabeth assured herself they had not seen Ilona. Mary Ilona Walters Spenser was buried in Boston, and Elizabeth did not believe in ghosts. But no matter. The fact was that Richard's former wife was still there between them. Richard was still as married as if his wife were alive.

Elizabeth turned her face to the cold window glass and flung silent words to whatever was out there in the black night. "Why can't you leave us alone?"

CHAPTER 17

$\mathcal{T}$he next morning Elizabeth sat, staring at the murky contents of her coffee mug. Susan flew into the room, late for work, just taking time for a single gulp of orange juice. "I almost forgot to tell you. Gerald rang."

Elizabeth caught herself just before asking who Gerald was. "Does he want me to call him back?" Her voice reflected her distaste for the task.

"No. He said you shouldn't bother. He's going to be gone for the weekend."

Elizabeth wasn't certain whether she felt more relief—or more guilt over being relieved. Gerald was simply a complication she didn't need right now.

The screen door banged at Susan's departure, and the room filled with silence which Elizabeth had no desire to disturb. Silence could be a most comforting companion—as if in its own emptiness of sound it understood the void within her.

She groped through the mist that was her mind. "Work!" She commanded herself. Her feet, as of their own accord, carried her to her room.

Like an automaton she turned to her desk and the Elswyth

Thane letter file. Nothing could take her mind off her own situation like visiting bygone days through the experiences of another. Meeting Thane's friends and favorite books was exactly what she needed. She turned to the letter her hand drew from the file—written on notepaper with a picture of a little blue bird lounging in his nest, his wings folded behind his head:

We are all more or less in this laid-back state here, tho perhaps not so comfy or happy-looking about it—but we have all been having the most thundering colds and coughing our heads off for days, with "something that's going round" while the most glorious fall weather is on. Elmer and I have been simply prostrated with it, and it takes a lot to lick him! Jody is, however, in excellent health, I am happy to say, and eyes us anxiously as much as to say, "What is the <u>matter</u> with you?" while we cough and gag and hold our heads. They say it lasts 3 weeks, which is cheerful news, and we have done two of them so far!

Then a paragraph of literary gossip about Edna Ferber, liked by Thane, "she knew what she was doing"; Margaret Drabble, disliked, "a Johnny-come-lately"; and Arnold Bennett, much admired, "he had his facts right, he always did." Elizabeth had read Bennett on Thane's advice, but she found him hard to get into. Apparently Elizabeth had mentioned some of her own pleasure reading in a previous letter, because her correspondent continued:

Haven't read the Mary Stewart Arthurian trilogy, but only

for lack of time. I just can't read everything and run
this house!!

I think you are right, that it is good for my books that I
never know myself how they are coming out. Yet I never
seem to write myself into a corner, as so many writers
claim to do. I am always fascinated with the soul-surgery
professional writers seem to enjoy about their work! There
seems to be something the matter with me! Just the same as
I can't understand—or tolerate—the who-am-I syndrome. I
always knew who I am!! "Finding myself" seems to me utter
nonsense. Where else are you? Right here!

I also am afflicted with these friends who have to "get away
from it all" and have that "anywhere out of here" feeling. I
recently suggested to one of them that what she had better
do was to get off the earth entirely, if she didn't like the
climate, or the people, or the living conditions, or whatever, where she was!! Always on the run, trying to be better
off somewhere else!!

Already it is dinner-time! It has begun to get dark so
early now.

Elizabeth had to smile. She felt as though she had been delivered a
lecture from the past. She wasn't a victim of the "who-am-I
syndrome" nor the "anywhere but here" feeling, but she had
certainly given in to the mopes. And all so silly, really. Just because
some young woman out for a late-night stroll bore a passing
resemblance...

She bounded to her feet and headed to the kitchen. A nice pot
of tea. Strong, with milk. And then she would settle in to a solid

DONNA FLETCHER CROW

day of work. She could pretend she was in one of those lovely, isolated studios at the MacDowell colony.

The tea kettle was just starting to sing when the phone rang. She hesitated before picking it up. If it was Gerald what would she say to him? "Hello?" It came out as a timid query.

But Richard didn't seem to notice her hesitancy. And perhaps he had likewise delivered himself a lecture on the nonsense of giving in to passing specters, because he sounded completely normal. "I need to interview a backwoods New Hampshire poet we're considering publishing. None of Kamnachandra Uri's sophistication but supposedly the Genuine Article. Real Grandma Moses and folk wisdom... Anyway, I'd like your company."

Elizabeth smiled at her noble resolutions of a few moments earlier for a day of focused productivity. "Funny, that. I'd like to be your company. One seldom has an opportunity to meet a Genuine Article these days. We have cowboy poets out home, of course."

By the time Elizabeth had scribbled a note to Susan and run a comb through her hair the doorbell rang. Fortunately she had chosen to put on her red sweater today. That should be warm and comfy for the backwoods.

To her surprise, and perhaps somewhat defiantly of any lingering specters, Richard took her hand, and, swinging their arms to match their long, jeans-clad strides, they walked to the car like carefree teenagers in the sunshine.

Neither of them made any reference to the previous night's ghost. In the bright light of day the whole thing seemed just slightly ridiculous. Mary Ilona was dead and buried. She had to be —otherwise Richard was a married man. Besides, they didn't make mistakes like that these days.

Since ghosts couldn't lob chunks of granite through glass windows, Elizabeth told Richard about her alarm of earlier in the week.

He seemed truly perturbed. "You're sure you weren't hurt?"

"Not a scratch."

"Did you call the sheriff?"

"Of course. Not that he could do much. Our best theory is that it was a disgruntled pal of some shoplifters Susan failed to keep out of jail. But there wasn't any proof."

Their drive took them up Route 35, near the road they had been traveling the night before. Elizabeth looked at the man beside her, his long frame at ease, his hands easily holding the steering wheel, his plaid cotton shirt comfortably open at the neck. *Pooh! What did Scrooge tell his ghost? "You're a bit of undigested beef—a blob of gravy."* Their ghost had been an undigested sea scallop—a bit of lemon bar. She turned to talk brightly, if superficially, about Richard's new Robert Frost.

"Is his poetry any good?"

Richard shrugged. "Good is in the ear of the beholder. Those who have had their consciousness raised to the level of T. S. Eliot may find he lacks a bit of obscurity; on the other hand, a generation raised on Edgar A. Guest will find him over their heads. That's why marketing wants a report on the man himself—can they do a media hype and develop a new folk hero?"

"But isn't that..." she hesitated, "crass?"

"Not if he's authentic. Creating false images is crass. Making the most of what's really there is creative marketing."

"Yes. I suppose so. But I can see why you have moments of wanting out of the publishing jungle."

"More than moments."

"Well, Dr. Richard Spenser, just wait until I'm head of the English Department at Rocky Mountain, and I'll take you on to teach my modern poetry seminar."

"Best offer I've had today. How long do I have to wait?"

She sighed. "At the rate I'm progressing on my doctorate, none of the poets you're publishing now will qualify as modern." It was a pleasant thought, though.

They drove on through gently hilly countryside, thicketed

with red and gold woods, the fields and pastures outlined with stone walls, accented with white-steepled churches, red barns and green-shuttered farm houses. Tucked in protected valleys and draws, tidy farms nestled their families around them like mother hens. They passed a verdant rolling pasture dotted with black-and-white Holstein cows. Richard said, "Did you know Vermont claims to be the only state in the Union with more cows than people?"

Elizabeth watched the placid creatures contentedly chewing their cuds and occasionally flicking a tail to ward off a disturbing fly, some of them even lying down on the sunny slope while continuing to eat. "That must have something to do with the unrushed order one senses here—like people are living a more natural, simpler life."

Richard nodded. "Farming keeps one in touch with the natural rhythms of seasons and soil."

"That's it. People here seem just to take life as it comes—more tolerant of delay and frustration." She recalled Elswyth Thane's observation of the Vermonter's absence of bad temper with perverse inanimate objects: He just registers a "resigned sort of curiosity as to the worst that can happen, and a humorous contest of ingenuity against cussedness in the mending of it," she had written. But before Elizabeth could quote it to Richard a covered bridge appeared ahead of them—a white one with open lattice-work on the sides.

It brought back to Elizabeth the similar one they had crossed on their way to Dummerston. Such a short time ago, but it seemed like years. Something that had happened on the other side of the mountain—before the ghost of Richard's dead wife made her appearance. Their tires made a hollow sort of rumbly sound as they entered the secluded enclosure of the wooden structure.

Still, Elizabeth refused to let the shades of last night cast a pall over their outing. She forced a light tone. "It's absolutely charming. I just can't believe they're still *using* bridges like this. I feel like it should be preserved in a museum somewhere."

"With a statue of a headless horseman riding out at you?"

"Statue nothing. I want the real McCoy." Actually, another apparition was the last thing she wanted, but she was determined to keep up the banter.

"Then you'd better not consign our historic treasures to musty, dusty museums."

They emerged into the full light at the end of the passageway with tires singing a gentler, more solid tune. Over yet another autumnal wooded hill they approached a tiny village. "I can't believe it—that's at least the fifth house I've seen that has its Christmas decorations up. Do they really start that early here?" Elizabeth twisted in her seat to be sure she had actually seen a green-and-red wreath hanging on the door of a white clapboard house and a string of colored lights stretched across the green porch roof. It seemed a jarring anachronism behind the mound of bright orange pumpkins at the foot of the lawn.

Richard laughed. "Not already up. Still up. It's too cold to get out and wrestle them down right after Christmas. And everyone's too busy once spring comes. So why bother now? It's only two months until Christmas, and this way they're ready early when it comes."

Elizabeth shook her head. "Vermont's answer to avoiding the Christmas rush."

On the other side of the village Richard stopped at a roadside stand set beside a stone wall at the foot of a long, rolling lawn. "Want to stock up on blackberry jam and crabapple jelly?

"I'd like to get some maple syrup."

"You'd be lucky this time of year. Need to come back next spring after the sugaring. It's autumn produce now." He opened her door and held out a hand to her.

Three overall-clad children were playing ball on the lawn with a black-and-white collie that bounded to greet the newcomers.

Elizabeth looked at the colorful jars of preserves but recalled the ones she and Susan had purchased when she first arrived. "I'm afraid I don't need any jam. I don't suppose you have any maple syrup?"

The oldest boy shook his head. "Sorry, lady. How about some honey?" He held up a jar filled with amber liquid. "We don't keep bees, but our neighbor does." Elizabeth reached for her billfold. "Our syrup went really fast this year. It was nice and light 'cause of the sunny days and freezin' nights we had. Besides, my Pa's the best boilin' man in these parts."

"You do your own boiling right here?" Richard asked.

"There's the sugarhouse." The boy's younger sister pointed proudly to a long, low building just up the hillside behind the farmhouse. "I got to help with the buckets this year. Got outuv a whole bunch a school."

"That sounds like fun." Elizabeth smiled at the girl.

"Was. All except washin' the buckets. Pa's awful particul'r 'bout the buckets."

"And rightly so," Elizabeth replied. "You don't want old sap polluting the fresh clear stuff."

She added a cake of fresh honeycomb to her purchases and continued the sugaring topic. "Do you have a double bush here?"

"Sure do. This lower part of the pasture runs early. On up the hill's slower to start. That's why our syrup's the best—mixin' sap gives it more flavor."

"I'll tell my cousin to be sure to come here to get her syrup next spring," Elizabeth said as Richard ushered her back into the car.

"I didn't realize you were so knowledgeable about sugaring," he said.

"I'm not. Just what I picked up reading Thane's experiences in *Reluctant Farmer*. Simple book-learning—none of the real earthy experience like those children have."

The scenery changed subtly as they drove north. It became

more rugged and mountainous with less rolling green farmland. And now there was very little autumn color. The trees had shed their glory, and bare branches stood against the blue sky. This part of the state was ready for the snows that would be coming soon. They passed a small abandoned marble quarry, and Richard pulled to the side of the road so they could get out and enjoy the view. The quarry had long ago filled with water, and a stand of silver birch trees, a few yellow leaves still clinging to their branches, grew around the edge.

The small pond was home to a family of ducks that swam across its mirrored surface, making a row of V's across the white-and-gray marble wall reflected there. "Can't believe they're still here. They'd better get on their way south soon," Richard said. "We could have snow by Halloween. Sometimes the ski resorts open the middle of November."

But today the sun was warm, and Elizabeth was enjoying every moment. She reached out and tugged at a birch branch bending near her. "'One could do worse than be a swinger of birches,'" she quoted. And turned back toward the car. Best to keep moving. Too much dawdling could be dangerous.

At Thetford they turned east across the Connecticut River and entered New Hampshire. Glancing once or twice at his hand-written instructions on a piece of paper on the dashboard, Richard drove through the tiny town of Lyme, along a small foaming river rushing from the White Mountains through banks of slate gray chunks of granite. At a clearing in the woods Richard stopped before a neat, but plain, red-brick building with a water wheel at the back dipping its ladles perpetually into the flowing water. "This must be it. He's supposed to live in an abandoned textile mill."

As soon as their car door slammed shut, the weathered door of the old mill swung open, and a surprisingly young man came out to meet them. He wore the to-be-expected beard, but it was well trimmed. Instead of a more picturesque lumberjack plaid he wore a dark green flannel shirt, unfaded jeans and loafers. Elizabeth bit her tongue to keep from whispering to Richard that he'd have to get his poet into woodsman's boots. Their host introduced himself as Albert Ross, and after shaking hands all around, he offered them mugs of coffee and thick slices of apple cake with maple sugar icing.

"This is delicious. Did you make it yourself?" Elizabeth asked.

"Oh, no. My wife Nancy made it. She wanted to be here to meet you, but both our son and daughter had dentist's appointments, so she had to go into Lyme."

Elizabeth grinned at such middle-class goings-on. *He probably drives a station wagon, too,* she thought and looked around the room: wide planks of the old mill floor scrubbed almost white, the comfortable furniture arranged around the large rag rug with its gentle, muted tones, and the abundant green plants filling every corner and tumbling from macramé hangers extending from the open beams high overhead—everything looked as if it had just grown there. Authentic, indeed. Through the open window at the side she could hear the rhythmic creak, swish, drip of the water wheel. "Are you a full-time poet?" She asked when they were seated.

"Only in the summers, I'm afraid. I teach school in Lyme—to keep the kids in shoes."

His soft New England accent was pleasing to Elizabeth's ear, and she instantly warmed to his twinkling deep-set blue eyes. "I wish I could say I'm an admirer of your poetry, but I haven't had a chance to read any yet."

"A melancholy situation, which we can only hope some *deus ex machina* of a publisher may choose to remedy." The poet's humor danced in his eyes, emphasized by his beard. He casually handed Elizabeth a portfolio of his poems picked up from a nearby bookshelf and turned to answer Richard's first interview question.

Elizabeth listened to the men for a moment but then was

drawn into the pictures his poem "Autumn Hawk" made in her mind:

You circle down, dive,
and Clutch me. Rapting me up
And back.

Back to wood smoke:
Swirling leaves of autumn scent
First heaven sent with gusty breaths
Then drifting down with the official
Notice of Winter

Elizabeth looked out the window just as a gust of wind sent a few late-falling leaves tumbling down.

Back to fields:
Fallow corduroy, each wale
As true as I could make it
(With eye on and off the pole star post,
But glancing the fencerow for pheasants).

Back to orchards:
Almost hidden in memory's tall grass
Ready to be trampled by
A boy, a lot like me, stealing
Tart pleasure in abandoned Eden.

A soaring bird
To grip my awkward, ground-bound

Fancy and snatch it; flying over
Barns and schools, springs and summers
Back to every autumn.

The nostalgia of the picture gripped her, and she knew, with a small crimp at her heart, that when this experience was "almost hidden in memory's tall grass," as the poet said, this autumn would live forever. Every fat, orange pumpkin, every russet leaf, every dusty rural lane would carry her heart back to New England.

She turned next to "Dawn Dancer," a snapshot of the poet's young daughter.

With the dawn she mounts the stairs
While Phoebus climbs the skies;
As light slants through the house
Her voice—a piercing ray—bids all to rise

And join the welcome to the day…

Elizabeth glanced at the timber stairway in the corner of the room. It was in shadow now, but her imagination imbued it with rays of morning sun slanting through the western window, making a halo of the small girl's curls.

Dawn dancer now she treads the hall—
Followed by her blanket train—
And leads the family to the ball.

The men's conversation penetrated Elizabeth's consciousness, and the fragile scene evaporated. "I'm sorry, Mr. Spenser. I'm very flattered by your house's interest, but if people like my poetry, they can read it. My poems are for sale; I'm not. When would I write if I spend all my time running around the country riding the celebrity syndrome?"

"I understand what you're saying, but—"

Richard's protest was interrupted by the implacable poet. "If my poems are good, I should stay home and write more. If they aren't—why would anyone need to see me?"

His logic was impeccable.

"The way I see it is, my Creator gave me a gift of creating order with my words—of going first with my imagination so others can see the way. I've seen Johnny Carson—the Creator gave him a different gift. He probably wouldn't be a very good poet. I sure wouldn't be a good talk show host. Or guest. That's the way Providence planned it, and I have no intention of upsetting the scheme of things by getting out of place."

That was unanswerable. Elizabeth and Richard shook hands with their host, and Richard thanked him for a most refreshing interview. Back in the car Richard shook his head and chuckled all the way back across the river to Thetford. "Hoist by my own petard."

"Well, you wanted authentic."

"But who thought he'd turn out to be so authentic he wouldn't play the game?"

"So does that mean you won't publish him?"

"Oh, I don't know. Marketing might have more fun selling a mystery image than working with a warm body."

"But either way marketing rules?"

Richard shrugged. "That's the bottom line."

Richard drove on in silence, the chuckles stilled. Elizabeth observed the creases forming in his forehead and knew he was thinking deeply. "A penny for them."

He sighed. "I'm not sure you'd get your money's worth." After a moment he continued. "It's sobering, really—meeting backbone of that caliber. If I had his gumption I wouldn't be doing what I'm doing."

"Maybe. But you didn't agree to step in and keep the family business afloat for your own greed, did you? I got the idea it was an emergency situation. You had your parents to think about and stockholders surely."

He grinned. "I'm not sure I can claim such nobility, but thank you."

"You'll know when it's the right time to make a change."

"You don't think I'll be caught in the rat race for the rest of my life? That's comforting."

They drove through a small town, its wide street lined on both sides with big old wooden houses, their screened front porches shaded by now nearly leafless elms and maples grown taller than the houses. Richard pulled up before a pale yellow house with a wooden signboard in the front lawn: Thetford Inn. "Hungry for some authentic backwoods cuisine?"

"More of the Genuine Article? I'd love it."

They crossed the wide porch, and the bells that tinkled when they opened the screen door summoned the host, a large man, probably well into his sixties, wrapped in an enormous white chef's apron. Elizabeth and Richard were his only patrons, but it was apparent they would have been received with the same personal attention if the room had been full. Their host took them to a table covered with a snowy cloth. "Will chicken and biscuits be all right?"

There was no menu, but both guests agreed instantly to the offered choice.

The innkeeper disappeared to do something mysterious in his kitchen, then reappeared to set their table, complete with antique, crescent-shaped bone dishes at the top of their dinner plates. Elizabeth was delighted. "I must find a set of these in an antique shop to take home with me."

"What will you use them for? Salad plates?"

"Certainly not. I'll use them for bones, just like God intended. It's such a practical idea, I can't imagine why it went out of style. You never know what to do with the bones when you eat fried chicken."

In a surprisingly short time the host/chef/waiter returned bearing a tray laden with fried chicken encased in a crisp, golden batter; smooth, well-seasoned gravy; and garden-grown vegetables. The towel-lined basket contained warm biscuits. "Your marketing department should come here. He has to be the quintessential New England innkeeper."

"Who undoubtedly saw that Carson fellow on television once and thought, 'He don't fry chicken. And I don't do talk shows.'"

They ate in companionable silence until Richard paused halfway through his second piece of chicken, the drumstick still in his hand. "Are you a good cook?"

Elizabeth laughed. "What a leading question. I'd like to be, but cooking like this takes years of experience. Maybe when I finish my Ph.D. I'll be able to move to an apartment with a better kitchen." Of course, she would need someone to share her cooking with. Cooking for oneself was no fun at all. Would she be inspired to cook for Gerald if she had more time? She wondered.

She was spared following that perturbing train of thought by their host's return. "Is everything all right? Can I get you anything else?"

"Everything is delicious," Richard replied.

"I love your biscuits. They're so light and yet still moist in the center." Elizabeth smiled up at the large man.

"I'm glad you like them. I'll make you some more." And before Elizabeth could protest that she was already full, he picked up the basket and returned to the kitchen.

Elizabeth couldn't imagine how he could produce a fresh batch so quickly, but when the basket returned emitting irresistible smells, the biscuits were piping-from-the-oven hot. Almost burning her fingers, she slathered one with butter and honey and closed her eyes to savor every morsel.

Licking her fingers, she pushed her plate back and surreptitiously undid the snap on her jeans, then gasped when their host set a thick slice of apple pie, likewise warm from the oven, in front of her. "Apples off the trees out back," he said.

Elizabeth laughed and picked up her fork. "It's hopeless."

A short time later they drove home through the deepening evening in a quiet serenity that Elizabeth valued all the more because she knew how very fragile it was. Happiness, it seemed, was a delicate cobweb laden with crystal dewdrops—to be enjoyed to its fullest while the sun shone on it, but easily destroyed.

And Elizabeth herself inadvertently gave the first puff. "I didn't think a day like today would be possible after last night."

Richard was quiet for a moment, eyes glued to the road. "I don't see why a silly mistake has to make any real difference to anything."

"I don't either. But it does, doesn't it?"

Richard drew a deep breath and let it out slowly. "Yes. I suppose it does. Not the ghostly vision, but my reaction to it."

Elizabeth considered agreeing that the fact that he could even think he saw his dead wife was proof enough of the power she still held over him, but she held her tongue.

CHAPTER 18

*A*fter a restless night Elizabeth awoke the next morning to the reassuringly commonplace sounds of clattering dishes and rattling silverware. She pulled on her robe and went out to the kitchen. Susan, her blonde hair still damp from the shower, was setting bowls of flaky cereal on the table, and the coffee pot was bubbling. "I was hoping you'd join me."

Susan pushed the milk pitcher toward Elizabeth, but her eyes focused attention on an open letter on the table. "Mail already? Do you get two deliveries on Saturdays?"

"Special delivery." Susan held the letter for Elizabeth to read the signature at the bottom of the closely-written page.

"Donald? Do I know a Donald?" Elizabeth frowned. "Oh... I remember. Oh!" Her eyes flew to her friend's face as she recalled Susan confiding to her that Donald was the one man she had ever been serious about—a major factor in Susan's coming back to Newfane to practice law. But he had inexplicably vanished.

"Read it." Susan inclined her head.

Elizabeth obeyed, then handed the letter slowly back to Susan. "I don't understand. Just like that? No explanation of why? Or where he's been for three years? Just 'It's so wonderful to be back.' And he wants to see you again?"

"Took him a lot of words to say that, didn't it?" Susan played with her coffee mug but didn't drink. "What do you think? What should I do?"

Elizabeth considered. "Do you want to see him?"

"Yes. No. I don't know."

"Then I'd say you'd better see him. How will you ever know what you want otherwise?"

"Good point." Susan picked up the letter with the Boston phone number scrawled across the bottom.

Elizabeth stuck her dishes in the sink and disappeared into her room to give Susan privacy. *Like life needed another upheaval,* she thought. But the best antidote was always work, so a few minutes later, dressed in comfortable clothes, long black hair pulled back in a ponytail, and sitting at her desk, Elizabeth assumed her most disciplined working manner and drew a letter from her file:

Dear Elizabeth—

This is a most inadequate response to your letter enclosing pictures, etc. But I am laid up with the prevailing germ— however, I did enjoy hearing from you and strive to deserve it! It has settled in my eyes and for the first time in my life I cannot see straight!! Anyway, thanks for writing, and best wishes.

E.T.B.

The note was undated and the initials at the bottom badly

scrawled. With a pang, Elizabeth recalled how this letter had signaled the beginning of the end of their correspondence. Her notes reminded her that in late October she had called to find out how her friend was feeling: "This bug is going around. As soon as you get over it, it comes back two or three times. This is my second time. It's left me kind of wonky. It's nice of you to call."

"Well, I hadn't heard for a while."

"I know you hadn't. I have a nice long letter from you waiting here, but my correspondence just piles up. I enjoy your letters so much…"

Elizabeth's eyes misted. The words read from her notes had a plaintive ring that she hadn't remembered hearing in person.

"I'm reading your *Washington's Lady*."

"Yes. Isn't she a lovely lady?"

"Yes, she is…" The notes revealed repetitions in the conversation that showed the author was tiring, perhaps her concentration wandering a bit. "How is Elmer?" Elizabeth asked next.

"About the same. He's had it too, but I think he's over it. I guess you can tell it's in my throat a bit."

"Yes. But maybe you're through now."

"I do so hope so. It's so nice of you to call. And I do enjoy your letters so much. Don't quit."

Elizabeth didn't quit, and at Thanksgiving time she received a slightly more hopeful letter, sharing reminiscences of two of the authors Elizabeth had mentioned she was reading at that time:

I have been laid up with the prevailing Germ, and my correspondence has gone to the dickens, but I am trying to at least let people know why I have not replied! Your lovely letter has been lying here since Nov. 6, and a lot of others too—I am trying now just to say that it is here and had been so much appreciated.

I have at present a very helpful houseguest, which takes some of the burden of daily chores off poor Elmer, who had begun to feel the strain!

Our guest up from D. C. improved our Thanksgiving enormously, tho I was far from up to par.

So glad to find another Angela Thirkell lover—I am afraid she isn't read much anymore. Too tame by present standards! As for Wells—H. G.—he was an experience, even for a woman turning 40! Dear little man—but wanted (needed) careful handling socially! A bright and roving eye. I saw something of him on the sets of Shape of Things to Come in England before the war. Everything happened to me before the war!

Elizabeth smiled as she recalled the fun she had preparing a special Christmas present for her friend. Cold ceramics were the craze of the moment, and she found a wonderful whitewear piece of a Cocker Spaniel. Using Thane's snapshots as a model, she painted a replica of the much-adored Jody and mailed it surrounded with many inches of Styrofoam packing and many fervent prayers that it arrive in one piece.

Two days after Christmas her telephone rang:

"This is Elswyth Beebe." Elizabeth remembered the thrill of hearing from her friend, who said repeatedly how delighted she was with the ceramic Jody. "It is on the living room TV, and everyone who comes in is enchanted with it. It arrived in perfect condition."

Elizabeth breathed a prayer of thanksgiving. Then Elmer came on the phone to ask how she made it. Elizabeth explained that painting ceramics was something of a hobby of hers and that she had several good pictures of Jody to work from.

Elswyth Thane came back on. "I put the two together and will send you some pictures. Jody was very intrigued, as he'd never met a dog like it before—he kept sniffing it, but it wouldn't move.

"A neighbor down the road has been sick and Elmer over-worked, and we have had Christmas company, and I didn't know when I'd get a chance to write, so I called, because I didn't want to let it go any longer."

"I'm delighted that you did. It was lovely to talk to you!"

Elizabeth sat smiling over her notes, recalling how pleased she had been with the phone call—what a lovely way it had been to start a day.

The promised letter arrived the morning of New Year's Eve:

Dec. 31, 79

Dear Elizabeth—

Your "Jody" has caused a sensation here, and I have been searching the file for your letter hinting at its arrival for any clue that you were contemplating such a thing! The file is a mess, and I find nothing—but neither can I find words for such a gift!! It has been moved from place to place in the living room as we try to decide which is best for it and has caused coos of delight from all of Jody's friends who behold it. Jody himself is frankly puzzled—we put it on the floor beside him to take the pictures which will follow this to you as soon as they come back from the shop, and he sniffed it with the most <u>puzzled</u> expression and then made a tentative lick at its head—it didn't even <u>taste</u> like a dog!!

Anyway, you have given us all the most fun and pleasure possible, and I can never thank you enough!

This is otherwise a rather sad Christmas here, with everybody holding on like mad and trying not to show it. Of course my Christmases in NYC in Dr. Beebe's lifetime were always fabulous. Now we can do nothing but "adjust," and the process is painful.

Thank you, again, and I can't <u>wait</u> to send the pictures on— they are slow, of course, to deliver!

Elswyth Thane Beebe

But the promised snapshots never came.

On February 22 Elizabeth wrote again, asking how her friend was feeling and telling her about an old movie she'd seen on television about Alfred the Great—his wife's name was Elswyth of Mercia. And this time the reply came quickly:

Feb. 26 (I guess)

Dear Elizabeth—

I have more or less lost track of time, after a week in the hospital, which revealed a wrong medication and a complete resolution everywhere, but am gradually getting back to what is supposed to be normal (for me!). Anyway, it will be spring soon even in these mountains, and I hope things will begin to straighten out again.

Your letter this morning with enclosures was a delight to

my somewhat foggy brain! You are the only person I have ever come across who knew who Elswyth was! It was the original form of Elizabeth, I am told. Where did the movie come from? England, obviously, I would like to know more about it.

The weather here is crazy too—we have had almost <u>no</u> snow—in the skiing country, and the lodges are falling right and left. They had to <u>make</u> snow for the Olympics, which was not far from here—did you see the TV? Some of it quite fascinating. Just next door, as it were, to Wilmington.

Elmer has run down to town to get the makings for dinner and will be back soon—so this letter isn't really an answer to yours and your fascinating enclosures—don't give up on me. According to my very grave and gloomy, but highly thought of doctor at Bennington hospital, I will be all right in a few weeks more! I was on the wrong mediation, and it upset me something awful! We'll see what <u>his</u> medication and a week in the hospital can do!! I hope never to see <u>that</u> place again!! Very highly thought of, I'm told, but he is one of the <u>gloomy</u> kind that always makes you feel as tho he had barely rescued you from the grave! (But don't count on it!)

Blah. I am getting better in spite of him, I think, but poor Elmer has had a gloomy time, looking after me since I came home, and Jody has been ailing, too, and had to go to <u>his</u> doctor!! Both of us mending now.

E.T.B.

185

Elizabeth's file revealed copies of several unanswered letters she had written. Then, on May 16, she telegraphed flowers to Elswyth Thane for her eightieth birthday.

My Dear Elizabeth!

However did you manage to produce this delightful bouquet out of the air! I had a phone call from town that there was a "bouquet" waiting for me, and should they send it or would I call—I said Send and this amazing production arrived via the village drugstore, where deliveries are sent, to be picked up when we go into town. It is sitting in the big window now, looking just too beautiful, and I have thoughts of trying to take its picture for you but doubt if I could manage it now! I find I must do less and less, in order to do what has to be done, if you follow me, but both of the village girls who have been coming in to change beds and gather laundry and dust etc. have been ill, and I have had nobody but Elmer, whose job those things are not, tho he is willing to try anything— but by the time I plan and list the two meals a day—he gets his own breakfast! (and he can do a roast chicken better than I can—these French-Canadian children are brought up in their mothers' kitchen)—he also has all the outside work to do. I try to run the house still! Jody, too, is getting old and ailing, and we are watching him anxiously from day to day. His appetite is still good, and he still trails Elmer devotedly, but he is reaching the age limit for spaniels, and we know what must come, when he can no longer enjoy his life as he still does. He is really a member of the family, and it will be a sad day when he goes. I say we must get another, housebroken, as soon as possible if we lose him. Elmer thinks a young dog would be too much for me—but we must decide when the time comes.

Meanwhile, summer has come at last, I am thankful to say. And thank you <u>again</u> for thinking of me.

Elswyth

And that was her last letter. Elizabeth had written again that summer, then in the fall and again the following year. But the mailman brought her no more delightful letters full of memories of famous people and happy events of days long past or reading advice and opinions on the art of writing for the budding literature professor. Elizabeth was on her own now.

Richard had told her that Elmer died in May.

Elizabeth had caught her breath at the news. "I didn't know! That must have been dreadful for her!"

Richard agreed that it was but assured her that his godmother had born up very well—as Elizabeth knew she would have.

And then Jody had died that summer and been replaced by a dog that had something wrong with her and had to be put to sleep. She was followed by the final replacement—a little dog Elswyth Thane showed much fondness for but Richard vowed was mentally ill. "Everyone tried—I even took a hand in it—but that animal *never* house trained."

Elizabeth worked the rest of the afternoon and late into the evening organizing and outlining the notes for her final chapter until she was at last driven from the typewriter by insistent hunger pangs. She wondered when Susan would return from Boston, but Sue probably didn't know the answer to that herself.

After her hasty tomato soup and cheese sandwich supper Elizabeth was back at her desk, everything else forgotten in the exhilaration of bringing all her thoughts together in the home sprint as she filled each successive sheet inserted into her typewriter with her own analysis as well as professional critics' evaluation of Elswyth Thane's lasting contribution to American literature.

When her mind and her eyesight finally blurred to incomprehension on the last paragraph she tumbled into bed, too far gone even to check what time it was, much less set her alarm.

The sun was straight overhead when she awakened the next day, chagrined to realize she had slept through church and surprised that the ringing of the bell hadn't wakened her. She wandered around the house aimlessly, checking for signs that Susan had returned in the night. Finding none, she brewed herself a pot of nice strong English Breakfast tea and took it out in the backyard with her stack of rough draft manuscript pages. She sipped, read, scribbled a note, read, sipped, corrected a typing error... read, sipped... read... A cloud passing across the sun made her shiver, and she realized the air was more chill than she had at first thought, but she stayed with it, reading through to the end.

Yes. This was ready to show to her advisor. He would undoubtedly ask for revisions, but she was satisfied with her first draft. Weeks, maybe months of polishing were sure to follow. References had to be double-checked, holes filled here and there, but the first draft of her dissertation was in hand. And she could see—if she had ever doubted—the correctness of her advisor's insistence that she do on-location research to give the work freshness, immediacy and her own personality. Already it was good. With a few rewrites it would be excellent.

So why did the thought depress her? All those years of intensive classroom study, a year of planning and research, now her degree within her grasp—why the deflated feeling?

She looked at the sheaf of papers in her hand and knew. Her passport had just expired. Her excuse to remain in Vermont was gone. Of course, Susan would be happy to have her stay on. She wasn't scheduled to begin teaching again until next term. But if she stayed on she would have to admit to herself that it was for no other reason than because of her feelings for Richard. And that would just prolong the agony.

CHAPTER 19

*S*usan still wasn't back from Boston—which probably meant things were going well with her old flame. Which meant she would no longer need Elizabeth's company. Definitely time to be moving on.

Elizabeth hadn't seen baby Allison for days. She would just drop in on Julia and say good-bye. Walking down the quiet, shady street, Elizabeth refused to admit this was her last chance to find an excuse for extending her stay—for finding someone who needed her.

Excited noises from the back garden told Elizabeth not to bother ringing at the front door but just to go around back. "Oh!" Rounding the corner she walked full-face into a large bubble, which broke and showered her with tiny droplets. Tommy and the dachshunds raced to greet her with a chorus of unintelligible shouts and yaps. Then, just as quickly, they turned, and Tommy blew another blast of bubbles.

"Tommy, don't let the puppies drink the bubble liquid," Julia called from her lawn chair under an almost bare elm, where she was nursing her tiny daughter. "Pull a chair over," she greeted

Elizabeth. "Tommy has gone through two batches of bubbles every day since you and Richard got him that big ring."

"Batches? You mean you make it?"

"With my eyes closed: one-half cup dishwashing liquid, two tablespoons water, and a blop of salad oil."

Elizabeth laughed as she placed her lawn chair next to Julia. "My goodness, the things a mother has to know."

Julia ran her hand softly over Allison's peach fuzz head, inserted her finger between the rose bud mouth and her nipple to break the suction, and held the little pink-and-white bundle over her shoulder, rubbing and patting softly. When a satisfying bubble sound emerged Julia snuggled the baby in her right arm. Allison took the offered nipple and began making tiny, contented squeaks and slurping sounds. "Little pig," Julia said fondly, her eyes liquid soft. "I think this is my favorite part of mothering."

"Is she sleeping through the night yet?"

"Goodness, no. You hear tales of babies that do that at two or three weeks, but I never met one. It's no bother, though. I just pull her into bed with me. If I had to get up and warm a bottle I might not be so complacent."

"I came to ask how everything is, but I can see it's just great." Elizabeth sturdily resisted any impulse to feel let down. Under no circumstances would she want Julia or anyone else to be unhappy just so she could stay longer. And she could see nothing that could be done for the one person who obviously needed help. "I finished the rough draft of my paper, so I'll be packing up soon. I brought Tommy a present. I haven't found just what I want to give Allison yet, so I'll send her a package when I get back to Colorado." She called to the other side of the lawn, "Tommy, want to see what I brought you?"

That brought him tearing across the grass at a speed even Jessie and Joey had trouble keeping up with. Tommy tore into the brown paper sack as if it had been sealed. "Wow! Stickers!" He held the Stuck on Stickers book out for his mother to see.

"What fun. What do you tell Auntie Liz?"

"Thanks!" He plopped down in the grass and began arranging the dragons, dogs and UFOs Elizabeth had chosen to start his collection.

Elizabeth stood up. "I haven't made my plane reservation yet, but I'll try to get off day after tomorrow. I can't believe how much I have to pack. I think my files gave birth to quintuplets while I was here. I'll stop round to say good-bye when I know for sure."

Tommy looked up with big eyes. "You're not *leaving?*"

"Pretty soon, Tommy. I have to go home."

"Oh." He returned to sticking the green dragon on a yellow-and-purple-striped page, but he did it more slowly.

Elizabeth walked homeward more slowly, too, making herself focus on all she had to do to get ready to leave: Airline reservations, call Gerald to see if he could pick her up at the airport, call Richard to say good-bye... It all sounded so simple. Why did it feel like performing do-it-yourself open-heart surgery?

She had always hated leaving a job undone. She told herself she should have a sense of accomplishment over her dissertation. And she did. But even though her own research had been successful she hadn't turned up a single clue to the mystery of Mary Ilona's obsessive research. And she had failed miserably in her goal of helping Richard break out of his grief.

She stopped stock still in the middle of the sidewalk at the next thought. What would she have done if Richard *had* been able to put the spectre of Mary Ilona behind him and move on? The possibilities were too much—and too painful to contemplate. She must simply close the door on that fantasy.

She forced herself to carry on walking and tried to shut out all thoughts of Richard. As far as she could tell she was leaving things worse for him than they had been before her coming. It seemed that her presence had opened the Pandora's Box of Richard's loss. Now the best she could hope for would be to shut the lid by leaving.

Just as she turned on to Susan's street a departing scarlet streak caught her eye. The elusive Donald? Goodness, little red cars had been almost a through-line of her time here. Perhaps Vermonters had a fondness for them, because they showed up well in the snow—like Rudyard Kipling's red golf balls.

"Sue? I'm here!" she called as she ran up the steps and through the front door.

Elizabeth stopped abruptly and gasped at the sight of her friend. Her shoulders were slumped, her eyes tired behind her glasses, her step slow. "You look like the jury voted to hang your client *and* his lawyer."

Susan sank into the nearest chair. "Just tired, tired, tired. Donald and I talked most of the night, then I spent the rest of it trying to make sense of what he'd said. I still can't figure out what happened."

"What do you want? Coffee? Talk? Sleep?"

"All of the above. In that order."

"Right." Elizabeth returned in a minute with two steaming mugs to fill the first order. As she sipped she realized that her own nutrition for that day had so far totaled a pot of tea and a cup of coffee—good thing she drank milk in her tea. But food could wait. "Okay, your witness."

"I don't know where to start."

"With exhibit A—tell me about Donald. How did he look, for example?"

"Tall, blond, tanned, confident, gorgeous."

"Did your heart do flip-flops?"

"More like a roller coaster."

"Is that good?"

"I hate roller coasters." Susan set her mug down with a bang.

"Come on. Talk. Where had he been? Why did he disappear? What was he doing? Why did he come back?"

"He's been in the Caribbean and South America—on business. Some sort of investment opportunity. He left suddenly, he said, because the opportunity opened up unexpectedly. He was so sorry to have missed my homecoming and all that. He didn't write, because he was moving around a lot, and it was necessary to keep the business quiet: competition, industrial spies, whatever. He has come back because the investment has paid off and..."

"And?"

"And he wants to take up where we left off."

"Presumptuous, isn't he? Did you really talk all night and not learn anything more specific than that?"

"Well, I was reminded of a lot of things I'd forgotten. How addicted he is to cokes. What a smooth talker he is. How my stomach squeezes when he smiles at me. How fanatical he is about his car..."

"But nothing of real importance?"

"I think that was the exhausting part—I've never met a witness I couldn't get an answer out of—and he answered everything I asked, seemingly straight forward. Then when I thought back over it all, I really hadn't learned anything of substance."

"What are you going to do?"

"Sleep on it. If my feet will take me to the bedroom."

Elizabeth pulled Sue to her feet and led her across the room. A light shove, and Susan sprawled on her bed, kicking off her shoes in the process.

Elizabeth stood for at least a full minute outside Susan's door, thinking of her friend's dilemma. Was this something she should postpone her departure over? Then, shaking her head, she turned to the task of getting her files in order. That had to be done no matter when she left.

Hours later, surrounded by tape measure, bathroom scales and cardboard boxes, Elizabeth was close to tearing her hair. "Now, let's take it again from the top, boys and girls. The airline will let you have four extra pieces at $10 apiece if they don't weight over seventy pounds apiece and if, when you measure the height, width, and length of each box, it doesn't total more than sixty-two inches." But even talking aloud to herself didn't help Elizabeth's focus.

Her cramped muscles screamed when the phone rang, and she pushed herself to her feet. She didn't know whether she was pleased or dismayed to hear Richard's voice, but he sounded surprisingly chipper. He wanted to arrange a date for tomorrow evening. "What would you like to do better than anything else in the world?"

She considered replying "Fly to Paris for dinner" but gave the question serious thought instead. How did she want to spend her last evening in New England? Dinner at the Newfane Inn? A final drive to Wilmington? A show in Boston? Then she knew. "This is going to make me sound frightfully dull."

"Well, let's have the worst."

"Sit by a fire and read."

He gave a surprised laugh. "Would you believe we have a library—and a fireplace in every room in this house? Just think, I could entertain you every evening for—quite a long time—and take you to a different place every night without it costing me a cent."

"You're forgetting the price of firewood."

"Nope. Homegrown."

"Well, in that case, I accept." Much better to say her good-byes in person rather than over the phone.

"You're certainly the easiest lady to please I've ever met."

"Not if I get hold of a badly written book."

"In that case, be sure you bring only your favorite authors. On second thought, don't bring any books. I have a surprise for you."

After the call Elizabeth returned to her calculations. She finally concluded that she could get everything into the four extra boxes if she weeded her notes carefully. But she wouldn't throw anything away. In case she miscalculated, Sue could look it up for her. That just left calling the travel agent in the morning.

CHAPTER 20

The agent at the other end of the line assured Elizabeth there would be a seat for her on a United Airlines 767 the next afternoon at 1:10, direct to Chicago O'Hare, only a 37-minute layover, and then direct to Denver, arriving at 5:44. Six and a half hours back to her old routine. It felt like a lifetime away.

She turned from the phone when Sue walked into the room. "Well, you're looking better this morning." The lawyer's short blonde hair gleamed, and her eyes were bright behind her over-sized glasses. Her pin-striped power suit was freshly pressed.

Susan gave her briefcase a swing. "I told you I was just tired—sick and tired of riding a roller coaster. Besides, I have to be on my toes because Maxwell Barton, Esquire, of Barton, Barton, and Franklin will be in today."

Elizabeth blinked. "Oh, I remember. The bigwig Boston attorney that everything stops for."

"Everything moves for, you mean."

"I must say, you take his demands very gracefully."

"Part of the job."

But Elizabeth wondered. She'd like to get a closer look at this Maxwell Barton, Esquire.

Sue paused at the door. "You're really packing? Are you *sure* you have to go?"

"Very sure."

Rain spat against the windows in small gusts. The trees that had been such fiery displays of autumn glory when Elizabeth arrived, now waved their bare branches in the wind. The first snow would come any day now. Definitely time to be getting on.

By the time she needed to get ready to meet Richard she had tied, labeled, taped and locked everything but one bag and her overnight case, which she would do tomorrow morning.

She put on a light sweater and the wide-legged pants that would make for comfortable sitting before the fire and was just clipping on small gold earrings when she heard Richard and Susan enter the house together. They were still shaking the rain-drops off their slickers when Elizabeth entered with a bright, if forced, smile. She started to give a casual greeting, but Sue spoke first. "I've been trying to convince her to stay, but I can't do a thing with our stubborn westerner. Maybe you can be more persuasive, Richard."

Richard looked at Elizabeth in astonishment.

"No fair, Sue. You stole my big scene." She spoke lightly, but actually Elizabeth was relieved to have it out in the open. "We're celebrating tonight. I finished my dissertation. Well, rough draft, at least."

Richard's heavy eyebrows drew together in a hint of a frown, and his mouth looked grim, but his voice was even. "Congratulations. In that case, we'll have to make this an evening to remember."

He helped her into her raincoat and opened the door. Elizabeth was on the threshold when Susan, looking at the mail on the table, stopped them. "There's a letter for you, Elizabeth."

"Don't tell me my creditors have caught up with me. Definitely time to be moving on. Just leave it on the table. I'll see to it when I get back."

Richard opened an umbrella over her head, and they went out.

The miserable weather made the Spenser library feel all the more snug. Firelight reflected on mellow old wood and burnished the brass accessories. Elizabeth gave herself up to the comfort of the overstuffed sofa in front of the fireplace and even put her feet up on the coffee table after Richard assured her he always did. Before he sat down he pulled a volume from the shelves. "I've got something special for you."

She took the book from his hands. "*Bound to Happen*! Richard, how on earth could you have known that's the one Elswyth Thane novel I never could find? She practically dared me to find it, but it was written in the '30s and long gone. You're a magician!"

"No magic at all. You told me it was the only one you hadn't read."

"I did? And you remembered?"

"Certainly. And, as a matter of fact, the book isn't long gone. It was reprinted in 1976. Oddly enough, we discovered it was the only one of her works missing from our own collection. So I bought two of them."

"Wonderful." Elizabeth's pronouncement covered the gift, the evening, the arrangements. She began reading instantly, with Richard on the other end of the sofa likewise absorbed in a book.

Occasionally her reading would be interrupted by a deep chuckle as Richard came across an amusing passage. Then she would turn again to be lost in the endearing tale being told in the unmistakable voice of her friend and favorite author—the hero and heroine, surrounded by the beauty of his family country estate, but caught in a hopeless situation...

"Listen to this," Richard pulled her back to the present. He read a short descriptive passage from his book to her. "Isn't that great? What that man can do with words."

Her smile and attention were forced, her eyes drawn almost

magnetically back toward the pages she just left. Then she gave herself a little shake to focus on her host. "What are you reading?"

"*Pastoral*, by Nevil Shute."

"You surprise me. I thought you stuck to biography and literary criticism for pleasure reading."

"You're mostly right. I have to read so many bestsellers for work—Besides reading the *Caudex* line I have to keep up with what the competition's doing—so it's a relief to be able to sink my teeth into something more classic. Sometimes I tell myself I'll never read another popular work if I can ever get out of this business."

"Why are you reading Shute?"

"Background and perspective are important in keeping a solid line at the house. Shute is one of the writers who's made the novel what it is today. It's important to know how we got where we are in order to try to see where we're going. It makes a change from just reading sales figures."

"Of course I've read *On the Beach*, but I'm not a Shute expert at all."

"I prefer his aviation stories: *Landfall, In the Wet, The Rose and the Rainbow...* But his underlying theme is always the same —fidelity."

"Fidelity. What a wonderful, out-of-fashion word," Elizabeth mused.

"Yes, that's what I saw in *On the Beach*—not a commentary on nuclear war, but a study in faithfulness in the face of certain extinction: Planting oak trees and spring bulbs, taking a secretarial course, refusing to have an affair—staying the course." He paused.

"Sorry. I invited you up here to read, and then I spend the evening lecturing."

"I'm not sorry in the least. Pity you're stuck in that office. I can see you'd make an inspiring teacher." She returned to her book. The novel was short, set in large type, and Elizabeth was a fast reader—her profession demanded it. At the end she didn't look up, not wanting to break the spell of the happy ending. A happy ending, yes, but gained at great price and sacrifice. And a question she would have to ponder—was the world well lost for love?

"Aren't you two hungry yet? Or are you too famished to be able to call for food?" Annie walked in carrying a large tray.

Richard jumped up and took it from her. "Annie, you're a dream. We're starved, aren't we?"

Elizabeth agreed that, indeed, they were, but Richard continued. "Looks like it's do-it-yourself, though." He took two antique, long-handled bed warmers from their hooks by the fireplace and put oil and popcorn in them. They sat side by side on the braided hearth rug and shook the pans over the glowing logs in the oversized fireplace. Soon the kernels popping in the copper pans drowned out the sound of rain against the windows. Butter sizzled in its own little warming pan by the fire.

"Don't use it all," Elizabeth protested as Richard doused his mound of white popcorn with the golden liquid.

He poured an equal amount on hers. "Salt?"

"Just a tad. Mostly I like the butter flavor."

Richard poured lethally rich hot chocolate from a high-necked cocoa pot and pulled some large toss pillows off the sofa and chairs for them to lean against.

"Will you marry me?"

Elizabeth gasped. Could she possibly have heard right? "What?"

"I said—"

At that moment the door across the room opened. "That's all right, Annie, we'll bring the tray back late—" Richard turned and stopped with a strangled sound.

Ever afterward the horror Elizabeth's mind held of that moment wasn't from seeing the beautiful woman enter the room but from feeling the coldness emanating from Richard. It could have been a frozen corpse beside her rather than one that entered the room.

"Oh, dear. Annie said you were busy, but I didn't quite realize —Oh, well, I wanted to make a dramatic entrance. After waiting three years for it, I'd hate for it to be an anticlimax."

Richard didn't move. Was it only shock that held him rooted? Had he felt a momentary flash of joy at beholding his old love? Somehow, Elizabeth found words. "Ilona Walters, isn't it? I've read your books."

"Ah, there's someone who knows what to say to a writer." With a light laugh she crossed the room and took the hand Elizabeth wasn't holding out to her. "Actually Mary Ilona Walters Spenser. But I expect you know that. And you are...?" Light flashed on the wedding ring Mary was still wearing.

"Elizabeth. Elizabeth Allerton."

Mary Ilona whirled gracefully and threw open her arms to Richard. "Aren't you happy to see me, darling?"

Elizabeth didn't wait to hear his answer. Whatever it was, it was between Richard and his wife. "I know you two have a lot to catch up on." She was across the room and out the door before Richard could reply.

The force of her exit line carried Elizabeth to the front hall, where she realized she was without transportation. She was hesitating over calling Susan at that hour when Annie appeared with her coat. "I could drive you, Miss Allerton."

All the way home, with only the swish of the windshield wipers to break the silence, and then all the time it took her to pull off her clothes and get into bed, she couldn't shake the ridiculous feeling that this was somehow her own fault. She was the one who had come here, insisting on digging up every fact about Elswyth Thane and William Beebe. She had challenged Richard to help her. She had determined—however futilely—to get to the bottom of Mary's obsession. She had vowed to lay the ghost haunting Richard to rest. Well, fine work she'd made of all that.

Shivering, she pulled the quilt up to her chin. Sleep was out of the question, no matter how much she might need it before her flight. She tossed and turned as each unanswerable question presented itself.

Should she go with her dignity intact and rebuild her old life? Or should she accept the humiliation of pretending nothing had happened between her and Richard? That she hadn't heard his words to her in that moment before the world shattered? Whatever she did, Richard was lost to her, but should she stay long enough to clear the air between them? Smooth the way so Richard could rebuild his relationship with his wife?

When a faint glow of morning finally showed around the edge of her curtains Elizabeth forced herself to move. With her feet feeling as though they didn't quite make contact with the floor, she walked to the telephone. "United Airlines reservations? This is Elizabeth Allerton. I want to cancel my reservation."

CHAPTER 21

*E*lizabeth was just emerging from the shower when the doorbell rang. She toweled off quickly before stepping into the skirt she had kept out to wear on the airplane that day and pulling a sweater over her head. Somehow she wasn't surprised to open the door and find Richard standing there. His features stood out against the darkened hollows under his eyes and sunken cheekbones, but his lean frame and broad shoulders were even more stiffly upright than ever. It was clear he was holding himself in tightly—doing the right thing.

She couldn't begin to know all he was feeling, but uppermost must be confusion. The confusion of facing a long-buried, but still grieved-for wife. Even a shock of joy could be as hard to assimilate as one of grief.

Well, whatever he was feeling, it was apparent he was in crisis, and she wouldn't let him go through it alone. He needed a friend. She couldn't take him in her arms as his love, but she could hold his hand as a friend.

She stepped back, holding the door open. "Let's have some toast and coffee, and you can tell me all about everything." Elizabeth led the way to the kitchen and busied herself filling the coffee pot and popping slices of bread in the toaster. When she could delay no longer she turned to Richard, seated at the table. "So—how is it she's alive?"

He ran his hand through his hair, then shook his head. "It seems she had planned to be on the plane with James, even had some of her luggage sent on to load. Then a call from her agent made her change her plans. She sent her secretary on in her place to get things ready."

"So that's who they buried as Mary Ilona? And nobody missed this other woman?"

"Apparently she was something of a loner and didn't have any family." Richard looked as bewildered as Elizabeth felt. "Everyone thought Mary was on the plane as planned. Mary said it was quite a shock when she read of her own demise in the paper."

"Understandably. But then she decided to play dead? For *three years*! And what about her family? What about her husband? Didn't she give a thought to anyone else's pain?" Elizabeth's anger rose with each question. This was unbelievable. "People don't just play dead! What's she been up to?" She realized she was almost yelling and turned away.

Richard's voice rang hollowly in her ears. "Much as I had guessed, her reasons for wanting to go away in the first place—she wanted to be free to do her research unhindered. Unhindered by me, that is. I knew I had put too much pressure on her. She was so driven by her career, and I wanted to start a family..."

To which Elizabeth wanted to reply *Phooey!* It might have taken a few heated discussions. Arguments, even. But if Mary Ilona had told him she wanted more space he would have come around in time. She didn't have to escape from the whole world just to get time off from him. Something wasn't right here.

Elizabeth took a deep breath and forced herself to answer calmly. "I don't know. It's hard to imagine you being that unreasonable."

"So unreasonable a woman would rather be dead?" The look of guilt in his eyes tore at her. How could any woman be so callous?

Didn't he realize how little sense this all made? She wanted to shake him, but this was a moment for calm. She needed to get the facts—or at least the lies Mary was presenting as facts. "So, where has she been?"

"Bermuda, mostly. South America some."

The answer set bells ringing in Elizabeth's head. Of course. If she hadn't been so wrapped up in her own emotions she would have seen it long ago. Donald had just reappeared after kicking around the Caribbean and South America for two and a half years. Just too, too coincidental. "And what was this big project she was willing to spend three years in hiding just to be able to research? Buried treasure? A lost manuscript?"

"Nothing so melodramatic, just honest, creative work. She had a vision of doing a whole series of young reader adventure books that would become to this generation of kids what the Hardy boys were thirty years ago."

Elizabeth didn't know whether to laugh or scream at a story of such a selfless Pollyanna, doing it all for the children of the world, but she managed to keep a perfectly straight face. "I suppose I can understand dedication to a creative urge. But do you really believe it was worth all that?"

"Obviously it was to her." He paused. "Since I had made her feel it was her only way."

Elizabeth bit her lip to keep back an unladylike epithet.

He continued, "And even by objective standards, if you think of movie rights, a television series, book clubs…"

Aha, now you're talking business. Elizabeth smiled wryly. "And she has returned with the book written?"

"Books. Twenty-five of them."

"So she chose this moment to return because…"

"Because she had finished the series. She's ready to publish."

Elizabeth raised her eyebrows at such productivity. And such crassness. "Are they any good?"

"Fantastic. I read three last night. They're even better than she says. The richness of the background detail could only have been written on the spot, and the pace of the adventures makes 'Raiders of the Lost Ark' look slow."

Elizabeth was amazed that he could be so objective. But maybe that was a defense against examining his own feelings. "Fine. But what does all that have to do with Dr. Beebe, other than the locale of his explorations?"

"Simply that. She used his writings as sort of guidebooks to hidden beaches, caves, rugged mountainsides..."

How convenient—all so innocent. So pat. "I can see that, but what is there in any of that for you to find objectionable in the first place?"

Richard ran his long fingers through his hair again and gazed at the floor. "That's what I've been asking myself over and over. It must have been some sort of communication problem between us. I was in England a lot of that time, you remember. Or maybe I was overly protective for my godmother. The earlier biography attempts on Dr. Beebe made her very unhappy. I didn't want anything like that again, especially when she wasn't well."

Elizabeth nodded. That must have been just before her own correspondence had dwindled due to Elswyth Thane's poor health. "And now she's come back for you to publish her Great American Adventures and make her a Great American Celebrity?" Elizabeth didn't really mean for her voice to sound *quite* so sarcastic.

"The marketing boys will go crazy! What they can do with her fragile looks and a three-years-in-the-jungle story."

Right. Fragile looks and jungle instincts. But Elizabeth merely said, "Better than any New Hampshire poet anyone could dream up?"

"Much better." There was a long pause. A long, awkward pause while Richard took a deep breath. "And she says she's ready to start a family."

Excellent for promotion. Then Elizabeth had another thought. *Was Mary Ilona pregnant with a child she wanted to pass off as Richard's? Was that the real reason for the timing of her return?* But again Elizabeth curbed her catty reply and made an attempt at humor. "Well, aren't you lucky I didn't accept you? I wonder if they could have gotten you on bigamy charges for being engaged to one woman while married to another? We'll have to ask Sue—just as academic curiosity, of course. Breach of promise, perhaps?" She gave an excellent imitation of a bright laugh. "Not that you really promised anything, of course. You just asked a question, which the lady saved me the trouble of answering."

She turned her back on him to pick up the coffee pot. "Here, your coffee is stone cold."

Richard stood. "No. Thanks. I've got to be going. Mary is anxious to get the contract signed. We would love to have the first one out in time for Christmas, so we're picking up her agent and catching a shuttle flight to Philly this afternoon."

"Lots of lost time to make up for." Elizabeth couldn't believe how carefree she sounded, even to her own ears.

"I wanted you to know what happened." He took a deep breath. "Elizabeth, I..." Another breath. "You understand, I..."

He walked toward the door with jerky motions, then paused. "You'll be here when I—we—get back? Late tonight or early tomorrow?"

Elizabeth clenched her fist to control her desire to fling the coffee pot at him and scream that if she never saw him again it would be much too soon. But the truth was, she was far too curious to know what was *really* going on. "You think I'd walk out in the middle of the launch of the new Robert Louis Stevenson/George Lucas/Alice in Wonderland? I always wanted to go to Cape Kennedy for a shuttle launch. This should be much better."

There was no way she would put down the thriller without reading the last chapter.

But she was aware of the danger. She was not reading Dick Francis, who always kept her up all night but never failed to deliver a happy ending. She was reading Desmond Bagley, who kept her up all night but might, in the wee hours of the morning, devastate her with an unhappy ending.

Richard gave a final nod and pulled the door closed behind him.

Elizabeth turned back to the kitchen table and pushed the empty coffee mugs aside. In an attempt to distract herself she reached for the letter Susan had left there for her last night. She had forgotten all about it until she glimpsed it when she sat down with Richard.

She gasped at the sight of the Princeton University Library return address. Goodness, how long had it been since she sent that query regarding Dr. Beebe's papers? Was it possible answers to her search had been within her reach all this time?

She ripped the letter open and, with fingers clumsy from haste, pulled out photocopies of William Beebe's correspondence. With the rapacity of a treasure hunter she was immediately absorbed in reading—hunting for her own particular kind of treasure—clues to the *real* reasons for Mary Ilona's disappearance.

Snatches of the letters painted a vivid picture of Dr. Beebe's world and of the man himself. "I was intensely mortified to find that my man had not sent you the few electric eels I was able to rescue..." She scanned the page and turned to another. "I am very anxious to study and to have on hand for your reference papers on the colors and color patterns of moths and butterflies..."

She read on, absorbing every detail of his notes on the flora and fauna of the Caribbean until at last she put a paper down with a sigh. She had been so sure there would be something here— some clue to Mary's fixation.

She picked up another letter, this to Carl Van Doren. Elizabeth's eyebrows rose. Van Doren, critic, academic, and Pulitzer Prize-winning author, who, with his brother Mark, helped establish the credibility of American Literature in the world. In a way, this man was one of the founders of her own profession. "Use anything of mine you want. Hope the rest of the Anthology is better than my stuff! Sincerely, Will Beebe."

She put an X in the margin to remind herself to work that into the next draft of her dissertation, probably as a footnote. She would need to locate the anthology.

But for now she ploughed on through the letters. Interesting reading, but if there was anything there to her purpose she couldn't spot it.

There was a review by Dr. Beebe of a book called *The Mysterious Sea*. Beebe liked the book, but Elizabeth was getting near to the frantic point as the stack of papers dwindled.

She picked up another bundle of clipped photocopies. Not letters or reviews, but seemingly manuscript pages headed *Nonsuch*. Nonsuch, the Bermudan Island where William Beebe had his laboratory. "I found an easier descent and climbed painfully over the needle-sharp points, rough carved by the acid of the water and sharpened by the emery of shifting sand and wind. A projecting pinnacle gave suddenly, and I tore my shirt and skin within... I was neck deep under the sea. I reached out and swished the water back and forth, and something stuck between my fingers. I plucked at it and palmed it and climbed back up on the only material in the world which was not water. Bracing my toes into convenient crevices, I shook the water from my eyes and gazed mistily, unbelieving, at what I held..."

The room tingled with silence. The paper in Elizabeth's hand seemed brighter, as if the mere photocopied words were illuminated from within. Elizabeth knew that if she were being depicted in a comic strip, the cartoonist would show her with her hair standing straight out from her head. Her scalp was tingling and her eyes bulging as she read on. "I have named it the cave of

Opulentus Thesaurus—the riches are incalculable, and yet I hesitate to exploit them. I shudder to think what teams of spelunkers and treasure hunters would do to the natural habitat."

Elizabeth stood up. This had to be shared. Besides, she needed another mind to help sort it all out—a mind trained to cool, rational analysis. "Hello, Sue?" She tried not to yell into the receiver in her excitement. "I know it's the middle of the working day, but could you possibly come home? I think I've got something really hot here."

Susan was with her in less than half an hour. "Actually, I was looking for an excuse to leave the office. Donald said he'd call. This way they can tell him I'm out with no fudging."

Before Susan could even take her coat off, Elizabeth thrust the photocopied manuscript page at her. "Tell me what you make of this."

Susan sank into a chair and read. Then she raised her eyes to the top of the page and read again, more slowly this time. At last she let the sheet fall to the table. "I can't believe it. This sounds like William Beebe did find treasure." She drew a thoughtful breath. "A cave filled with water much of the year off a remote island in the Bermuda Triangle." She shook her head. "That's so exciting it's almost a cliché. Are you sure Elswyth Thane's husband didn't write fiction, too?"

Elizabeth nodded. "I know. That's how I reacted too. But that must be what Ilona found. That's a vision that could easily lead one to an obsessive act. Especially someone with gold-digging tendencies." She approached her next question more carefully, but the fact was, she had called Sue for more than her analytical skills "Where do you think Donald ties into this picture?"

"Donald? What does he have to do with this?"

Elizabeth sighed. "Maybe nothing. I'm probably seeing bogeymen under every rock. The only thing I'm sure of is that something isn't right." She recounted the story Richard had told her.

Susan was shaking her head and laughing by the time Elizabeth was finished. "Can you believe how gullible men are? I do think they'll swallow anything a beautiful woman tells them."

"You should try it in court and find out."

"If I had big, round, blue eyes I might be tempted." Then Susan was quiet, and Elizabeth could almost see the wheels turning in her head. At last she nodded. "Yes, given the time of his disappearance and the locations he admits to, Donald probably does tie in somewhere. But I can't see how."

"Were they friends? Before?"

"Donald and Mary?" Susan thought. "Not exactly friends that I was aware of. Acquaintances, maybe even distant cousins or something. I can't really remember, but I have vague memories of Donald introducing her around at a couple of parties." She reached down and opened the briefcase she had set on the floor. She pulled out a long, yellow pad.

"What are you writing?"

"Drawing up a scenario, listing what we know and what we have reasonable cause to believe. Or doubt."

Elizabeth read over Sue's shoulder: *Mary Ilona researching background for adventure books, reads Beebe's explorations, becomes obsessed with the idea of a treasure cave. Richard, protecting E.T.'s privacy, puts his foot down. Hard.*

Elizabeth started to protest at the last word, then recalled his harshness with her when he thought she was following a similar line. "Right. Go on. The biggest question mark in my mind is the three-year hiatus. Ilona was obviously writing all that time. She has the manuscripts to prove it. But why stay dead to do that?"

Susan was quiet for several minutes. "I'd like to know if she had any life insurance and what happened to it."

"But she wouldn't need money from insurance if she found buried treasure."

"I don't know, divers and equipment—that could be a pretty expensive operation."

"But presumably during nice dry low tides lanterns and shovels would do the job. Will Beebe wasn't down in the bathysphere. As he described it, his head was out of water much of the time. He was more just wading."

Susan seemed not to hear Elizabeth's comment. She sat gazing into the middle distance. Then she gave a small gasp. "Of course. There would have been probate proceedings. I'm going to do some checking."

It was evening before Susan returned, and Elizabeth felt she had worn a groove in her brain going over the same ground again and again, asking the same questions. She looked at her friend expectantly. "Yep! I got the goods." Susan waved her notepad triumphantly. "The clerk of the court in Boston will send me copies of all this tomorrow, but I got the gist of it over the phone: One Donald Lamont filed the probate petition, citing himself as next of kin—not so distant a cousin, it seems. Lamont was appointed to handle the estate of Mary Ilona Walters, including a $150,000 life insurance policy."

"Wait, what about Richard? Wouldn't her husband be next of kin?"

"Apparently all this was set up before her marriage and not changed afterward. They weren't married very long, were they?"

Elizabeth considered. "Less than a year, as I remember. And Richard said he was out of the country on business a lot of that time."

"Right. And nobody ever keeps their wills up to date. So when the estate was closed and final distribution made after payment of all bills, everything was turned over to Mr. Lamont as sole heir."

"And don't tell me—it took six months to close the estate."

"How did you know?" Susan raised an eyebrow above the frame of her glasses.

"Elementary, my dear Watson. That's why Donald stuck

around for six months before taking off to join her. What a holiday they must have had."

"May I offer you a bowl of clam chowder in celebration, Mr. Holmes?"

The two women sat around the table eating ravenously and congratulating themselves.

Elizabeth was on her second bowl of chowder when she paused with her spoon halfway to her mouth. "No. We didn't really crack it, you know. We've answered some pretty tricky questions. At least we've formulated some great theories. But we have no proof. We haven't really solved anything."

CHAPTER 22

*E*lizabeth stared into her chowder as if she might divine an answer there. Susan toyed with a packet of oyster crackers. "Maybe if we face them with what we do have they'll tell us the rest."

Elizabeth grinned. "Like the big Perry Mason courtroom scenes where the guilty person always breaks down and confesses? I think I liked you better as Sherlock's sidekick."

"I need some more chowder." Susan stood to refill her bowl.

"Give me another scoop, too." Elizabeth held her bowl out. "We haven't had chowder since my first night here."

Susan shook her head. "Which was so dramatically interrupted by Sheriff Norris's untimely appearance."

But fresh bowls of chowder did nothing to move their reasoning any further forward. Even after she was in bed that night Elizabeth continued thinking about all that had happened since she came to Vermont: What a bad start she got off to with that hit-and-run accident... How nervous she had been that day in court... It all seemed like months ago...

She was just drifting off to sleep when she jerked upright and flung her covers off.

"Susan!" She burst into her friend's room.

"Glumph?"

Elizabeth grabbed Sue's arm and shook her. "I've got it! Well, maybe, anyway. At least, I've got an idea. Can you hear me? Are you in there?"

"I don't function well at three-thirty in the morning." Susan yawned.

"Well, I do. At least this time I think I did. Listen, remember when I had to wait for my case to come up in court and the one before mine was something about an unclaimed property statute —somebody found something in an abandoned house—and the judge said it had to be held for two years or something like that in case somebody claimed it. Do you remember?"

"I don't think I was in the courtroom with you then, but I know about unclaimed property laws. There was a lot about them in the papers last year when treasure hunters in Florida wanted to —Oh! I see! Clever, clever girl! And in the middle of the night, too."

"Do you know anything about Bermudan law?"

"Not much. It's based on English Common Law, but their Parliament enacts its own laws."

"Would they have a found property law like we do?"

"Probably. Likely. I can check." Susan sat up straighter in bed and leaned against her headboard. "You can bet they wouldn't let any treasure out of the country until the taxes were settled on it."

Susan yawned, and Elizabeth was about to start back to bed when she stopped. "But then, who's to say someone who was willing to play dead would be that worried about the letter of the law?"

The next morning Elizabeth found Susan already digging through books when she came out of her room rubbing her eyes. "What are you looking up?"

Susan indicated the encyclopedia open in front of her. "Nonsuch Island. The article mentions William Beebe's bathysphere decent, all right. But it's been a wildlife preserve for about twenty years. No one is even allowed to land there without a permit."

Elizabeth poured herself a mug of coffee and sat down. "So I think it's fair to assume whatever our friends were doing there was likely outside the law."

"Or maybe Mary Ilona got a permit to be there as a writer, but not as a treasure hunter."

"I'm not sure that gets us very far."

Susan went to the phone and called her office, issuing instructions to her secretary about some correspondence and telling her not to put any calls through to her unless they claimed an absolute state of emergency. "Oh, except Max, of course."

"Max, of course?" Elizabeth mimicked. "Susan, what's going on here? When did you start calling Boston's most prestigious lawyer 'Max'?"

"Since I accepted his invitation to dinner two nights ago."

"You sly thing. And you didn't tell me!"

"Well, you were a bit preoccupied with your own problems."

"Yes. But—isn't this sudden?"

This time Elizabeth noticed the special light in Susan's smile. "He'd been asking me for a long time, but I wasn't sure I wanted to get involved. Seeing Donald was the best medicine possible. It helped me realize what I really want."

"But this—Max, I only got a glimpse of him. My impression was that he's very distinguished. But, isn't he, er—well, old and grayish? My guess would be that he's on his third wife."

"Sounds irresistible but not quite what I had in mind when I said I realized what I wanted. He *is* very distinguished and has been a widower for something more than a year. I rather hope he'll soon be on his second wife and that he'll stop there."

Elizabeth started to ask more, but the phone rang. "It's all yours, Sue. It's undoubtedly *him*."

"Hello?" Susan almost purred into the receiver. "Oh, hi. Just a minute." She held the phone out to Elizabeth. "Wrong *him*."

Elizabeth took the phone. "Richard? When did you get back?" Her eyebrows rose at his invitation. "Certainly. Tell your grandmother I can't imagine the circumstances that would cause me to turn down taking tea with her. Yes, I think Sue's free, too."

Elizabeth put down the receiver and turned to Susan. "Seems they returned from a most successful meeting in Philadelphia, and Alexandra Spenser is serving tea in celebration." Then she realized—"Oh, no. I haven't got a thing to wear. Everything's still packed. And wrinkled."

"Dig out that two-piece moss-green dress. I'll plug in the iron."

Elizabeth started to obey, but the phone rang again. "Popular, aren't we? Want me to get it?"

"Please," Sue called from the laundry room.

When she emerged Elizabeth held her hand over the mouthpiece. "Doesn't sound like any Boston lawyer I ever met, but then, what do I know?"

Susan took the phone, then rolled her eyes. "Hello, Donald. Yes, I do have plans." She stopped to flash a conspiratorial smile at Elizabeth. "Tell you what—I'm going to Mrs. Spenser's to tea, but I understand she's inviting a group. I'm sure she won't mind my bringing a guest if you'd like to join us there... Great. Three o'clock." She hung up with an air of triumph.

"Susan! What audacity! You can't just invite someone to Mrs. Spenser's party. Especially not that sleazeball."

"Great, huh? It's just like the final scene where Nero Wolfe always gathers all the suspects in his parlor."

"Yes, but Nero Wolfe does that after he knows all the answers. We don't know anything."

"We know quite a lot, and I can't think how we'll learn any more if we don't confront the suspects."

"Do you have any idea how ridiculous we'll look if everything is as innocent as Mary Ilona claims it is? Apparently Richard has accepted her story whole cloth."

Susan looked her in the eye. "And have you?"

Elizabeth's look spoke clearly what she thought of Mary Ilona's yarn.

CHAPTER 23

A short time later Susan swept around the circle drive in front of the Spenser home and pulled up next to a bright red Porsche. "I see Donald arrived ahead of us," she said.

At last the image clicked in Elizabeth's mind. "That's Donald's car! You're sure?"

Sue laughed. "I could hardly be mistaken. I doubt there's another of these in New England. And don't scrape it when you open your door. He's so fanatical he carries a touchup stick in his glove box."

"That's the car that followed me the day I went to Wilmington. I'm sure of it. I thought something looked familiar when I saw him leave your house the other day, but I only got a glimpse."

"Followed you? What are you talking about?"

Elizabeth told her about seeing flashes of a small red car repeatedly the day she visited Elswyth Thane's home. "But I thought I was being paranoid, so I dismissed it."

Susan started to walk toward the house, but Elizabeth called her back. "Wait." She took a deep breath. "As long as I'm being paranoid let me say this. Then you can tell me how ridiculous I'm being."

Susan frowned but waited for her to continue.

"I was thinking little red cars might be a New England thing, but if there aren't many, maybe I've been seeing the same one lots of times. That is definitely the color of the streak Sheriff Norris found on your car. The evidence of the accident I could never believe I had."

"Are you saying *Donald* hit my car? On purpose?"

"I'm guessing he hit your car with his touchup stick. The dent Sheriff Norris saw on the other car could have happened anytime."

"And then Richard was the complaining witness to this put-up job? Are you suggesting Richard and Donald are in cahoots?"

Elizabeth sighed. Put that way, it certainly sounded less than likely. But she wasn't ready to throw in the towel yet. "No. Donald could have been waiting behind another car and when I backed out, he scraped two pieces of metal together or something in hopes someone would look. If some passerby hadn't observed his charade he would have made the complaint himself..." Oh, dear. That did sound far-fetched. "Well, maybe from where Richard was it just looked like I hit the other car. It was a tight space..." She ended with a sound between a sigh and a laugh.

But Susan didn't laugh. "Then he saw Richard writing down my license plate number, so he knew he had a schill?"

"Yes! That's exactly what happened. I'm sure of it." Elizabeth could have done a happy dance right there. She *knew* she hadn't hit anything.

"Why?"

"Hm?"

Susan was more emphatic. "Why? Why would Donald go to all that trouble?"

"Well," Elizabeth thought. She knew she was grasping at straws. "Well, maybe he wanted to get your attention. Maybe he didn't know you weren't driving. Then when he dropped the charges you'd be all grateful and—"

Susan just shook her head and walked toward the house.

All the principals were gathered in Alexandra Spenser's parlor by the time Elizabeth and Susan arrived. All gathered, with Mary Ilona the center of attention in a rainbow-shaded chiffon dress that emphasized her tiny waist, then swirled in a fluff of cotton-candy colors with the entire effect crowned by hair like dawn's first sunbeam striking a cloud.

Well, Elizabeth was glad she had pulled her own hair back with a tortoiseshell clip. She ran her hand over her own tailored skirt. *I told myself the best way to fight a ghost was to give it substance, but this wasn't quite what I had I mind.*

"...My little cabin actually had a roof thatched with banana leaves, just like you see in pictures." Richard and Donald were both hanging on every word Mary spoke. Even Elizabeth felt drawn to her charm. "And it was right on the beach by the most incredibly blue bay. You really can't imagine the depth and clarity of the color without seeing it..."

"I'm amazed you were allowed to build there," Elizabeth said. "Especially since one is required to have a permit even to land on Nonesuch Island."

Mary was completely unruffled by Elizabeth's challenge. "Oh, yes, it's so important to preserve the habitat. But my credentials were never questioned, since I was granted permission because of my work on Dr. Beebe's papers. He's still very revered there."

Elizabeth would have liked to get a look at her documents, but she went on. "If you were right on the beach didn't your cabin flood in high tide?"

Mary smiled in delight at her expanded audience. "Oh my, yes. And the thatched roof leaked in the rain. So I simply threw every-thing into my little runabout boat and moved into Hamilton— that's the capital of Bermuda, you know, and very, very British and charming. It was an excellent arrangement. Gave me just enough variety. And then there were the jaunts to the other islands for background research. And clear down to South America—especially the jungles of Brazil. Absolutely breathtaking. If I've just been able to communicate even a little of this in my books..." She turned wistful eyes on Richard.

"You certainly have. No doubt about it."

"But then the dry season came, and you returned to your typewriter at your seashore hut?" Elizabeth didn't want the conversation to get too far afield.

"Oh, yes. Always. A writer's job is essentially a lonely one— even for a writer of adventures."

And that's just what it was to you, wasn't it? A glorious adventure, leaving Richard guilt-ridden and grieving. "So you did your work exploring in the cave at low tide, rather than going in with diving gear?" Elizabeth maintained her innocent tone.

"Oh, yes—walked right in on dry ground like Moses crossing the Red—" Mary Ilona's mouth snapped shut mid-sentence. She just sat there, her big blue eyes narrowed as they assessed Elizabeth.

"Well, come on and tell us. I'm dying to hear about the treasure. It isn't any secret is it?" Elizabeth longed to see how Richard was responding to this, but like a mongoose with a snake, she didn't dare let her eyes waver.

Ilona's bright laugh did her recovery powers great credit. "Of course it isn't a *secret*. I'm just not talking much about that yet, because I want to write a personal experience book based on my whole adventure, and sometimes these things can lose their impact if one talks about them too much first."

"Oh, but you can tell us—your publisher and some of your most avid fans." Elizabeth quelled her conscience by recalling that she did like the book she had read to Tommy.

As Elizabeth hoped, Mary Ilona found the invitation irresistible. "Well it really was unbelievably thrilling—just like something out of a movie. The cave was practically full of them—stuck in niches, on rock ledges—a few fallen into the water, but most were right where they'd been for hundreds and hundreds of years."

Richard spoke for the first time since the brief greeting he had given Elizabeth and Susan. "Mary, are you saying you found a cave full of ancient statues or something?"

The author gave a silvery laugh. "Oh, darling, how trite! I would never have thought you so cliché ridden! The cave was full of *Opulentus Thesaurus*, the world's rarest underwater plant because it grows underwater three months of the year and on damp rock the rest of the time and produces the most *glorious* colors in semi-darkness. You won't *believe* the pictures I got for my book."

For a moment Elizabeth was as stunned as Ilona must have been when she discovered that the treasure William Beebe referred to was a wonder of nature—the only kind of treasure he would truly have valued.

Of course, Ilona carried it all off as if she had known all along. But then, she'd had three years to readjust to the fact that the golden treasure she thought to find was of the botanical variety. And, being Ilona, she had figured out how to turn it to her own advantage.

Elizabeth struggled to make the pieces fit. "But I don't understand. If it wasn't real treasure, why did you have to wait for the unclaimed property statute to run before you could leave?" Elizabeth believed so firmly in the scenario she and Sue had developed that she quoted it as fact.

Ilona gave her a look that clearly asked how she knew all that, but her survivalist instincts for keeping the unflappable upper hand led her to answer in the most casual manner. "Oh, it was just sheer idiocy that some lawyer tried that one on. He simply couldn't find anything on the books to stop me with, and his environmentalist-Nazi clients got a court order to impound my pictures, because they were worried about the impact this would have on the local flora and fauna if herds of tourists and scientists started pouring in.

"Of course, they have all their visitors' restrictions anyway—which is why I won in the end. But it was a ridiculous hassle."

Elizabeth was still racing to keep up with the revelations when Sue, her voice dripping with honey, spoke up. "How fortunate that you had Donald there to support you through your difficulties. But tell me, how is your book going to deal with the insurance scam?"

Finally, Ilona was speechless.

Elizabeth heard a sharp intake of breath from Richard. For the first time she allowed herself to turn and look at him. She hadn't taken her eyes off Mary Ilona for fear of losing her focus, but a corner of her mind—and heart—had stayed tuned to Richard. What must he be going through to hear all this?

Elizabeth's brief glance told her nothing though. Richard's features could have been chiseled from Vermont granite. It was clear he was holding his breath. Was his wife a fraudster?

"There won't be any need to deal with it at all." Donald came in so smoothly that Elizabeth couldn't help admiring what a good team he and Ilona made. "Television and movie rights to the adventure books will easily sell for more than the policy paid, and we'll return the money."

"What are you talking about? What insurance money? Give what back? Donald, you're daft!" It was clear Ilona didn't know whether to be amused or outraged.

"From the airplane crash, of course. It came to me as your next of kin. Where did you think I got the dosh to finance your great adventure?"

Mary Ilona blinked. "I—I guess I didn't think." She bit her lip. "Wasn't that illegal or something? You knew I wasn't dead."

"Of course it wasn't illegal. It was a loan," Donald insisted with belligerence.

The air was vibrating with unanswered questions when the

door opened and the attention in the room shifted to Annie. "Mrs. Spenser says are you ready to have the tea brought in, Mr. Richard?"

"Yes, Annie. We certainly are." His words were as cold as if Mount Wantastiquet had spoken.

Susan jumped to her feet. "Let me help you carry things." She almost ran out of the room.

Elizabeth glanced at Richard's stonily inscrutable face. Wherever things went from here, she had laid the specter. Her work was done.

CHAPTER 24

*I*n a few minutes Susan returned, not carrying a tray of tea cups, but flushed and triumphant with the news she bore. She looked at Donald, then spoke to the room in general. "I've just talked to the prosecuting attorney's office. Charges are being filed as we speak. Sheriff Norris should be here in a few minutes to make the arrest."

Donald shot to his feet. "Ridiculous! I explained it was a loan. You don't arrest people for borrowing money."

Susan was at her professional courtroom best. "You committed a crime. Paying the money back would be restitution, but you still broke the law. If restitution prevented prosecution, every time someone got caught they'd just say, 'Well, I'll pay it back.' An involuntary loan is fraud. How many embezzlers have thought they'd pay it back?"

"And what about setting me up?" Elizabeth broke into the brittle silence. "What were you playing at with that red paint trick on Susan's car?" Donald took a step backward as she advanced on him. "Why did you do that?"

"I—I didn't mean any harm. I just wanted to discourage your

research. It was common gossip that Sue's guest was here to look into Elswyth Thane. I didn't want you stealing Ilona's thunder."

"As I did." Elizabeth tossed her head triumphantly.

"I'm far more concerned about that plane crash, Donald." Susan took up the reins again. "I shall be asking the FAA to take another, closer look at the circumstances. Did you choose to profit from a tragic accident, or did you play a far more sinister role? I wonder."

"I will not listen to any more of your fantasizing." Donald pushed forward, knocking Susan aside.

But Richard blocked the door. "I believe my grandmother invited you to tea. It would be rude to leave now."

Donald sank into the nearest chair. "Milk or lemon, Mr. Lamont?" Alexandra Spenser had seated herself quietly at the tea table.

The cakes went largely untouched, but Elizabeth was on her second cup of tea when Annie ushered Sheriff Norris into the parlor. "What a nice surprise, Edward. Will you take a cup of tea?" Mrs. Spenser asked.

"Thank you, Ma'am, but I'm afraid I'm here on business."

"Can I sign as a complaining witness this time?" Elizabeth's smile was so broad she could hardly get the words out. "Just doing my civic duty, you understand." She caught a flicker of amusement in Richard's eye as well. His one glimmer of unbending the whole time.

Sheriff Norris escorted his charge from the room. Alexandra Spenser offered to refill their cups, but Elizabeth did not return to her seat. "Thank you, but we really must be going. I'll have an early plane to catch tomorrow."

"I'll see you out." Richard moved toward the door.

Susan went on to her car, but Elizabeth and Richard held back. "So you're off. I hope your research was everything you'd hoped it would be." Richard's voice held a shade of warmth, but he was still holding himself in a stiff grip as if a careless motion could shatter shelves of glass ornaments.

"All I hoped and several times more. Incredible, really." Elizabeth forced a smile. She was determined to play this as a casual friendship. Maybe someday she would believe it herself.

"Yes. Incredible, indeed." A long silence grew between them.

"Well, your wife will be wondering where you got to." Elizabeth put only the slightest emphasis on the third word.

Richard nodded wordlessly.

"And remember, if you ever break free of the publishing world and want a position as a lowly English professor I might know a head of department I could recommend you to."

"Gerald?"

"Depends on how long it takes you." She gave him a saucy—if forced—grin. "Gerald might find he has competition for his job once I finish my doctorate."

But Richard didn't pick up on her jocular tone. "If that ever happens, Elizabeth— Dr. Allerton, what a nice ring that has— I think we should agree now that it would be a clean slate."

"Make a fresh start? As if none of this ever happened?" Elizabeth thought, then gave a decisive nod. "Sure, why not? Buried under a sea of forgetfulness." She stood on her tiptoes and kissed his cheek before turning swiftly and crunching across the leaf-strewn driveway.

Somehow she managed to keep her head up and to simulate a carefree walk all the way to Sue's car. She sank onto the seat and Sue, remaining blessedly silent, started the engine. They turned down the drive. Away from the house. Away from Richard. And Elizabeth realized she was shaking. There had been such comradeship—gaiety, even—working with Richard to solve the mystery and make sense of it all. They had been engulfed in the—dare she say romance—of it all.

But their revels now were ended. The vision she had been almost subconsciously forming of a life with Richard—before his wife reappeared—was, indeed, baseless and melted into air, into thin air—an insubstantial pageant faded.

In the cold light of reality she had to face the fact that Richard was a married man. As he would be even if her schoolgirl fantasy of him turning up at Rocky Mountain should come to anything. Fine words: clean slate, fresh start, the past buried in forgetfulness...

But she knew her heart would never forget.

AUTHOR'S NOTES

My husband and I lived in New England for three years while Stan attended Harvard Law School. The lovely village of Newfane, Vermont, was one of our favorite getaway spots. It was not, however, until I had returned to Boise, Idaho, and become the mother of small children that I discovered the books of Elswyth Thane and engaged in the correspondence that is part of this novel. I read every author Elswyth Thane recommended and found the experience to be extremely formative in my English literature continuing education, picking up where my college degree left off: John Buchan, Rudyard Kipling, Angela Thirkell, D. E. Stevenson, and, of course, William Beebe.

All quotations from Elswyth Thane's letters are as she wrote them, except for substituting Elizabeth's name for mine, and all references to the work of Dr. William Beebe are historical—except the fictionalized *Opulentus Thesaurus*.

Like Elizabeth, I never got to meet Miss Thane—except through her books and letters—which is perhaps the truest way to meet any author.

The original manuscript of *The Flame Ignites* was first written in 1984, shortly after Thane's death, and resurfaced in the archives of the Boise State University library to become a prequel to my Elizabeth and Richard literary suspense series.

A special thank you to my lifelong, friend Gaymon Bennett—truly a Genuine Article—for introducing me to his college roommate, who subsequently became my husband, and for allowing me to use his fine poems "Autumn Hawk" and "Dawn Dancer."

ELSWYTH THANE, 1900 – 1984

One of the most beloved American writers of her day, Elswyth Thane was known for her romantic adventure novels and histories, both fiction and nonfiction.

Thane was born Helen Ricker in Burlington, Iowa. Her family moved to New York when she was 18. There Helen Ricker changed her name to Elswyth Thane and began her career as a freelance writer. Her first novel, *Riders of the Wind*, was published in 1926.

When she was 27 years old Elswyth married 50-year-old naturalist and pioneering deep-sea explorer William Beebe. They were married on a friend's yacht, and Mrs. Theodore Roosevelt, widow of the former President, was one of the guests at their wedding. Thane was emphatic, though, that none of her novels, "especially that one about a woman who married an explorer (*From This Day Forward*) was in any way autobiographical. The sole exception being *Reluctant Farmer*." (her autobiography)

The Beebes were friends with Rudyard Kipling, who features in her books *England Was An Island Once* and *Reluctant Farmer*. The latter was written after the Beebes purchased a small farm in rural

Vermont and Elswyth set about turning it into a home and refuge during the turmoil of World War II.

A devout Anglophile, Thane spent much time in England researching her novels, even spending time there in the early days of World War II. Thane's love of England comes through all of her writing, but perhaps most clearly in her best-known work, The Williamsburg Novels. This series of seven novels (which she originally envisioned being one book) traces the generations of two families, living on both sides of the Atlantic from the American Revolutionary War (which she calls a "family feud") through the early days of World War II.

BOOKS BY ELSWYTH THANE

Fiction

Riders of the Wind

Echo Answers

Cloth of Gold

His Elizabeth

Bound to Happen

Queen's Folly

Tryst

Remember Today

From This Day Forward

Melody

The Lost General

Letter to a Stranger

The Williamsburg Novels

Dawn's Early Light

Yankee Stranger

Ever After

The Light Heart

Kissing Kin

This Was Tomorrow

Homing

Non Fiction

The Tudor Wench

Young Mr. Disraeli

England Was an Island Once

The Bird Who Made Good

Mount Vernon is Ours

Mount Vernon: The Legacy

The Fighting Quaker: Nathaniel Greene

Reluctant Farmer

The Family Quarrel

Washington's Lady

Potomac Squire

Virginia Colony

Mount Vernon Family

Plays

The Tudor Wench

Young Mr. Disraeli

ABOUT THE AUTHOR

Donna Fletcher Crow is the author of 50 books, mostly novels of British history. The award-winning *Glastonbury, The Novel of Christian England,* an epic grail search covering fifteen centuries of English history, is her best-known work. She also authors three crime series: Lord Danvers investigates, Victorian true-crime novels; The Elizabeth and Richard literary suspense series; and The Monastery Murders. Donna and her husband of fifty plus years live in Boise, Idaho. They have four adult children and fourteen grandchildren. She is an enthusiastic gardener.

To read more about all of Donna's books and see pictures from her garden and research trips go to:

http://www.donnafletchercrow.com/.

You can follow her on Facebook at:

https://www.facebook.com/Donna-Fletcher-Crow-Novelist-of-British-History-355123098656/

BOOKS BY DONNA FLETCHER CROW

The Elizabeth & Richard Literary Suspense Mysteries:

The Flame Ignites

Elizabeth and Richard's stormy first meeting

in a New England autumn

The Shadow of Reality

Elizabeth and Richard at a Dorothy L Sayers mystery week high in the
Rocky Mountains

A Midsummer Eve's Nightmare

Elizabeth and Richard honeymoon at a Shakespeare Festival in Ashland,
Oregon

A Jane Austen Encounter

A second honeymoon visit to Jane Austen's homes turns deadly

A Most Singular Venture

Murder in Jane Austen's London

The Monastery Murders, Clerical Mysteries

A Very Private Grave

Legendary buried treasure, a brutal murder and lurking danger—

an itinerary of terror across a holy terrain

A Darkly Hidden Truth

Ancient puzzles, modern murder and breathless chase scenes

through a remote, waterlogged landscape

An Unholy Communion

An idyllic pilgrimage through Wales

becomes a deadly struggle between good and evil

A Newly Crimsoned Reliquary

Murder stalks the shadows of Oxford's hallowed shrines

An All-Consuming Fire

A Christmas wedding in a monastery—

if the bride can defeat the murderer prowling the Yorkshire moors

The Lord Danvers Investigates,

Victorian True-Crime Mysteries

A Most Inconvenient Death

The brutal Stanfield Hall murders shatter a quiet Norwich community and pull Danvers from deep personal grief into a dangerous investigation.

Grave Matters

Lord and Lady Danvers's honeymoon in Scotland is interrupted by the ghosts of Burke and Hare-style grave robbers.

To Dust You Shall Return

Catherine Bacon is murdered in the very shadow of Canterbury Cathedral but Charles and Antonia are overwhelmed with their own problems.

A Tincture of Murder

William Dove is on trial in York for poisoning his wife while Lord and Lady Danvers struggle to assist in a refuge home where fallen women continue to die mysteriously.

Where There is Love Historical Romance

Where Love Begins

Where Love Illumines

Where Love Triumphs

Where Love Restores

Where Love Shines

Where Love Calls